THE CHILDREN OF ALBION

JILL TURNER

Illustrated by Katie M. John

DEDICATION

To The Children of Albion

www.thelittlebirdbookstore.com

ACKNOWLEDGEMENTS

To those who've been part of this journey. You know
who you are.

Respect to some writers and artists, long gone,
Who in some way fed my imagination.
Aubrey Beardsley, Edmund Burne Jones,
Charles Dickens, John Keats,
And Alfred Lord Tennyson.

THE GREATEST STORY EVER TOLD.

This is the greatest story ever told. I think someone else said that once but as far as I'm concerned, they're wrong. This story is. I know 'cause it's mine. Well ours. All of ours.

As to a beginning, where to begin? Me, I s'pose. Robert George Terry is who I am, well, Robbie to my mates – and to everyone else really and all. Birth? Well I can't tell you much about that. Don't remember it, see? It was in the hospital. St Edmund's, except we call it St Ed's. Sneds really by the time you finish. It's the big one. Fuckin', big, grey, ugly lump by the roundabout. Over the dual carriageway from where I live.

Me, I come from the estate. Me, Mum and my sister Sam. Sned's estate it is. Quite funny really. Get born, cross back over the dual carriageway, then back one day and that's the end of you and you're buried up the end by Sned's church. Dunavta travel far round here, do yer? Yeah, it's kind of funny when you think about it. Sort of.

Well, born I was but I can't tell you much about it. Don't remember it, like. Date of birth? Well I've said it enough times to coppers to know it alright. Born in August. My sister Sam says that makes me a Leo, in the horoscope; things that tell you what your future is. Don't know what that's about but she says that means I'm a lion. King of the Beasts that's me. I like that. Sounds hard. You can work out the year yourself. I'm eleven anyways, so's you know.

Well the day it all started, my story, she'd really pissed me off – Mum that is – so I decided to go up the back. Mum was doing that thing again. Picking up these useless geezers from the pub and bringing 'em back. Then, when they piss off, she gets pissed off and then she gets pissed. Fuckin' great!

I love her and that – she's my mum, ain't she? – but she's fuckin' awful then. All crying and hugging me, and calling me her baby. The smell of drink off her is something rotten. Sam's no good: no help. She just goes to her room and turns the CDs, or fucks off out, so it's me that has to get Mum up to her bed. Does my head in, but someone's got to look after her, don't they?

But that day, she was really wrecking my brain, so after she conked out and I made sure she was alright, I went up the back with a can of lager the geezer left behind and ten fags I'd nicked out of his coat pocket earlier. I lift stuff off her blokes a lot. They're always so pissed by the time they get home with her, they never know – and I reckon they fuckin' deserve it anyway, just for messing with my mum.

The back where I go, is just over the road from my block, Bluebell. Dunno why they called us Bluebell. But on our estate everything's called something like that – Daffodil, Snowdrop, Crocus. It's a laugh. The only fuckin' flowers I've seen round here are in those picture cards they had round the top of the wall in primary – the alphabet ones with the word written out underneath in big black type so all the little nippers can learn to read.

Anyway, it's somewhere I go when I want to get away – the back. It's just a coupla streets of old houses left over from after they built the estate, I s'pose. It's funny. Our blocks are all grey and concrete like, but the houses on the back are all red with proper tiled roofs and that. They are like a little row of soldiers standing on the edge of the estate – except they're all falling down.

To get to the back you have to go past Marigold House and out into Hotspur Avenue, then slip through this corrugated iron fence. You can get through this bit where the pins have come out - well, actually I pulled 'em out - and there you are.

I've got a place there. It's just a house. One of the old terraces. Like, *really* old. There used to be loads of 'em round here. Built for the dockers. Back to back, two up two down. No bogs and that, just a shed in the yard for a toilet. Sounds dirty but my nan said they used to be nice in the old days. People used to look after 'em proper. *'Pride in the place and that,'* she said. She said, *'they went and cleaned their windows and even their doorsteps. Washed 'em even. Not like now. And the council didn't do nothing in those days either, so it was just people doing it themselves and keeping it nice.'* That's what she said, anyways.

So they were quite nice back then, Nan told me. But then, it all started getting a bit rundown round here and things changed. The work went and the families moved out and things went to shite. The houses became real dumps. Slums they were. No one really cared about the people that lived there. And a lot of them didn't care about themselves. Then there were the riots – something to do with the blacks and the police, I think, and it was pretty tasty with police cars being set on fire and gangs attacking the coppers with petrol bombs and that – and after that, anyone who could, moved out. The place was pretty much left like after a battle in the war, like. All burnt out and falling down and boarded up. And that's when the real shit started moving in 'cause it weren't like anyone else would live there.

The landlords let the houses that you could still live in to students; packed 'em in like rats. And then found even less fussy people to cram in on top of 'em. The immigrants. They'll live fuckin' anywhere 'cause most of them are illegals anyway, aren't they? That's what they say round here. It became the crappiest place in town to live, which is why the junkies started coming and the whole place became one massive shithole.

Then the council started bulldozing the lot and rebuilding new places. Big concrete estates like mine, with grey blocks of flats that look just like the fuckin' hospital 'cept with littler windows so you can't even see out – not that there is much to see round here except more shitholes – and little brick houses with tiny gardens out front. I mean *tiny*. You couldn't grow nothing there. Just a bit of grass, really. They spent a million and a half quid trying to persuade people the place weren't crap, but it still was even if it looked different, and everyone knew it, so even though they made all these new places, called them Bluebell and Daffodil and Crocus and shit, trying to make them sound nice, the only people who stayed were the junkies, the illegals, and people like my mum, who can't afford to go nowhere else.

Of course, it soon got clogged up with the crap that comes with crap people. Crap people always get loads of crap around them like crisp packets, and cans, and dog shit, and graffiti, and broken stuff thanks to little fuckers like me when I was a nipper, riding round on bikes and smashing things up. And 'cause no one cared, no one did nothing about it. Not even the council. I guess they felt dumb after they'd spent all that cash and it was still shite. But you'd think they'd be bothered and do something, wouldn't you? But they're not. And they don't, so it's a dump round here. Just one big fuckin' dump. But I don't mind it.

It's *my* dump.

Anyway, I do like it up the back where the old houses are. I like the buildings. It looks like Coronation Street, except with no people, although the hard lads on the estate still use the pub that's round the corner, *The Moderation*. It's still left standing right out on its own in a pile of rubble. It's not that far from the school where I go, which is funny really 'cause most people round here spend their time as kids in the school and then their time when they're grown up in *The Moderation*. Like I said before, no one travels very far from here – hospital, school, pub, cemetery. That's it.

A few of the old houses are still there, still standing properly with rooms and roofs and windows and doors and everything like real homes, and haven't even been smashed up yet. This old lady lived in the one I go to. My nan and my mum knew her. I asked Nan about it once. Nan never knew about me going there and Mum don't know either. No one does. But Nan always liked gassing on about shite from the old days so she never asked no questions about why I wanted to know.

Anyways, this old lady had lived there since she was a girl and she wouldn't leave – not even when the junkies moved in and the place stank of piss and all her mates went and told her to get out, too. But she didn't. Then the council tried to shift her when they were building all the new places but she still wouldn't go. She told them the only way they would get her out was in a coffin. Nan said, '*she told the council wankers to fuck off when they came round with their bits of paper saying she had to leave.* ' Tough old bird. I like that about her. And the council couldn't do nothing about it neither. They couldn't knock the street down with her still in it, so she won.

In the end she died, didn't she? She was in there for ages. Then someone noticed the smell, so the cops had to come and get her out, so she stayed 'til she wanted to go, well not as long as she wanted maybe, but you know what I mean. Like the police or the council didn't make her move or nothing, did they? She took her time, like.

I feel sorry for the old dear really. She weren't no trouble or nothing except to the council, and who gives a shite about that? I'd say she was pretty sound.

And she was right and all. The only way they got her out was in her coffin.

Anyway, then the street was left for fuckin' ages, which is pretty stupid since the council had moaned about needing to knock it down, and then when they could they didn't even bother. They went and boarded it up instead.

They stuck up these great shields of corrugated iron everywhere to stop the tramps getting in. But it don't take long for someone like me to get it off again, so they came and stuck them up all over again. Stuck a warning on and all with some cartoon bloke falling over with writing under saying something like, *If you go in here you'll fall over and die, which* is bollocks and everyone knows it.

So a few days later some fucker – not me – ripped all the corrugated iron off again along with their nancy sign. It went on for a while before they clocked on they were wasting their time sticking stuff up if someone was going to pull it down again, so they put these heavy duty metal sheets all over it. Armour-plated it was and it's only a dump of a house. You'd think they wouldn't be bothered. They don't seem to be bothered about much else round here.

That was nearly the end of that. The other fucker gave up pulling stuff down and decided it weren't no use. But I didn't. It wasn't long before I found another way in. I ain't saying exactly how 'cause I don't want loads of other fuckers going in there. Like I said, I go there to get away and I want to keep it like that.

It's my place. My den. For me.

Which was why it was so weird. That day. When it all started.

Like I said before, she pissed me off that day, Mum, so I went off up the back with my can of beer and my fags. It's a bit of a scramble over the waste ground behind the flats and then the houses are just standing there. I go round the back and wriggle through where it's all overgrown and then through the gap I made. When you get to my house, the old lady house, there's a bit where the boards've gone rotten and the metal plates don't reach – only I know where that is – I'm little enough to wriggle under and then I'm in.

It goes to what was the back room or something, I guess. It stinks in there. Kind of musty and that. Smells like old ladies but also some other damp, cold, mouldy smell like the outside sheds at school and like earth. It gets in your nose and ain't nice but you get used to it after a while. The fags help.

There's no furniture or nothing, just a little brown fireplace with kind of bathroom tiles on the sides of it that ain't seen no action for, like, ever, and pale green wallpaper with big pink roses on that look like mutant cabbages. I never stay in that room 'cause of it smelling funny. I head up the stairs to the big room at the front, which stinks the least and is the lightest cause it's got two windows where the metal's slid down a bit but it's too high for anyone to get in. I've got a blanket there to sit on and an ashtray and all. There's a fireplace there, too, just like the one downstairs with an old-fashioned grate and the tiles on the sides.

It's not a palace or nothing, but it's quiet. It's dark, too, apart from in that front room 'cause of where the builders boarded it up.

Which was why, once I got in, I was startled when I did

see a light. A fag lighter flicking quickly. Across the room. A flame. And a face. Bloke's face. Lighting a fag. Pale, pale skin. Bit like a girl. Long white fingers holding the fag in the way girls do, the other hand clutching the lighter. Older than me, fourteen or fifteen maybe.

But he didn't seem nothing like me. Kind of soft looking, with longish hair and a kind of lazy, sleepy way wiv him. Not sharp, quick, like me and my mates – know what I mean? He was dressed strange, too. Tatty clothes. Like he'd been sleeping in them. Big clumpy boots, jeans and some big overcoat – all black – with some girly-looking shirt underneath. Weren't that cold either. But it's cooler in the house than outside 'cause the sun don't get in there. I was just in my trackie bottoms, T shirt, and my hoodie and cap. I like to look the business.

When I saw him, I tensed, I did. You would, wouldn't you? But he just lit his fag and looked at me. He never moved, though. He was sitting down on the floor, writing in some book, and I was standing by the door, so I figured even if he got up and he was loads bigger than me, I could leg it before he got sorted. He looked bigger than me in a tall way but he didn't seem that *big*. Tall, yeah, but dead skinny and soft-looking. I could work that out even by looking at him sitting down, so I reckoned if he was some kind of mad perv or something, I could smack one on him at least, and then run like fuck if I had to.

I got up on my toes ready but he didn't do nothing. Just looked at me. Not staring funny like, screwing me out or anything, just looking; like you'd look at a picture and that, or a really cool sky at sunset when it's all red like blood, or at something you'd want to remember for a very long time like when you get a birthday cake, or that time Mum took us to see the big Christmas tree in town.

I didn't like him looking much, 'specially not saying nothing. It made me feel funny – nervous, like – so I said to him.

'What the fuck are *you* looking at?' I figured I'd give it a go since he weren't doing much. But he just said, *'Hallo.'* That's all. *'Hallo'*. Just all calm, like. I mean, what the fuck d'you do with that? I just kind of looked at him. I wasn't quite sure what to do, how to play it.

'This your gaff?' I asked after a while. I thought he might've been one of the junkies with an eye on the place to turn it into some smackhouse or something. But to tell you the truth, he didn't have that look on him – you know? That dirty, whingey, sick-dog look with mucky little fingers and those horrible glinty eyes they get. I looked into his eyes to see but they were clear. Funny colour, though. You know you get blue and brown eyes – well that's what you get in people, don't you, blue or brown? Well, his were kind of grey, a bit like the smoke coming off his fag.

He blew out a load of smoke. And then he said something. His voice was kind of posh like those fellas you get on the telly sometimes. Didn't talk like no one round here, anyway.

'No it's not mine. I just wanted to be here for a while,' he said.

I was a bit pissed off 'cause as far as I was bothered, this place was mine and I s'posed now I'd have to scrap him for it. I didn't really want to but that's what you have to do. Only, even if I did, it wasn't gonna do me much good, I figured, cause he'd still flipping cough about it to everyone, so I was a fucked either way.

Then he said, 'Do you mind?'

'Eh?' I think to myself. 'What the fuck's he on about? Do

I mind? Do I fuckin' *mind*?' No one ever asked me, do I fuckin' *mind* before. It's always do this and do that and *'fuck off out of it you little bastard.'* I thought he might be being funny or something so I said, 'Nah,' carefully, waiting to see what he did next.

He smiled slightly at me, then. 'Sit down. Do you want a cigarette?' He fumbled in his pocket for the packet. Players Special, Black. I quite fancied one 'cause the ones I got this morning out of the fancy man's pocket were low tar and it's like smoking air. Nothing to them. Horrible things.

'Yeah,' I said to him. I thought again and, just in case, I said quickly, a warning, like, 'I'm not gay or nothing,' and waited to see how he took it.

He gave a short laugh then. 'Heh. Neither am I,' he said, and looked me straight in the eye. I could see he weren't lying. Then he said, 'And even if I were, I wouldn't fancy you.' And he grinned and I laughed.

Nice teeth he had. Posh kids' teeth. White and straight not like mine. They're a bit knocked about from fighting now and one's dead so it's gone a kind of brown colour. Mum said they look like a broken fence and we'll get them fixed when we win the lottery. I'm quite glad we've got no money for stuff like that. I'm not a big fan of dentists. Or needles. Especially not needles.

It's funny 'cause when you think about what he said about not fancying me you could say he was starting on me – being larey, like, but I knew by the way he said it, he weren't. And it felt like he'd said something nice to me. Sort of teasing. Like when Mum's in a good mood – which ain't that often – and she calls me 'skinhead'. She knows I'm not. She's just joking about my hair. My number two crop. But the way she says it is nice. We'll be sitting there watching telly and she'll look at me and just say, *'Little skinhead.'* Nothing else. And for no reason. And I'll say something like, 'Gerroff' and then she'll say it again. *'Little skinhead.'* And then we'll look at each other and smile. It feels nice.

And when he said that, for some reason it was the same. I grinned at him. I decided to take the fag. 'Cheers,' I said. But I lit it myself.

I still had my can in my hand. It felt rude to take a fag and not offer nothing back so I held it to him. 'Want some?'

'Thanks,' he said, and he took it from me. He knocked back a good old swig straightaway. He didn't even wipe the top with his sleeve or nothing. I hate it when people do that; it's like you've got a fuckin' disease or something, so I liked that about him, and all.

As he leaned forward to take it, his coat sleeve shifted up his forearm and I could see this big red slash. 'You've gone and cut yourself there,' I said. He smiled and pushed the sleeve up to show me properly.

It was ace. I could see why I thought he'd been cutting himself - or someone had cut him. Right across his forearm was this big red slash. Scarlet. Then there was another slash, about the same length, cutting across it nearly from the inside of his elbow to his wrist. It looked just like blood. But when you looked closer you could see it was a tattoo.

'St George's Cross,' he said. 'England.'

'Quality.' It did look pretty cool. Just like a wound as if someone had done him. Or he'd sliced himself, like I said. I've just got a tattoo I did myself. On my arm. Did it with a pen and a needle out the domestic science drawer at school. Skull and crossbones. But it went a bit wrong. It's got funny teeth and the crossbones are all bent, so it looks really shite. Took fuckin' ages and all. And it hurt. But his was sound.

Then, I thought to myself. I mean, I like England same as anyone. Course I do. My country, ain't it? But there's weird fuckers around, and I don't want nothing to do with them. I mean I hate France and that. Argentina. Germany. 'Course I do. I'm English, aren't I? It's natural. But that don't mean I wanna do stuff to French people or nothing. It's like you hate them and you don't. Not the people. Just the thing.

See I'm English and proud of it I am. It ain't racist and it ain't BNP. Like I said, it's natural. But the way they go on about it, you think it were wrong, just saying what you want about being English. And they put you in prison for it they can these days. One of the cops told me once after I got done for shoplifting in the Paki shop. That annoys me. All these people living in my area - Chinese, Irish, Muslim, Scottish, black. All of them can be proud of what they are. But not us. Really fuckin' pisses me off, and the more I think about it, it really fuckin' pisses me off even more. But like I say, I don't have nothing against no one. I hate those muppets who go and firebomb the Chinese chippy or the Paki shops. That's just bollocks. Leave them alone. Everyone should leave everyone alone, I reckon. But it just don't work.

And before anyone thinks anything, robbing out the Paki shop ain't racist neither. It's just 'cause he's a bit of a muppet and never sees you so it's easy. Not to do with him being a Paki. Round here you just rob what you can get away with. Nothing to do with where anyone's from or what colour they are. Except you don't rob off old ladies and single mums. Not unless you're a real twat.

But England's a fuckin' mess, ain't it? And it don't work – all these people with no one getting on 'cause they're all too different? And then you got them suicide bombers flying about and all, which is really shite. But still, I hate them

British Bulldog boys. The fat fuckers you see in the pub and the politics ones that get on the telly. So, just checking, I ask him,

'You ain't BNP are you?'

'No. Just England. I mean, I'm part of it,' he stretches his forearm out to show the tattoo, 'and now it's part of me.' He smiled, kinda to himself.

'Football fan, then?'

'Well, yes, of course. My country. But it's a bit more than that. This isn't just about football'.

'Ain't it?'

'No.' He stopped then and looked away. I could see he wasn't gonna tell me but he weren't BNP. Dumb of me to think so really. He didn't look like he could fight his way out of a crisp packet. Maybe he felt the same about shit like I do. Anyway, for a minute I said nothing to see what he'd do.

Then he says to me. 'Why are you here?' I didn't mind him asking. It wasn't like – you know how most people just ask you stuff for what's in it for themselves. Why are you *here* and not somewhere else not wrecking my head? But it was just about me. He was interested, I could tell. And he'd given me fags, so I told him, 'I just come here to get away sometimes. I live on the estate.'

He looked at the wall and picked away a bit of peeling paper. Then he said, 'Mmm. I come here to get away, too. I've had enough, you know? I just don't want to live in their world anymore. Out there. I think I want to live here now.'

Not dangerous, then, I thought to myself. Just a bit looney-tunes. He didn't say anything so I said, 'What, all the time?'

'Yes. Maybe.'

Fuckin' weirdo, I thought, and I told him, 'You're a

nutter. You can't live here. I mean there ain't no proper toilet for a start and no lights. It's dirty and it smells funny. There's no sofa. No telly. You're having a laugh, ain't you?'

'Maybe.'

He goes kind of quiet again and the silence is making me feel a bit funny. Uncomfortable – nervous, like – like I did before when he was looking at me, so I says, 'Listen. I gotta go mate. Got to get on. Stuff to do and that.'

I hadn't but I felt like going back out onto the street. I needed to get a bit of the buzz back – noise, people and that – know what I mean?

He nodded.

'Bye,' he said.

'I'll see yer,' I said and legged it down the stairs and out through the gap, checking no one saw me getting back out onto the wasteground to the street. Then I headed down the rec near home to see if anyone's about.

I was just turning the corner into Galahad Grove when I see the white van. Only I didn't see it quick enough and they clocked me before I could leg it. Shit!

''ere sonny, can I have a word?'

Bollocks. The truancy patrol. I turn to face them and sigh. Caught. Bang to rights. There's nothing I can do. The sergeant knows me anyway so there's no point in doing a runner. They'll be round my house before I get there myself.

They come over to me. The sergeant. A woman copper. And the education welfare bloke. I know them all now. And they know me. But we still have to go through this stupid fuckin' panto.

'What's your name, love?' says the woman copper. They always call you *love*. The fellas call you *'son'* or *'sonny'* – or *'sunshine'* when they're getting pissed off with you. I look at the sergeant. He knows me, my name, my address and every piece of bother I've been in since I were a nipper. But we still have to do this. Every fuckin' time.

'Robbie. Robbie Terry.'

'And how old are you, Robbie? When's your birthday?'

I'm thinking, listen love, I know how old I am without having to work it out from my birthday. I'm not some div, so I give them the old date of birth spiel – the ten- oh-eight stuff – with a big sigh like they're really wasting my time, which they are. Even though I've got nothing to do, I can still do without this shite.

'Ah, so shouldn't you be in school today?'

I look at the old Education Welfare. Scribbling away he is on his little clip board. Funny. He's a nervous little muppet. He's speccy with funny greasy hair and looks like that bloke Hitler out of history. The one with the 'tache. This education welfare guy I've met before and he's such a twat he makes me want to shout 'Raaaaaah' at him, suddenly and dead loud, just to see what he does. Thing is, he's scared of us kids. You can tell, which seems weird to me. I mean if you're scared of kids, why work in Education Welfare? Seems mental.

I can't be arsed with him. He don't scare me, and even the coppers think he's a prat. You can tell that and all, just by the way they kind of pretend he's not really there, like when some shit kid at school is desperate to be mates with you and you and your mates try and ignore him all the time 'til he fucks off.

'I'm sick,' I tell them.

The sergeant rolls his eyes. He knows the score but Education Welfare just stares at me through his big milk-bottle specs and keeps writing.

'You don't look to bloody sick to me,' says the sergeant. 'What's wrong with you, then?'

'Bellyache. I was puking everywhere. Everywhere. Disgusting it was. Puked my guts up. There was puke on the walls and that. Then I got the runs. Well bad, it was, really bad. I –'

Just when I was beginning to enjoy myself, especially as Education Welfare had started to go a bit pale, the sergeant cuts me off, putting his hand up. 'All right, all right, sunshine, so why are you out and about and not lying in your sick bed? If you're so sick, that is?' He leans back and folds his arms, staring down at me under his cap. He knows I'm lying like shit and I know he knows, but that's all part of this game.

'Well,' I says, 'then, when I've puked everything up and I've had the almighty shits, I feel a bit better, so mum sends me out to the shop for her. To get some shopping.'

'You've passed the shop,' the sergeant tells me. He's trying not to smirk, the smart arse. He's just messing with me now.

'They didn't have what she wanted so I'm just going up the parade. The other shops,' I say, quick as you like. We could go on like this for ever. He knows it and so do I. Education Welfare's just scribbling. He don't know anything at all.

'We'll have to talk to your mum, Robbie,' says the woman copper. 'You know that.'

Shit. Bollocks. Not now.

'She's sick, now, too,' I says. 'Came on quickly when she asked me to go to the shops. She's in bed. Bad.' I nod heavily to make me story seem more true. It doesn't work.

The sergeant looks at me and sighs. 'Well, we'll have to talk to her sometime,' he says. 'And you, you have to be in school. You know that.'

'School,' Education Welfare parrots, nodding his head up and down like a toy dog. The sergeant looks at him like he's annoyed with him and wants him to shut up, then carries on to me. 'It's the law, son.'

It's all a big familiar game to both of us now, me and the sergeant. We do this all the time. Me truanting, him catching me, me lying, him sighing and then all of us going back up the school – including Mum – for more meetings and more forms to be filled in. The next bit is they have to take me home and talk to mum. Or take me to school. But I get a touch of the smarts. I can see Education Welfare's watch. Three thirty.

'School's over now. Half three, so it don't matter. Do it? I'll see yer, yeah?' I turn to go. Education welfare starts to panic and looks at the copper.

The sergeant sighs. 'All right, all right. Just make sure you're in school tomorrow. We'll be following it up, Robbie. And we'll be talking to your mother. You know that, so don't think this is over.'

I wave at him like he's just given me a party invitation. 'Yeah, sure. See yer,' I say and I'm off. The sergeant watches me go, still standing there with his arms folded, and I know this is only starting.

THE WASTELAND

I'm heading for the rec still. I've got some fags left and I reckon I might be able to swap them for a few swigs of something if there's anyone hanging around. I don't wanna go home yet. Not 'til later. Maybe after mum's gone to bed.

Bollocks to that lot, anyway. They know and I know it's a fuckin' farce. All except Education Welfare. The muppet; he believes all that shite, all the forms and all the, *'we tell you to do this and you do it and this is the rules'* and that crap. Even the coppers get pissed off with him so sometimes, I even feel sorry for him in a way. We all know it's a bunch of shite, whatever they do. But I can see some lads over by the swings so I head over there and forget about it all.

I didn't go up the back again 'til a few days later. The sergeant was right and fuckin' Education Welfare followed it up so Mum had to go down the school again and make it like I'd be there all next week. I said I would, more to get them off my back than anything else. Mum moaned at me a bit for not being at school. But not much. I think she likes having me around. It's a bit of company for her since she stopped working 'cause of the depression. She got the depression after dad left, Nan told me, but it got worse. And now she has it real bad. Except when she's drunk.

See these fuckin' Education Welfares, they don't understand. There ain't no time to go to school. It's not so bad for me – I mean I'd be lying if I said I was always off looking after Mum on one of her bad days. Most often, I'm just skiving 'cause I've got better things I want to do for myself. But Marty Malone upstairs from us, he's got seven younger brothers and sisters and with his dad gone and his mum out all day, who's gonna get them up and get them their breakfast and their tea and make them go to school and that? Marty does that since his dad left. And then these knobheads come round and try and get him into school instead. Daft it is. He's fourteen now so they've pretty much given up. Except when they get some new officer all keen, busy-bodying about with their stupid clipboard files. The old ones know to leave him alone. It's just a waste of everyone's time, in't it? Soon I expect they give up on me, which will be doing us all a big favour.

But I had to play the game this week else Mum gets fined. It is fuckin' stupid though. There's no point in me going to school; 'cause I ain't been so much, I dunno what they're on about in their lessons anyway. Half the rest of the kids are the same and the others don't speak English. It's a joke. We don't learn anything; we hate being there and the teachers hate being there even more. Even more than they hate us. But still, we all have to go through it over and over *'because it's the law'* as they keep telling me.

I always hated school. Since I was a nipper. Didn't like being shut up like that. I used to leg it out the door as soon as I could and go flying down the road. The headmistress was into keeping me in, so she used to grab me and lock me in a classroom all day just to have me there. Prob'ly so old Education Welfare wouldn't be after her. Although when you think about it, it's a fuck of a lot worse to lock a kid in a classroom all day than just let him go home. Anyways, that didn't last long. I found out how to open the window, so then they locked the window, so then I put a chair through the window. And after that, they gave up. To be honest, the teachers don't want me there anyway. Disruptive they say.

And I've been known to have the odd dust up. Bit short tempered, you know how it is. Someone says the wrong thing and off I fly. Whoooom! So it suits us all if I don't go at all. Everyone's happy. But every now and then, like the other day, they have to ruin it all by coming after me and writing lots of forms and then I put in the odd appearance 'cause I don't want Mum to have to go to court for me. However much she pisses me off sometimes.

Anyway, it was a few days later when I went up the back again. I'd been out that night down the rec. Billy Hughes had nicked a moped from somewhere and we was having a brilliant laugh riding round and round, trying to do doughnuts on the footie pitch and pulling mega wheelies off the side. Then the Amery boys turned up – Gavin and Dave. They're Dean Amery's brothers and they're nutters. No one'll touch them though 'cause they're his brothers and they know if they do, he'll do them. And he's the bollocks round here, Dean Amery. If the estate had a boss, he's that bloke. You wouldn't wanna mess with him. He runs the place. Big lad. 'bout thirty. Been in and out of inside since he was about fourteen and deals everything you want and more. He even kicked the big black dealers off the estate. There was war over it – and he won.

There ain't nothing goes on round here that Dean Amery don't know about and if you cross him – well, just say, I wouldn't want to be you. No way, mate. All the Amerys are hard. And when I say hard I mean, like, psycho. You don't wanna go there, so Gavin and Dave pretty much do what they like and they ain't nice to be around, so once they turned up and started pushing everyone about, I legged it. It's not worth getting in a row with them 'cause they don't care what they do. Gavin Amery burned his granny's house down once.

So I decided to home and get some dinner. Get to bed before mum came back from the pub. But there were lights on and music, so she was back already. And as soon as I got to the door I knew.

I could smell the fags and the aftershave and the drink as soon as I opened the door. Yeah, Yeah. She'd picked up some wanker again. A different one from this morning. There he was in my front room, watching my telly and playing my CDs. He looked at me, sitting back on the sofa there like some fat knacker, pleased with himself; big hairy belly poking through the gaping bits between the buttons on his shirt, legs all spread out, giving it the big 'un. Gave him a look, I did, but the fucker just smirked back. *'Doing your mum,'* his fat smirk said to me. *'And there ain't nothing you can do about it, you little shit.'* And the thing is, there weren't. And I hated it. And the shite knew it and all. He was laughing at me, he was.

I wanted to get out of there and tried to sneak past, but mum grabbed me. She smelt of drink and fags all covered up with some sickly perfume. It don't hide the smell. It just makes it thicker and breathing it in is like suffocating in some big sweet pudding. Catches in your throat like when you tried to stuff too many sweets in your gob when you were a nipper and you can't get your breath.

'And this is my baby.' She plants a big snog on the side of my face. It's all sticky with lipstick and leaves a bloody mark. I wipe it off and try to wriggle away from her. 'My baby,' she goes again. 'Isn't he beautiful?'

I fuckin' hate it when she's like this. Especially in front of some fat Charlie Big Potatoes like Jabba sitting fatly there on the sofa.

'Oh yeah,' he says with that same shit-eating grin. 'He's

really pretty ain't he? A real little darlin'.'

He said it kind of funny. Like it was nice but I knew he were getting at me. I give him daggers but Mum still had hold of me. She was swaying slightly, which ain't a big surprise seeing the tarts' trotters she had on her feet and the amount of drink she must've stuck down her neck.

She laughed. That stupid high, shrieky one. Pissed women's laughing. I began to feel like there was some big wriggly worm in my belly, moving about. I couldn't get away though. She had me tight. If she was a fella, I would have clocked her one. But she ain't.

Then this shite goes, 'Real pretty. Just like his mum.' He looked at her then. Made some horrible noise in his throat, like a dog growling, 'Worrr. Come here, sexy and let me get another slice of that gorgeous arse.'

I felt sick. He put out some big hairy arm towards her. She was loving it. Dirty cow. She was wriggling more than I was trying to get away from her and laughing all high pitched, 'Oh, oh, oh!' like she's pretending she's shocked. He grabbed her wrist and pulled, and I saw my chance. A little gap in her clutches and I pulled away and was out the door, I tell you. Didn't look round. I knew what they'd be at. Rolling on the sofa and all. Disgusting.

I heard her call after me, 'Take some money out my bag, love. It's on the side. Get yourself some dinner. Stay out as long as you want.'

Too right. I know what that means. *Fuck off and don't come back 'til we've finished messing.* Well don't worry, mum. That's something you can count on, missus.

I could hear them behind me, his rumbly voice, hers all girly. I got the money – a bit and bit more – and legged it fast as I could, slamming the door behind me. I had their noises ringing round my brain as I careered down the stairs and out into the night.

Thought I'd go up the chipper, down at Sned's Parade. Everyone hangs out there and I might run into some mates. It's alright, the parade, somewhere to go. Me and Danny Sears – he's like my best mate round here, well I'd hang about with him more than anyone else – we often just hang out down there. There's all what you need, the offy, the Spar, bookies if you're into that – think it's a mug's game myself – and the chippy. There's a chemist and a kebab, and another chippy run by Chinese guys, but I don't go there no more after I got a donner for my dinner one night and was sick as a dog for a week. There's a few big concrete sort-of-flower-pots outside, like huge round window boxes. But there ain't no flowers in them anymore, so they're all just filled up with fag ends and empty cans and that. It's an alright place to hang out though. Somewhere to have a fag and see what's going on, who's about, so that's what we do. 'til the Chinese guys get windy about it and phone the cop shop. Then plod 'll come along and move us on. It's fuckin' annoying but the Chinese guys keep getting done over, so they get a bit worried when there's a few kids hanging about. It's fuckin' stupid though when they ring the cops. 'cause they do that, it *makes* people wanna do them over. Don't seem to make much sense to me, I tell you. Still, I think they're alright. In spite of the donner.

Sometimes, there's a row. I've been trying to keep out of it recently. But you know how it is. Something just starts up and sucks you in. It's exciting when the big fights go off. I got some copper on the side of the head once. With a full can of cola. He went down like a tree – but I felt a bit guilty. Waste of cola, too. But I was Charlie Big Potatoes round the estate for a while, which felt quite nice. All these kids started kind of looking at me like I was something. Even the big lads give me the nod now. I saw Dean Amery and his mates outside The Moderation once when I was going home. That night, after the cop thing. I'm walking past and Dean goes, *'Alright, Robbie.'* I didn't even know he knew my name. And his mate goes, *'Hey look out, lads. It's the cop killer.'* And they all laughed but it felt kind of good, you know 'cause those guys are the business and normally you're just a cheeky little shit to them. Though, don't get me wrong, that didn't mean we were mates or nothing. I wouldn't dare give Dean Amery any cheek or I'd find myself on a one way trip, know what I mean? Most people round here wouldn't even dare say 'Alright' to him in case he took it the wrong way. You just don't talk to fellas like Dean Amery unless they talk to you, so I just grinned.

I still felt a bit bad about that copper, though I knew no one would grass me up. Not round here. But I didn't really mean to get him that bad. Didn't kill him, though, or nothing. Not really. 'Cop killer' was a joke. There was just a lot of blood; a fuck of a lot. But he was a cop. And he knew the score, didn't he? Or else he wouldn't be a cop in the first place, would he?

Anyways, cause of that 'cop killer' thing I still get loads of respect from the little kids. There's a bunch of nippers outside the chippy, getting their tea and all.

'Alright, Robbie,' says the cheekiest one. I know him. Ginger out of our flats. Well his name's Graham really but everyone calls him Ginger 'cause he's got hair that looks like his head's on fire. He's got a lot of bottle for his age 'cause he's only about six. I give him the nod, like I see Dean do if people do say, 'Alright' to him and I can see his little face all light up like he's now the big man 'cause I give him the nod.

Funny, ain't it?

Then I go and get my dinner.

The chippy was packed and stank of stale fat as usual. I had to shoulder it through the usual hard lads hanging around the door smoking and I get the expected smack on the head as I go past. Divvies. Think they're hard picking on kids. But I let it go 'cause I decided I wanted to go up the back and not get mashed in a fight with that lot.

And they let it go, too. One of them lives in my flats and knows me, see, so that was a result. No one went off on one, including me, which was good.

I got me chips and a sausage in batter. With the bit extra I'd taken out of Mum's purse just 'cause all that with Jabba had really pissed me off, I was flush. There was enough for a can and some fags and still a good bit leftover so I popped in the offy for some fags 'cause I could see the blonde bird was serving. The young fella was out the back and the girl always let me have them when I said they're for my mum. She ain't that bright, to be fair 'cause she ain't supposed to sell me them at all, is she?

Coming out with my little hoard, I'm wondering what to do. I don't really wanna go home. Not with those two messing about. But there's no one about so I feel a bit lost. Then I think of the back – and I think of that fella. In my place. My gaff. I kind of felt like going over there but maybe he's still there. I think of him living in the house, like he said. Maybe he was bluffing but I don't think so. He was probably some kind of runaway, a homeless or something. Maybe someone had done the pervy on him and he had nowhere to go.

But it was *my* place.

Then I realise: I don't even mind. He seemed alright. Sound. In fact, it'd be quite nice if he was there. I'd have someone to talk to who's not full of shite and doesn't treat me like a shite all the time.

I put my hand in my pocket to feel the shrapnel I got left. Enough. Maybe he hadn't eaten. Probably not 'cause he didn't look none too healthy if you ask me. Skinny. And there ain't much on me. And he didn't look like he'd be much cop at looking after himself to tell you the truth. I nip through the Jackie Chan crew again without much damage to me head and pick up the same again for him. If he weren't there, I could stuff it all myself, I think.

Then I head over the back. Had to wait about a bit 'cause I don't want no one to see me going in and there were a couple of pissheads outside *The Moderation* making dicks of themselves. By the state of them, they couldn't have seen their hands in front of their noses but you can't be too careful. Then the landlord comes out and boots them down the road to make their racket somewhere else and I see my chance. With a quick look over my shoulder to make sure no one was clocking me, then through the fence, over the wasteland and into the terrace. The house don't look much, standing there all silent in the dark with its metal shutters down. You couldn't see if anyone was in there. But that's the whole point, ain't it? That's why it's such a cool place to go. No one knows. If that kid was on the run or something it'd be the ideal place to be. He didn't look like a junkie, and didn't seem like the sort to have the law on his case – except maybe for looking like a weirdo. Maybe he's just got shite at home like me, I thought. I could savvy that.

Anyway, I snuck in round the side and went up to the top room where he was before. As I come up the stairs, I could see a flickering light, like off a telly. He was there. He'd lit all candles round the room and the shadows were jumping all over the walls like some kind of ghost movie. He was bending over one of them, that book in his hand again. The light made his face look kind of scary. All light and dark and nothing in between. He looks round quickly as I come in. *'You're not as dopey about watching your back as I thought,'* I thought to myself. He relaxed when he saw it was me.

'Hallo,' he said, just like before.

He looked like a magician in one of the books I got from school when I were a kid; all those candles around him made the place look like a grotto. Kind of pretty it were. It was sort of like when your mum took you to see Santa at Christmas but only in the posh ones in the big department stores where they make a bit of an effort. Not the crap ones down the shopping centre. There he was, lights all round him, his big coat – like a cape – still on him and that long hair falling all over his face. And, blimey, he was pale. Quite spooky. You would be creeped out if you didn't know he was alright. And I reckoned he was alright. And I'd know. I can always tell.

'Hallo,' I said, back. Now I was there, despite my brilliant idea that it would be a laugh and we'd get on and that, I felt a bit funny for a minute. Like maybe he had deep shite going on and maybe he wanted to be by himself. But, bollocks, I thought and got myself back, this is my gaff. And I stood there, holding my stash.

'Back again?' he said

'Looks like it, dunnit?' I said, all cocky like. I'm like that.

And we both grinned at each other across the room with the candles flickering up the walls.

'I got some chips.' I said to him. 'You want something to eat?'

'Excellent,' he said.

He was just sitting on the floor. There weren't no chairs

or nothing. I looked down. It was a bit dirty and the blanket I used to sit on seemed to have gone. He must have been using it to sleep with as I couldn't see anything else, just a few carrier bags in the corner. I knew there was a brush in one of the downstairs rooms. It was a bit chewed up like, like some dog had been at it but it were better than nothing and I weren't sitting down in that shite in me white trackie bottoms. You've got to be joking.

'Hang on a minute,' I said.

I went downstairs and got it and swept the floor. It was still a bit mucky so I took the chips out the placky bag and sat on that to keep me trousers clean. Then I unwrapped the chips and laid one of the big sheets of paper down like a tablecloth.

'Wait,' he said. 'We'll make a table. We should have a table.' He went to the carrier bags in the corner. I supposed that was his stuff. Not much of it. Couple of bags of clothes it looked like. That was all. He took out a big black pen and drew a big circle around my chips. What's he up to? I wondered.

'There's our table. Our round table. Now we can eat.'

'Nutter,' I said, but in a nice way and pushed him some chips as he sat down. 'What's all that about?'

'The round table. King Arthur and the knights. You know?'

'Nah, what's that? Something on the telly?'

He looked at me. 'No. Well, they did make films and things about it, but no. It's a story. True story. About a hero, a guy who lived in olden times. A long time ago.'

'A king, was he?'

'Yes, he was. But he was a leader of men. He fought England's enemies and had a band of knights who all had amazing adventures. Some a bit supernatural. They met giants and magicians and mythical creatures and people. Well, they say they were mythical but I know they were real.

'When they met it would be at a round table at their castle, Camelot, so there was no one at the head of the table, no most important seat; Everyone was equal. No one was better than anyone else.'

Sounded a bit daft to me so I said, 'Yeah, but he was the king, so he was better.'

'He didn't see it like that,' he said. 'To him everyone was the same.'

'But it don't work like that,' I said. 'Some people are better. Grown-ups and that. Clever people. Boss folk. Posh people. The guy that rules the estate round here. They're more important. They're better aren't they?'

'Are they?'

And then I thought about it. I'd never really thought about it before. I really thought about it. I thought about my dad, wherever the hell he is. I mean your dad's your dad, so he's supposed to be better. Someone to look up to. But if I had a kid I wouldn't fuck off like he did when I was a little and never see that kid, not even on birthdays and that, so maybe he weren't better. That didn't make him better did it? Maybe if he was a good dad he would be. But he ain't. Then I thought about Mum and what she does, which ain't great. And she don't look after us much like mums are meant to, so she ain't better. And I then thought about the Amerys 'cause they're boss round here, and they ain't really better. They just tell everyone they are and then kick the shite out of anyone who gives 'em lip, so everyone talks about 'em and treats 'em like they're special. Then I got confused because that's respect, innit?

But then I thought, well it ain't respect. People don't act

like that 'cause they respect them and think they're better. People treat 'em like that 'cause they're scared of 'em, so they're not better really even if they try and make everyone think they are. They're just total twats.

Then I thought of the cops and the teachers and the probation officers and social workers who are always ordering you around when really they don't know nothing. And you can forget *them*. Although, to be fair, a couple of the coppers ain't that bad. You can have a laugh with 'em. But, just 'cause they got a uniform that don't make them better, even if they think it does. And I thought of my sister. Like, she's older, so people might say that was better. But she's just a cow most of the time. So, not her neither, really.

And then I ran out of people to think about and I thought about me in the middle of it all. And it made me a bit cross, so I just said, 'S'pose not.'

The bloke wasn't talking any more, though. He was eating the chips and sausage, stuffing it in. It looked like he hadn't had any food for a bit.

I said to him, 'You living here, now?'

'Yes,' he said. 'I said.'

'Yeah, well, I thought you was taking the piss.' I shrugged 'That's cool.'

Then I said, 'You in bother?'

He looked at me. 'No. I just wanted to be somewhere else.'

'Cool.' I shrugged again.

He didn't want to say nothing more so I left it. But I wanted something to talk about so I said, 'Tell me about this fella. The king bloke.'

My belly was full now and if I'd been at home I would have wanted to be in front of the telly. But there weren't one, so I figured this would have to do.

He smiled and stretched back against the wall. 'Really? You want to know?'

I nodded. Like I said, no telly. He sighed – not a sad sigh, but like a happy kind of sigh. And then he started talking.

'A long time ago, hundreds and hundreds of years there was this man. Arthur, he was called. He was a warrior king, maybe in the fifth century, sixteen hundred years ago. Or perhaps more. At the time England – or Britain because it included Wales and Scotland. The Romans –'

I remembered them from school somewhere. The teacher must have been doing it one of the days I was in. 'I liked them. They were cool.'

'Yes. Anyway, the Romans had gone and the country was falling to bits. This king had stolen the crown from the rightful king – who he'd killed – and was doing a deal with the Saxons – who were from somewhere else, sort of Germany way – and letting loads of them into the country which people didn't like cause they thought they'd have too much power.'

'Kind of like us with the immigrants?'

'Yes, kind of like that. I suppose you could say that. In a way.' He screwed the chip paper up into a ball and dropped it onto the plastic before he carried on.

'Everything was falling apart. The leadership kept changing because although the rightful king's son, Aurelius, – he was the son of the one that was killed – took the throne back, he got poisoned by the Saxons –

'The ones what came in? The immigrant ones?'

'If you like. Anyway, no one knew what was going on –'

'Sounds like a bit of a mess alright.'

He didn't seem to mind me butting in. Just sort of ignored it and carried on. 'His brother Uther Pendragon took over.

And he was Arthur's father – Arthur was the king, the one I told you about before, the one who had the round table. Arthur was born at this place in Cornwall, down in the West Country. A big castle high up on the rocks over the ocean, right at the edge of England, Tintagel. Arthur's father died when he was fifteen and because of that Arthur became king, as a teenager. At about the same age as I am now.

'The country was still a mess with everyone fighting each other. But though he was only young to be a king, Arthur managed to bring peace back, stop everyone fighting, and made people proud again. Made England, really. Or what the core of England is....' he paused '...or should be.' He sighed again, that good sigh.

I said, 'Fuckin' hell. Some geezer. If he was a kid really. Like us.'

'Well, yes. He was young. But his elders had not done too good a job - '

'Made a real pig's arse of everything, did they?'

He smiled. 'That's right. Just because someone is older, it doesn't necessarily mean they are wiser, or that what they do is right.'

'Yeah. Well I know that right enough,' I said with a snort.

And that's the thing ain't it? When you think about it. You know what? I sometimes think I could do better myself. Than all of them. I mean, you look at guys like Educational Welfare and you've got to wonder. I don't know that I ever got any fuckin' education or any fuckin' welfare out of him filling in his stupid forms. And as for mum, she don't even cook or anything, and sure as fuck, a lot of what she does with the drinking and the blokes can't be right, can it? So I could see what he was saying and I understood what he meant by better – or not better at all. Yeah, I reckon we could do a better job than most of them sometimes.

Thinking of Mum made me wonder if it was alright to go home. All this brain thinking stuff was doing my head in a bit.

'Well, I best leg it,' I told him, getting up off the floor.

He shrugged. 'Okay.'

That was cool as well. He didn't want to know where I was going or anything and he didn't seem pissed off either. Actually, he looked a bit like he was the kind of bloke who didn't get pissed off about anything.

He just said, 'Thanks for the food.'

''S alright.'

I headed off back home but when I got there the lights were still on and I just didn't fancy it at all. Not with those two still up and messing about with each other, so I wandered back up the parade to see if there was anything going on. Gavin and Dave Amery were there and a few of their mates. They'd nicked a wheelchair from somewhere and were shoving the little kids in it and pushing them down the hill. They were having a right laugh but I didn't really feel like it so I just wandered up the town for a bit.

The town was kind of empty, like it is at night. Funny that. In the day like, it's all busy and shops, and people, and mums with kids, and blokes in suits, and noise, and cars, and cops, and lorries, and builders, and workmen, and buses - everything. Then nighttime, it's just black-and-glass-and-dirt-and litter, like the whole world is over and everyone left. There's the odd pub, with lights and noise, but behind glass, like a little cave of people. That's where I'd go if I could, and get a drink. But they won't let me in.

Sometimes, you can see people in their houses. They

leave their lights on and the curtains open and you can see in. Sometimes, I stand and watch them. It's like watching the telly. Looking through the window like it's a big plasma screen or the cinema, watching people eating dinner and talking and laughing or playing with their kids, or watching the telly themselves. And it makes me feel warm watching them, even though I'm not part of it, though I can kind of pretend I am. It's funny how light makes things seem warm, and dark makes things seem cold, when it's a different thing really, innit?

But tonight it just pissed me off seeing people in their houses, being warm and being happy together when I was cold and miserable and my home was shite and didn't look like that with warmth and smiling people all together.

Maybe I was just bored, I think. I couldn't think of anything to do 'cause I didn't want to go home 'til Mum and Jabba had gone to sleep so I didn't have to see or hear them, so I carried on just wandering about and I got to kind of thinking about the stuff the guy had said. It would be cool, wouldn't it, if you could just get some king to sort it all out for you? That would be great. If someone just came along and made everything okay. And you could just go, 'Listen, mate, I've got a problem' and they'd just sort it out. Someone who could bring back peace and make everyone happy, like that Arthur did. Yeah. That would be ace, that would.

I went back. Up the back. My gaff. I don't know why really. But I did. Maybe I just ran out of places to wander about. He was still there, that guy. I could see the lights. And it felt kind of warm. Kind of warm looking at it, a bit like the feeling I used to get when I looked through people's windows, so I went back in. He was just there, like before, in that room, reading a book, in his coat, looking weird. He just looked up at me like he'd been expecting me all along.

'Hallo, again' he said.

I stood by the door.

'What you doing?'

'Reading.'

'Yeah, I can see that, dumbass,' I said.

'I'm reading about Arthur. The King. It's good,' he said.

'Yeah? Go on, then. Tell us.'

He smiled again, and kind of shifts how he's sitting. He starts talking and his face lights up when he tells the stories – almost like he's a bit mad. But not in a scary way.

He took a big breath in and out before he started, like he was going to tell me something really important.

'Arthur was only a teenager,' he started, 'but he was a tough guy and a brave soldier and he fought the barbarians to make England safe again.'

And – you know what? No shit – it's kind of exciting and interesting when he talks. Not like school when the teachers are banging on about something and look even more fuckin'bored than we do, which you wouldn't think possible but, believe me, it is. Even though I don't get all his posh words, it doesn't seem to matter, so I sit down and say, 'Go on,' but he's kind of not listening to me anyway. It's almost like he's just talking to himself.

He goes, 'Everyone was happy and there was no more fighting. He built this wonderful court around him at Camelot, his castle, and even though he was in charge and had a team of knights, there were rules, ways of behaving. The powerful people looked after the weaker people instead of bullying them and making them afraid. The knights weren't allowed to just go round and beat people up. They had to look after the old and the women and children and if they fought it was always fair and for something they knew was right. It wasn't just being aggressive or showing off for the sake of it. And people all over the world knew of Arthur and what he had done to make things better.'

'What were the knights like? Sort of like X-Men?'

He looked away then, all dreamy. 'Oh, no. They were fantastic. They had the most wonderful names – Galahad, Gawain, Lancelot. Beautiful names.'

I thought I'd heard of that last one so I said so. 'He was wicked, weren't he?'

'You could say that.'

'So they were kind of like Arthur's mates? His gang? His crew?'

He thought. 'Yes, I suppose they were.' It was funny this way he had of thinking before he said anything, like it really mattered what he was going to say next.

'What happened to the King?' I asked. 'In the end.'

'He was killed in the end. He had a bit of … woman trouble, I suppose… then then his nephew, Mordred, turned against him and he ended up being fatally injured in battle and lay dying. He had a magic sword which was meant to protect him against harm but it ended up being used against him.'

'Oh.' Seemed a bit of a crap end to a cool guy. I shrugged, 'Women, huh,' and nodded. It was the sort of thing I heard blokes moan about outside the pub when I hung about. I didn't really know what it meant but it seemed the thing to say.

He got excited again, then, like he hadn't even heard me. 'But, the best bit is, it doesn't end there. Because then, when he was dying, his knights took him to the side of a lake and then, out of the mist, a barge appeared and on it a number of ladies all veiled in black. They carried his body on to the barge. Everything was destroyed, it was all over and he was dying, but he told them – ' and stopped then and said in a kind of posh actor's voice – '*I must go to the Vale of Avalon there to be healed of my grievous wound. But be you sure that I will come again when England has need of me, and the realm shall rise once more out of the darkness. But if you hear never more of me, pray for my soul.*''

They were funny old words and I didn't really have a fuckin' clue what he was on about, but the whole thing kind of made me go all shivery.

'They say he is only sleeping,' he went on. 'Arthur and his knights are still around, in a cave somewhere deep in the country – and when England needs him, Arthur will bring his knights back to save us.'

I thought for a bit. 'He'd better hurry up, ain't he?' I said. Then I sat back and said, 'Cool.' It was kind of what I'd been thinking before. That's kind of nice, innit? That there's someone out there going to look after you. Take over. Sort it out. It's kind of nice to think it, even if you know it's all a load of crap. I said, 'What did he look like?'

He went over to his bags and pulled out that weird, old notebook he always seemed to have every time I saw him. It was tatty with pictures of old paintings glued to the outside, one of a knight, all in armour 'n lying on a tomb. The writing was mad. He'd written on it THE CHRONICLES OF ALBION – whatever the fuck that meant. Inside, there was lots of mad writing and little drawings – done by him, I supposed. He opened it up and showed me. Mad writing but way better than mine. I can't do joined up at all 'cause I weren't in school for that. I used to try but it usually goes wrong so I gave up. His writing was funny, small and all over the shop like some mental inky-legged spider had gone on an acid trip all over the page. I couldn't read it – but the drawings were well good.

'You're kind of like, shit good, you are. These are fuckin' legend.' I told him. They were and all.

There were drawings of these blokes, olden times' blokes with all long hair and that. They were funny looking, bit like angels, except they had no wings and they had these big sad old eyes on them. Skinny and a bit girly they were in long dress-type things, although some of them had swords and armour over the top, so they they still seemed cool – despite the dresses. There was a blondey-haired one that came up again and again. He had the saddest face.

I said, 'This one looks like you, innit?' and he smiled a sad smile.

Some of the drawings were in these crazy countrysides with loads of trees and brambles and bits of river and that. They were kind of sad and creepy in a way but they were really good. Way better than stuff they put on the walls at school, and they only put the best stuff up there or stuff that hasn't even been done by kids but the school buys out of shops in frames and that.

So, I told him. 'They're well good. These. You should be on the telly or something. Or make posters and that.'

He smiled and pushed some hair off his face. He looked a bit shy for a minute.

'Except your writing's shite. I can't read that,' I said it to make him laugh. But he didn't, so I said, to make him feel better, 'Better than mine anyway. I can't write at all really. Can't read much either. But I think your book's well cool.'

'Thanks,' he said.

'Here,' I said – it seemed right to introduce myself properly now. 'My name's Robbie. What's your name?'

'Albion,' he said. Honest, that's just what he said.

'Yeah. Right,' I goes. 'What's your real name?'

'My name is Albion.'

'Okay,' I shrugged.

If that's how he wants it, Albion, it is. I already knew he was a bit of a weirdo, but, you know, I didn't mind. It was kind of interesting. And the book was well ace. But I couldn't call him Albion could I? It sounded like a fuckin' hatchback. Ford Albion or something. I decided he'd have to be Albie, to me anyway. Like Miles had to be Milo. Miles is Danny Sears's cousin and he had to be Milo 'cause Miles is a girl's name. Albie was an okay name. Kind of like a cross between Alfie and Albert. Sounded much better I reckoned. *Albion*, for fuck's sake! I ask you.

He was very quiet so I got the feeling then he wanted to be on his own and I didn't mind. I looked out the window at the clock on the school in the distance. It was two in the morning, so I figured it was okay to go home.

I said. 'I got to go home now. Your book's well good. Fuckin' quality it is.'

I got up off the floor. 'You gonna be alright, mate?'

'Yes,' he said looking right back at me with them big, old, funny-coloured eyes on him. He looked a bit like he might cry for a minute, but he didn't and he said, 'I'll be fine.'

When I was just about to head down the stairs, I stopped and looked back at him again. He was a bit of a state to be honest. Clothes hanging off him, hair a bit lank. In need of a few more good meals and a bit of a tidy up, if you ask me. I was a bit worried leaving him, actually. I mean he was bigger than me and that and fuckin' brainy but there was something about him that made me worry for him, you know. I didn't know how good he was at looking after himself. And you can't be too careful round here what with junkies and tramps hanging about and that. And the hooligans over the pub. They don't take too kindly to someone who looks a bit different. And that was him alright.

'You wanna be a bit careful, you know.' I said to him. 'There's junkies round here and all sorts.'

'I'll be fine,' he said again, but this time he smiled. He paused and then he said, 'Thank you.'

I decided I liked having him in my gaff.

The Chronicles of Albion.

The little rat boy came again today. He with the fighter's face and know-it-all smirk. He came with a gift for Albion, son of Brutus, brutal Brutus. I ate of his food as earlier I had drank of his wine. And outside, I heard the drunken archangels sing.

Ach. Who would see them any other way?

An army, marching on its beer belly. This Spartan army. Dressed in their sponsor breastplates, George cross a-dripping, colours nailed to their arms in stagnant green and bloodied-blue. Stouter hearts have none, but these days, my good sir, they draw their own front lines and choose their own battlefields. And there is danger there indeed.

GATHERING

The next day, I got some dinner for him again. I wanted to hear some more of the stories and more of them drawings and stuff and I was still wondering what he was up to.

I had to get some dinner for me anyways, so I thought I'd do him and all and take it round there to eat again. Mum and Sam were out when I got back. Sam lost the spare key ages ago so I couldn't get in. I had to climb over the bins and wriggle in through the toilet window with the bust catch, which is none too funny as the window ain't really big enough and there's a big drop on the other side as well. Then when I did get in, bashing my ankle on the basin for my trouble, there wasn't any fuckin' food in anyway, and no money lying around for me to get any tea, so I had to go on the rob. And I was well pissed off. And starving.

The shopping centre's always the best bet for nicking. Not the big new one up by the motorway 'cause there's too much security. There's big ugly fuckers like night club bouncers all around and they ain't above giving you a bit of a doing over if they catch you. I got my arm twisted up my back and a great big crack on the head the last time I got caught for it. I ended up in the juvie courts for that but I only got one of them order things. That just means you have to go up and chat to some bird up the probation office every week or so, which is a piece of piss. You know what they want to hear; how you're sorry and you won't do it again and it's really hard at home with your mum all depressed and without your dad and blah, blah, blah. Then they go 'poor you, poor you' and it's a laugh. Then you can do whatever you want.

The last one I had used to take me for tea down McDonalds 'cause I said there was no dinners at home. Me and this other lad got her car once and drove it round and round the probation office car park for a laugh. They were all watching out the window panicking and they ran out after us round and round, waving their arms trying to get us to stop. We did, but only when we got bored. And they never even told us off or nothing. They feel sorry for you, like. But, you know, at the end of the day, it don't do no one any good, none of this probation shite. I mean it didn't stop me robbing or anything, and it seemed to make the bird sad as well. She always looked sad when she was talking to me. But then, she seemed to be one of those weird people who like listening to sad stuff from kids. Fuck that! If I was sad I'd make sure I went and had a laugh. Go to Disneyland or Alton Towers and stuff. Not listen to kids out of the juvie courts all day.

Anyways, I decided to give the big shopping centre a miss after that. They can spot you a mile off when you go in and they know you ain't buying anything. I go to the old one on the other side of the rec. It's a bit near school for my liking but there's a couple of shite supermarkets there. They're run by a couple of Indian families. Little places stuffed with shite so it's really easy to lift something. The aisles are so tiny you can't even squeeze down without touching the side of the shelves so it's easy to knock a few things in your pocket or the front bit of your hoodie top if they ain't too bulky.

It's funny how much harder it is shopping for two, but I managed a small carton of juice, a couple of those flat rolls and a packet of ham. The cheese I could pay for. It wasn't much but it was better than nothing. There was no butter but I had an idea and dropped in the chippie on the way and ummed and ahhed, pretended I didn't know what I wanted and managed to lift some of the packets of mayo off the counter so the rolls wouldn't be too dry. It was the best I could do.

But when I got to the gaff, Albie wasn't there. All his stuff was there, so I reckoned he was still living there and had just nipped out or something. I made up the sarnies as best I could and I sat there by myself in the dark for a while to see if he would come back. But he didn't, so I went home. I left him a sarnie on what I reckoned was his bed – this pile of blankets and coats and stuff on the floor, so he'd find it alright. When he came back.

ÇHE ÇHRODIELES OF ALBIOD

Stand by me my apprentice. The urchin left me food. Climbed down from his chimney and brought me what he could. Left me food and in his heart a smile from that cracked mouth of his. Darkling, I listen and over the rooftops I can hear the quiet whisper, the silent scream of hundreds, nay thousands, more. Brush boys and wretched girls. Silent screaming. And what purpose be there in screaming, when thou knowest no one will come. But I will come my apprentice boys and serving girls. I will come.

THE BEAST

Everything really kicked off the night I got pissed, up the rec. Danny Sears was there and he had a two-litre of cider and the Baxter twins off our flats had a half-bottle of voddie so we mixed it up with a can of Red Bull I tea-leafed out the Paki shop and there we were. Tasted fuckin' rank but did the job alright. Later on, Danny's cousin, Milo, came down. Now Milo ain't really one of us but he's alright. His old man and Danny's are brothers but Milo's dad made a bunch of cash out of flogging cars and now he thinks he's dead posh and tries to forget he's really just a Sned's kid like the rest of us. Milo lives up the new estate where they have proper gardens out the front and a garage next to the house. Danny said they have a patio and a back garden with grass and a barbeque they cook nosh on. He says it's well good. Milo's old man is a bit of a wanker and his mum's a stuck up cow but Milo's alright as it goes. Milo ain't his real name. His real name's Miles, like I said, but 'cause that's a twat's name we call him Milo. He likes that.

Milo bought another half-bottle of voddie and it weren't the cheap stuff either. Pretty handy he is to have about to be fair 'cause he'll always bring something along. He nicks it out of his dad's drinks cupboard. They've got so much they never notice. Imagine. A cupboard in the room, just of drink. Except they call it a cabinet, Milo said, so we stuck Milo's bottle in the mix as well.

Anyways, that night we was drinking, just chillin'. Lying on our backs on top of the kids' roundabout and looking up at the sky, all blurry it was with clouds like smears. Zammo

Baxter starts spinning us which is a real buzz. Your head gets mangled trying to keep up as you go flying round and it's well mad. But then Milo started to feel a bit sick so Danny took him home and the Baxter twins decide to head off as well. They wanted to go over to Katie Hiller's to see if she was up for it.

I didn't want to go. Katie Hiller lives up the posh estate where Milo's from but you wouldn't think so since she behaves like a big old chavvy slut and lets anyone have a feel. Not me. I wouldn't want it. She's a total slag. I mean think of it, going where all your mates have been, *and* some of the chavvy scumbags and all. You might think I'm a bit young for that kind of stuff but, like I say, things are different round here.

I dunno what time it was. About one I suppose 'cause we saw the cop car doing the late night tour in the distance. Anyway, I stayed there for a bit just slowly spinning round and then I thought, *'I'll go home and go to bed'*.

I was pretty pissed out my nut. I find out when I tries to get up and it takes a long time and makes me feel a bit sick. I say, 'Laters' though and wander off. I've got the wobbly ankles thing and I can't keep a straight line so I have to walk all wiggly to get anywhere, which makes me laugh. My body's all mashed but my head's still buzzing from the Red Bull, which feels alright but a bit fucked up.

The lights are on when I get home and Sam's coming out as I go in. She gives me one of her looks and gives me that 'Ttttt' sound she's always doing these days as she passes. I dunno if it's at me or if it's at what's going on inside. With the lights on and the curtains half closed at this time, Mum's got someone in.

Sam always seems to be in a mood these days. Or most

times anyway. I can't talk to her any more. Sometimes, she's alright, like when she's chillin' out on the sofa and she'll let me play a song on one of her CDs or she'll read me my star sign out of the back of one of her magazines or out the paper, but then it's like she suddenly remembers she's not supposed to be nice to anyone and she'll push me away from her with her foot and start 'Tttt-ing' and tell me to, "Fuck off!"

It's funny, about Sam. You look at pictures of her when she was a kid and she was really cute. Well pretty with blonde hair, all curly, and a happy little smile. Miss Smiley Sunshine, Mum used to call her. But now she never smiles, always looks all cross and frowny and her hair is all dyed chip-shop-girl-blonde and kind of rough looking, not pretty and yellow and fluffy-soft like it used to be. I've changed, and all. In my old photos, I'm a funny, chirpy little nipper with big goofy teeth and a round chubby face on me. You wouldn't think it now.

Anyway, I go in. I want my bed. I open the door. Jabba from the other night is there on the sofa with Mum. She jumps up as I come in.

'Here's my little boy,' she says – or tries to and then falls back down. Pissed. He looks up. I can see he hates me, really screwing me out, like. And he's got all my CDs out again, all over the floor. I look back at him. Mum is still trying to get out of the chair. Finally, she makes it – which is a fuckin' miracle – and it's all, 'Let's get a drink for my baby,' and she's off wobbling on her slut shoes to the kitchen to get me a can. They've had a few already, by the state of her and the empties on the carpet. The way she's walking – Jesus, Fuck! And I thought *my* balance was fucked up.

I don't want anything to drink. I'm holding onto the door frame to keep myself from swaying all over the shop as it is and I'm really pissed off now, having seen that shit-head here again. She comes wobbling back with the can. It's that cheap stuff from the supermarket.

'One for my baby,' she says. She gives it to me but nearly misses my fuckin' hand completely 'cause the silly bitch can't see straight by now. Then she starts laughing. 'One for my baby and one more for the road.' She's singing, or trying to, some fuckin' old tune. Jabba's smiling at her, showing his teeth, but he's looking at me if you know what I'm saying, his eyes all gimley and mean.

'Come and have a drink with us, baby,' she goes, trying to pull my arm to drag me into the room and nearly hitting the deck herself.

'Nah. Going upstairs,' I mutter.

'Aw, come on, honey,' she goes again.

I try and move past her but it's hard 'cause I'm all levered off my face and so's she. She's grabbing me and I have hold of her to try and stop myself falling over. We're all over the place. We must look like decrepit old ones dancing.

Then *he* fuckin' butts in. 'Do what your mother tells you, can't you?'

What's it to him? 'What's it to you?' I go.

Mum stops then. She's looking from him to me and me to him and back again. Her eyes are all glassy with drink, but she's trying to work out what's going on. She's confused. I'm not. I know exactly what's going on, so does he.

He picks up one of my CDs. He says nothing but he doesn't move his eyes off mine. Still locked on looking at me, he balances the CD on one hand, his finger through the hole in the middle. Then he takes his fag, taps the ash all over the silver bit and then grinds the stub right in after.

I lose it.

'You fuckin', fat *wanker*!' I yell. And as I do it, I can see spit coming out of my mouth. I know I've lost it completely now but it's too late. It's like I'm looking at myself thinking, 'Don't be stupid,' as he's ten times my size after all. But it's done now and I've lost it. That's what always happens. Someone will do something to piss me off and it's like a switch flicks in my head and off I go.

I've still got the tin of beer in my hand so I chuck it as hard as I can at his big fat fuckin' head. It misses, but hits the wall with a dirty great thwack. As it does, a big arc of lager comes pissing out all over him.

'Mi Ralph Lauren!' he cries all high and cross as the beer lands down in a lash right across his shirt. As if it's fuckin' Ralph Lauren, anyway, and not some cheap market knock-off. But I've done it now.

He jumps up then and tries to grab me, but I'm too quick and duck behind the chair, shoving it into him and getting him a good one in the shins.

He yells, 'You little bastard! C'mere!'

As if I'm gonna. His big hairy arm comes over the back of the chair then, grabbing at me. Mum's still standing there, swaying and I can't get anywhere without shoving her into the stairs to get her out of my way and hurting her and I can't do that. Jabba gets hold of my arm and twists it real hard 'til I have to yell, even though I really didn't wanna; didn't wanna give him the satisfaction however much it hurt. And it well hurt, I tell you.

With the other fist, he clocks me a good'un on the side of my head. My ear's burning now, my brain banging like a ball bearing in a kiddie's toy while he's roaring at me, 'I'll teach you a lesson, you little shit!'

I relax a bit so he thinks he's got me and he gets close enough for me to get him back. As soon as he does, I lean over towards him, open my mouth as wide as I can and bite him hard on the arm, hanging on like a dog. He yells and lets his grip go. 'You dirty little bastard.'

But I'm away and out the door and legging it down the road before he even knows what happened. I go straight to the gaff to see Albie.

I run all the way, which is funny since I was so pissed before and couldn't manage it them. But I find when a scrap starts you can go from pissed to straight just like that. I crash my way in. He's sitting on the floor, writing in one of his little books as usual. He looks a bit surprised but in the calm way he has. I'm just standing there, panting and that, like some old black-lung tramp.

Then I feel sick.

And then I am sick. Real projectile vomit all over the floor. It nearly puts me on my knees it does, the force of it, and it just keeps coming. Albie jumps up and picks me up like I'm a sack of shite. He puts his arm right round my middle, with me bent over double with the puking. I'm so wrecked he has to carry me like that under his arm to the toilet as I puke my ring up everywhere. Over and over again 'til I think my guts are gonna come out my gob and all. And then I stop. I feel all cold but sweating at the same time.

'Sorry,' I say, when I've stopped retching.

I don't tell him what's happened and he don't ask me. Unlike them nosey probation wankers. But the funny thing is, it was like I didn't need to tell him. Sounds bollocks but it was like he knew anyway

You can just stay here now,' he said.

So I did.

THE CHRONICLES OF ALBION

Bursting through the door like a whirlwind and the skinniest one have I seen in all time. He was but a child, the ratboy, broken by those who were meant to give him safety and succour. He came to be helped, puking loud, like a fiend hid in a shroud. And one would not have thought so many undone. Only I knew. I always knew, my good sir. An unwelcome birthright perhaps but what one knowest, one cannot unknow. Socrates or the pig, indeed.

THE BUILDING OF CAMELOT

It was kind of nice in Albie's company. You could relax, you know. He weren't ever nasty. Just all calm about everything. Even though he didn't say much. He was the only person I ever met – 'cept my nan that you didn't have to watch your back with.

He gave me a blanket and I lay down on the floor next to him. I fell asleep straightaway. Imagine that. Falling asleep with some bloke you dunno beside you. You'd think you'd be staring at the ceiling all night blinking, wouldn't yer? But that's what happened. Honest to God.

Slept good, but the next day when I woke up I felt well shite so I went down the shop to get some Luco and some for Albie and some stuff to clean up all the puke properly. I managed to lift half of it and the dim bird was in the offy again so I took my coinage in and got a couple of cans to get rid of the jittery feeling.

Then I start on the house. I mean if I'm staying there, I'll have to get a few things sorted, like, 'cause it were a bit of a dump. Bed ferra start. There's a sleeping bag at home in Sam's cupboard so I sneak back real quiet to get in. The sleeping bag smells a bit musty but it'll be good and warm. My room, few clothes in my bag. I can hear this snoring through the wall and I know Jabba's in Mum's room. I try and pretend I don't hear it. Try and block it out. Hope his arm fuckin' hurts.

I take my CD player. Nan give me this banging one. We bought it together just before she died. Me and her, up the shopping centre. Nan. I liked her. Still miss her.

What else, what else? Sounds.

My sounds are in the sitting room. Still all over the fuckin' floor. The one he used as an ashtray is totalled, the twat, but the others, I clean up and put back in their cases all neat like I like 'em.

In the kitchen, there's nothing much. I take washing powder, biscuits and a bottle of whisky and a couple of notes out of Jabba's jeans pocket, lying on the floor at the bottom of the stairs. I get some milk and some teabags as well. You gotta have tea, innit? And I get a bucket and mop. I'll bring 'em back later. Not that they're ever used much in our house. I'm thinking hard. Lecky. I know what to do 'cause of mum's a bit useless.

Back at my gaff, water's not been turned off thank fuck, otherwise last night would have been messier than it were. The mains supply the primary school so everything was still working. It just ain't been used for a while. Lecky was something else.

I have a crackin' idea. I'm well proud of myself sometimes. I ring up the lecky people, tell 'em my Nan's moved and give 'em the address of the gaff. They say they'll do it that afternoon. Bob's yer uncle. Simple.

On the way round, I drops round MaccyDs and nick some packs of sugar and milk and some cups off the counter. I took some straws and some napkins and all. Dunno why really. They were just there and I thought they might come in handy. And then I pop into the supermarket and buy stuff for cleaning floors and toilets and kitchens and windows and sinks, and everything. It's amazing how much different stuff there is. I just get the cheapest, nuclear-looking stuff. Whatever we don't use, you could prob'ly flog off to the junkies and tramps to get off their faces. With what I had left over, I got a coupla tins of beans and some spuds.

Albie was a bit shocked to see me, armed with all my stuff – my cloths and buckets and that. I musta looked like some mental old Mrs Mops. But I put him to work and to be fair, he had a go, even though he was a bit useless and insisted on keeping his coat on, which was dumb cause it just got all dusty and he couldn't really put his back into the job.

I attacked the bathroom, which was disgusting. Horrible thinking about who was there before and how long it had been dirty for. But I attacked it hard and it looked pretty okay when I finished. You wouldn't want to sit on that toilet before, I tell yer. No wonder I was so sick the other night.

The kitchen was filthy, too. I got on my knees and cleaned out that oven but I had to throw out the trays and that 'cause they were filthy. Just fuckin' disgusting. Black gunk all over them. In the cupboard there was a few knives and forks and a bit of china left by the last person. I washed them a few times to make sure they were clean enough for us to use 'cause we had to have something.

That night, I cooked some dinner. The first. Beans and mash, I did. Albie tried to help me make the mash. He didnt really know what to do.

'Bleedin' 'ell mate. You ain't got a fuckin' clue, 'ave you?' I had to take over. 'You can wash up afterwards, you useless muppet.'

He laughed and flicked a bit of spud at me. It missed and hit the ground with a splat. 'On my nice clean floor!' I says to him. 'You can clean that up and all.'

We only had one saucepan so I cooked the spuds and made the mash first, then put it on the plates and hope it didn't get cold while I heated the beans. Then I poured the hot beans over. And if I say it myself, it were great.

We sat up late, just messing and chatting for ages 'til we

went to bed. Albie read stuff to me out his books. A lot of it I didn't really get, didn't understand half the words even. Didn't have a clue. But I kinda stored it in the back of my head to think about later. I didn't say nothing though 'cause I didn't want to look stupid. He didn't seem to mind. A lot of the time it was almost like he was talking to himself anyways; changing his mind half way through a sentence and then coming up with something new. And then scribbling, scribbling it down. I just liked listening and watching. Didn't matter, I didn't get half of it. It was just alright, you know.

CHE CHRONICLES OF ALBION

And then there were two. In our house in the middle of our street. Our castle and our keep. To find something, yea, where nothing grew and nothing fostered and nothing was fed. Somewhere under the concrete forests of Albion, something stirs and maybe even the one awakens. I sit awake and listen while my apprentice sleeps. May well he sleep.

NEW DAWN

Then it was morning. And that day felt like a new morning in a new life... like someone else's life even though I knew it was still me if you see what I mean. I'd moved in and it was the two of us from then on. Him with his mad ideas, and me.

And it seemed like I was the one who had to sort out the important stuff round the house seeing Albie's useless job the night before. I didn't mind that though. I fact, I quite liked it. But stealing for two full time was a lot harder than just the odd bit of nicking for yourself. I had to start thinking what I could pack in, not what I actually wanted. There's only so much you can stuff on you without being noticed. For a while we was living on chocolate and apples, which was a bit shite. The Paki families were getting a bit pissed off with me too 'cause I was in there so much without buying much and they kinda copped on to me. I decided I'd have to spread myself around a bit and go up the High Street.

I tried to get Albie in on it but he was worse than useless. I took him up the shopping centre - the big one. I figured it would be a bit easier as he looks kind of posh in that posh student way and we might fit in better than just me on my own. But it was worse. He was shite. He just didn't have it. Didn't have it at all; spent too much time looking at stuff and mooning about, or he'd think of something – nothing to do with what we were doing but just something out of his mental head – and come and talk to me about it when we were supposed to be working alone – for cover, like.

He did nick something a few times. The first time he was so proud of himelf, it made me laugh, but he was rumbled pretty quick. We had to leg it. He's not very fast, not like me.

Limps a bit and he's a bit mad looking when he runs, with his big boots on and his big coat flapping. I had to keep going back for him and ended up dragging him up a side lane up the back of the cinema so he could get his breath. He was laughing with the buzz of it all and leaning forward with his hands on his knees, trying to gulp some air in.

'You....smoke....too...much,' I said puffing back at him. 'What...you....get?'

He put his hand in his pocket – he still couldn't speak – and pulled out... some baby bath. Bubble bath, like, for fuckin' babies!

'You muppet!' I couldn't believe it. 'What the fuck you get that for?'

He laughed even more and I forgot to be cross and started laughing as well, thinking of us with nothing to eat but able to have fuckin' bubble baths for weeks. It was mad, the two of us standing there laughing and laughing even though we now had no dinner.

When I thought about it after, it was the first time I'd seen him laugh. He smiled a lot but in a kind of sad way as if he knew something you didn't, like something bad might happen. It's not really a nice smile. I preferred seeing him laugh.

Course the other thing about shopping with Albie was people stared at him. I'm not having a laugh. Honest, they did. Stared – 'specially the girls. It was mental and it wasn't just 'cause of the way he looked – and he did look like a total weirdo with his long black coat and big boots and these mental black old-man hats he had to stick on his head every time he went out anywhere, so everyone stared.

But the girls were something else. That was different. I mean I know girls look at you sometime when they fancy you or think they might do, but when they look at me it's a kinda sideways slanty one, narrowed eyes and that kinda checking you over, seeing if they might fancy you or not. Then if you catch 'em, they look away and maybe, if they like you, they'll look back at you again. If you're lucky, you might get a bit of hair twirled round the finger at the same time or even – maybe, sometimes – a smile. That's when they fancy you, girls. They do that. But with him, they just stared. And stared. And stared. All big eyed and fat bottom-lipped. Gummy looking. Nope. With Albie, they just stared. Struck dumb, they were, which is pretty amazing for the mouthy birds you get round our way. And if he smiled at them they'd be fuckin' delighted with theirselves, nearly wetting their pants they were. Don't never work for me though. It'd piss me off I reckon, if he played it. But he never did. Never seemed to notice it at all.

But, like I say, they noticed him alright. So, my ideas about him helping me blend into the scenery kind of backfired big time. I gave up after that and went back to working on my own. Lot better than going out with him, anyways.

I kinda took over the money side of things 'cause he was just fuckin' useless at the practical stuff. He needed me. He *did.* Fuck knows how he survived as far as he did 'cause he really was shit at stuff. Maybe he always had some mug like me to look after him, like. And of course, as things got bigger and bigger, it got harder and harder. But that was all later on.

What *did* Albie do you might ask? Well Albie was the ideas man, you could say. I learnt loads off him and that's why I didn't mind kinda doing the shopping for us and that. And, 'course, without Albie none of what happened would have happened at all. I mean, he made it all. He said once to me it were both of us what did it, but it weren't really, it were him.

It was funny, you know, that he told me all them stories about Camelot and that when we met. I never knew whether what came later was always his plan or whether it just happened.

I dunno.

You could get loads out of Albie when he was telling stories, but other than that, he was pretty much schtum about stuff. But the thing was, whether it were part of some big plan or not, Albie gave me a home.

I know that sounds weird 'cause I had my own home, but being with him was like kinda like being at my nan's. Being at nan's weren't like at home where mum was hardly ever there, or if she was, she was with a bloke, or drunk, or both, or hungover and needing looking after. And the house was always dirty and there was never no dinner hardly. And Sam would be in and out like a ghost, just ignoring me, and the best you could do was go to your bed and listen to CDs and try and block it all out and pretend you was somewhere else; anywhere else, just anywhere. But when I was at Nan's, Nan would get me cups of tea and talk to me. I could tell her stuff, like if I had a bad day at school or someone was a twat to me. She'd tell me when I was being a wanker and all – though she didn't use that word 'cause she was a nan, but kids need someone to tell them stuff like that 'cause you can't always work it out when you're a kid, can you?

If I was sick or something, she'd get me a hot water bottle and give me medicine or rub that stinky stuff on my chest that hurts your nose a bit when you breathe it in and comes out that blue pot. And sometimes, she'd let me stay up and watch telly with her, all cuddled into her on the sofa and that. Or she'd read me stories out of these old books, books that used to be my mum's when she was a kid. They weren't girls' stories either. Some of them were well good, magicians and knights and adventures a bit like the stories Albie knows.

Yeah, Albie is just like my nan, in a way.

I remember the first day I was there, after I moved in prop'ly, he goes to me, 'Would you like a cup of tea?'

I was like, 'What?'

He goes, 'I'm making a cup of tea. Would you like one?'

Well, no one ever says that to me in our house. It's all Mum lying on the sofa watching Jeremy Kyle still in her dressing gown going, 'Ah, luv, make us a cuppa, will you? For your mum, your mum who luvs yer?' Yeah, yeah, yeah. But even that's better 'n Sam who usually just stretches out a leg from where she's sitting and pushes me with her foot. 'Tea,' she goes. Just like that. No please or nothing.

So that's what I mean about Albie. He's proper nice. Like my nan.

And he learns me stuff like she did. Like once, we was walking down the street with some chips for us tea and I chucked my paper down, like you do – and you know what? – he goes, 'What are you doing?'

So I looks at him. 'Eh?'

He goes. 'What did you do that for?'

I dunno what he's on about. 'What you on about?'

'You threw your rubbish on the ground and there's a rubbish bin just there.'

'So?'

'Someone has to clean that up,' he says. 'Or else this place turns into even more of a rubbish tip than it already is.'

I'd never thought of it like that. I thought about my mum having to do the cleaning when she had her job before the depression and what it would have been like for people just chucking stuff at her and expecting her to clean it up. And I thought, 'Yeah, that's fair. s'pose he's right really.'

But I don't give in easy. I looked around. There was fuckin' crap everywhere, cans and crisp packets and fag ends and fag boxes and sweet papers and loads of other shite. There was even a dirty hairbrush and some toilet paper and some other stuff I didn't even want to look at.

'It's not like it's gonna make no difference,' I says. 'Look at it. It's a fuckin' shithole already.'

'Yes,' he says to me. 'And that's made by people like you throwing stuff down because they don't care about themselves, don't care about where they live, and don't care about anyone else.' He stops for a bit then he goes, 'I thought you were better than that.'

That's how he got you. Just like me nan used to, so I sighs and I goes back and picks up the paper and dumps it in the bin. And then we carries on like normal.

That's what I mean about Albie: Even when he's kinda telling you off, it's cool.

But we used to have a laugh together and all. I liked to make him laugh. Albie, though, like I said, he didn't laugh often. But I liked it when he did and I liked it best when he did it cause of me.

One night, it were really cold; all windy outside and ice on the roads and on the windows. We made up one bed and got in it 'cause it was the best way to stay warm. There really weren't nothing gay or nothing about it even though we was both blokes. It was just fuckin' cold, so we put the sleeping bags together and put all our clothes on that we could – 'cept shoes, him in his big coat and all – and got in with all the blankets on the top.

We still had that bottle of whisky I swiped out my house when I left. Albie said his granda' always told him a nip of whisky keeps the cold out so we just sat there in the bed sharing it and trying to keep warm. I ain't never had whisky before and it weren't very nice. Gave you the shivers when you drink it but it did the business and really made your belly warm as it went down. The whisky hit my head fast. I started talking shite. I told him he was my best mate, my very best mate out of everyone, and way more than Danny Sears who I didn't even see no more really. And he smiled and said he was glad. He said I was his 'second', which I thought was a bit off since I said he was my first best mate. But then he said he didn't mean like a second best mate. He said a second was your mate who was with you in a fight, on your side, like a boxing second 'cept better than that; your mate that you trust with your life. Then I thought it was cool being a second 'cause everyone needs someone on their side in the fight. And it is a fuckin' fight, ain't it? Life.

I said he was like that King Arthur in his drawings, 'cept he only had one knight, and that was me. I thought that was funny. I said I didn't have a horse or even a pushbike, but I had a fork – and I waved it in the air.

He thought that was funny. He cried 'Excalibur!' and waved his fag in the air along with my fork but then he dropped it in the bed and set fire to the blanket and we laughed some more as he danced about trying to put it out with his hands. We couldn't move much 'cause our legs were stuck in the sleeping bag so we looked like a slug having a fit, and that made us laugh even more.

I thought *I* was bad but Albie was fuckin' well pissed and waving the bottle in the air like a mad old alchie on a park bench. He was crying, 'I drink to Albion, its land and its people,' or something mad like that. That made me laugh more and then he laughed and then we were both laughing so much that tears were coming out of my eyes. We was hiccuping and gulping for air, like. It was brutal. And then one of us would look up and we'd be off again, snorting and giggling and just laughing, laughing, laughing.

But that was in the days when there was just two of us. At the very beginning.

THE CHRONICLES OF ALBION

How can a place of dew bright landscape of stout-hearted beasts and venerable magicians and dragon slayers diminish into this bitter concrete funeral pyre? And make asses out of lions and blind men of us all, wandering round in shrouds of our own choice and making? Indeed all cannot be buried under grey matter as the other grey matter will rise and the blood of the people will flow once more in their veins, if unblocked at the heart's source. For many maybe tis too late but the spirit in the children lives on.

I have indeed my own sword, a razor sharp wit and a will forged in iron. I have my apprentice by my side and in the distance I hear the mewling cries of thousands who will come. There is much to be done and much to be said.

RESCUE

It started really as an accident. Well I think so, but knowing now how Albie felt about things, maybe it was all part of his dreams. His big ideas. And I sometimes wonder whether it was that night, when we got pissed and he started going on about Excalibur and that which give him his idea or maybe he'd had it all along. To make his own Camelot. Here. In all this shite.

And it was weird, you know, that he even wanted to be here in this shite. I mean, I could tell like, from the way he spoke that he weren't like me – you know, better 'n me. Posh. Even though he said all that stuff about no one being better, you know what I mean about posh people. And then he knew all this history shit and could read and write loads better 'n me. He never said much about himself. I mean, I used to talk about my mum and my nan and that, but he never did.

So I went and asked him one night when we was just chilling in the gaff. I was a bit pissed so I didn't care 'cause normally you don't ask people stuff like that do you? But I'd wondered about it for a bit.

'Alb,' I goes. 'You're not from the estate are you? You're posh, enchya? You are, so why did you come *here*?'

'No,' he said. 'I'm not from here.'

'So where are you from? Why do you wanna live like this? Enchya got a nice posh home to go to?'

He sighed then. 'Well, yes I have in a way. I grew up in a big house. A little like this.'

He pulled out his book and showed me this drawing. Really good it were, but the house; it weren't like a normal house, it were like a fuckin' *castle*!

'There? Fuck me, mate. That's fuckin'... that's not a house.'

'No, ti's not a house. It's a school.'

'What were yer dad like? A teacher or sumut?'

He smiled. 'My father was a diplomat.'

'What's that?'

'Well, kind of like a politician, I suppose. He worked for the government and he travelled abroad a lot. My mother would go with him, so they sent me away to school. I didn't see very much of them.'

'You lived in a *school*? What, like Harry Potter? In the films?'

He smiled: 'Most of the time.'

'What, in the holidays as well?'

'Sometimes. Sometimes they would be home – they had a big house in London and another house in the country – and would send for me from wherever they were. They liked to have big parties, and when I was little, they used to like me to be there to show me off to their friends. I was quite cute when I was little.' He smiled, that sad one again.

'But then, when I got a bit older and I didn't look quite so cute anymore, they didn't want me to do that. They preferred me out of the way, so they got me to stay at school.'

'Two houses? You must have been well rich.'

'Well, yes, we were. But money isn't that important.'

Yeah, you can say that alright when you've got it, I thought. But my nan told me that, too. When I was bitching about something I wanted Mum to get me and Mum had no money and we weren't winning on the lottery ever, Nan would say to me, 'You don't need to be thinking about winning the lottery, Robbie. Your health is your wealth', so maybe in a way he was right and there are more important things than money. But to be honest with you, when I'm stressing about what we're gonna eat every day, I don't quite get that. But I didn't want to have a row about it, so I say, 'That school... is that where you learnt the stories? The ones about the knights and shite?'

'Sort of. Not that the teachers taught me. But they had a big library, a beautiful big old library and I used to go there. There were walls and walls of books, wonderful old books bound in leather reaching right up to the ceiling. You had to use a ladder to get to the top. And that's where I would go and find these books and just read, read, read. All by myself. When I wanted to get away. And these tales would fill my head and nothing bad would really matter anymore...'

He'd never said so much before, about himself and not some old knights or something, so this time, I didn't take the piss.

'Like me. When I need to listen to my banging tunes to stop the shite in my head. I guess it's the same.'

'Yes, Robbie, I guess it's the same.'

Anyway, what happened next was one night we were out. We were walking past the flats going home and Albie wanted to go in the shop. It was late, nearly midnight and they were starting to try and chuck people out so they could close up. But Albie wanted some fags so he wormed his way in and I just waited outside. It weren't worth starting a row with the chucker-outers and they hated me in the shop anyway. I always got hassle in there 'cause they were smart enough alright to know what I was up to most times I was in there, so I just waited for him and had a fag. I looked up at the flats. At our windows. I looked up and there was a light on but I didn't know if it was mum or Sam that was in. I could see someone moving in the room behind the nets, but I couldn't tell who it was. I sort of thought about going in to say hi 'cause I missed 'em sometimes. Don't get me wrong, I rang 'em sometimes to let 'em know I was alright. Left messages and that. I preferred to ring when I thought Sam would be at work and mum asleep and just leave a message. I didn't want mum all crying over me and that, and if she was pissed she might. And then I'd have to go back and look after her and everything and I didn't want to. I 'spect people would tell her that they'd seen me around. That's if she said she ain't seen me. But I hoped she was smart enough to say nothing 'cause I wanted the social after me like I wanted a fuckin' hole in the head.

I was just standing there, breathing in the smoke, like, and breathing it out. Kicking back. Thinking. Then – over all the noise of the cars and the panes overhead and the arguing outside the shop as the heavies tried to tell the piss-heads who's wandered over from the pub that they were closed – I could hear this little kid crying for its mum and I looked down and there was this nipper about three years old.

He was coming out of the doorway at the bottom of our flats looking for her, tears smearing dirt all over his little face. I knew his mum. She was a junkie, so she'd probably passed out somewhere or she'd gone out looking to score and left the poor little bastard on his own, hoping he'd be asleep all the time 'til she got back or more 'n likely, not even fuckin' caring. I was thinking about going over to him, but was worried people might think I was some kind of perv or trying to steal him or something, but while I was still thinking about it, Albie came steaming out the shop and just went straight over. You had to hand it to him. He kneels down on the ground by the kid – in all the dirt and shite and that – so the kid's not scared and asks him where his mum is. I wander over. I have to. He looks at me, Albie, asking me the same question with his eyes that he just asked the kid. But *I* dunno.

The kid's crying so much he can't say anything except in gulps but you kind of get the picture he woke up and she ain't in her bed or on the sofa and there's no one else about in the place, so I'm just standing there feeling a bit of an idiot but I tells Albie the kid's mum's a junkie and that I knows her, sort of. I tells it in a way that the kid won't know what I'm saying, just mime the needle in my arm and that. I dunno if the kid's old enough to understand the word junkie but I kinda didn't want to say it in case he was. Living with her, he prob'ly did know even if he didn't know he knew, if you know what I mean.

It's rank, innit? I mean I'll say that for Mum, she was never a junkie. There was a kid died in our flats of it. Younger than I am now, you know. His mum was seeing this junkie fella and while they're fuckin' passed out on the bed, the kid wakes up. He can't raise them so decides to play with all the lovely toys they've left lying around. The paper said he's seen 'em shooting up enough times to know what to. Maybe he did. Maybe it was an accident. But that's what he did. The mum found him the next day when she woke up. On the floor. All blue. With a spike in his arm... Fuckin' 'ell.... I ask you. What do you do?

Albie looks back at the kid and then up at me. I say, 'She's prob'ly off getting stuff.'

The kid looks up at me then. 'Allo, mate,' I say. And I give him a grin to show I'm friendly and so he won't be scared.

The kid's still sniffing and hiccupping and holding onto Albie's hand but he's stopped the roaring anyways. Then Albie says, 'We'll have to take him back with us.'

That wakes me up. 'What? You fuckin' mad or

somethin'?'

This fella goes past and says something to Albie like he reckons he's some sort of perv or something trying to touch up little kids but Albie just ignores him. I would have gone mad if someone thought I was trying it on with little kids but Albie's cool like that. He don't mind what people say about him. He just does what he does, and that's it.

The fella gives him an evil but he walks on and don't do nothing. You know how people are. Don't give a shit, do they? Good job Albie weren't a perv, weren't it?

Albie says again, 'We'll have to take him home with us. We can't leave him. He'll walk out on the road or something or someone… someone not right'll find him. And we can't go in, can we?'

I'm trying to think. We can't go in his house 'cause if someone finds us there we'll be in big shite. And that bloke's seen us now so he could come back. We can't call the cops 'cause they'll be after us and pass us and him onto the social. We can't talk to the neighbours – 'cause that'll mean the cops again.

And we can't leave him.

Albie stands up then. He's decided. 'We'll take him. We'll leave a note or something so his mum's not worried and we'll bring him back tomorrow. It's that or get the police.'

So that's what we did. We took him. I didn't like it. I didn't like it at all. But we had to do something and that's all we could do.

The nipper was well happy about that. He liked Albie. He held onto his hand tight as you like. And he kept looking up at him with his big blue eyes. Albie had to hold onto him dead hard because every so often the kid would trip 'cause he weren't looking where he was going but looking up at Albie's face instead. Ended up hanging off Albie's hand with Albie holding him up so he didn't hit the deck 'til he got his feet again. The kid didn't mind. He was just fuckin' fascinated by Albie. It was like the girls all over again.

When we got back to the gaff, I thought we'd better get him some food. That's what you do with little kids innit? Just feed 'em and find something for them to play with and let 'em go to sleep, so I got in the kitchen and made him some beans and mash and that, and gave him a drink. Lucky we had some milk left over.

I cleaned his face off after like my mum used to do with me. All mucky it was, even after you got the milk moustache wiped and the food off where it was stuck to his cheeks. His face was like it hadn't been cleaned in a long time. Prob'ly hadn't. Underneath, his cheeks were red but you wouldn't have known before. They were sort of grey with dirt and stuff, poor little bastard. Even after the teary stuff came off.

I did his hands as well. I took him to the toilet and cleaned his teeth for him with my toothbrush and then we put him in our room. I put some of my T shirts on him like a nightdress so he wouldn't be cold. Albie give him his sleeping bag doubled up as a mattress and some blankets and that, and a pillow out of one of my hoodies. It smelt a bit of fags and I thought maybe you shouldn't put a kid in a bed smelling of fags but what else could we do?

He weren't cold but he wanted to get up and sit on Albie's lap so we let him and he just sat there sucking his thumb and staring into Albie's face or playing with the sleeves on his big old coat. We had to get him off to sleep though. I mean it were nearly two in the morning by then, so Albie gets one of his notebooks out and shows the kid some of the pictures and tells him a few stories like a proper dad and the kid goes off to sleep pretty quickly after that.

I was still thinking, *'Fuck. This is kidnap ain't it?'* Even kids get done for this. I heard about it. They might say we tried to hurt him or fiddle with him and then we'd be in real shite. But Albie was right. What could you do?

You tell me what else we could have done. If we left him he could have wandered off anywhere looking for his mum and got hit by a car or met a nonce or something. And the thing was, there *were* loads of people around but no one else did nothing, like they never do 'cause that's what most people do when something happens. Just mind their own and get on with it.

But Albie says just 'cause everyone does that, that don't mean it's okay. You have to look in yerself and feel what you think is right to do and fuck everyone else. He says it's never okay to do nothing. It just ain't. And although I weren't that happy about it, I could see what he meant and I knew he was right.

He slept alright and even when he woke up he stopped being scared as soon as he saw Albie. We give him some more milk. We didn't have no cereal or nothing but I made him some more beans and he didn't seem to mind even though he had them before. Then we took him back. His mum was there, this time. Or someone was 'cause the lights that were on last night were off. We took him to the doorstep, rang the bell and then legged it and hid in the entry, leaving him there.

He tried to come back to us but we told him it was a game and he had to wait for a minute. Then she come out. She was a bit strung out and didn't even seem to think it weren't normal for her fuckin' little boy, who should'a been in bed, to be ringing her doorbell at eight a.m in the morning. I didn't want to leave him then, poor little fucker, but what could you do? Fuckin' 'ell. It's something my nan used to say sometimes, *'Need a licence to keep a dog in this country...'* I knew what she meant.

As we walked away round the front, I looked back and I could see him at the window, his little hands pressed on the glass and his little face in between them staring after us and watching us go.

Albie was quiet for a few days after that. Not himself, like. Thinking and scribbling and scribbling and thinking. I left him to himself and went down the rec. Bumped into Danny Sears and that and we had a bit of a kick about. More like old times. He asked me what I was up to these days and I just said, 'This and that'. He knew to leave it then. He's cool like that.

ТВЕ СВRОПІСLЕS ОЗ АLВІОП

Nary an infant, too. Tis a great task of care. But simple is as simple does and everyone needs a home. A place to call their own. Even a heart to call their own. Or a soul to call their own. Even their own.

But suit your action to the world and breed the fighters. The infant is born with his fist already clenched, ready. The child remains, yet a child but forced to be man. Without kith or kin, tribeless, sceptreless, nationless and unloved and unled, uncared for, abandoned, left and destroyed. And screaming with want. Streaming with tears uncried and unflowing. Weeping silently on filthy sheets as others exit stage left in ignorance and pursuit of selfish desires in the whore pits of the excrement-filled gutters, fixed on filling the bottomless cavern of their own want when perhaps, indeed, the solution to that, they have left behind where it breeds its own and the spiral continues ever downwards, ever down.

But, if you build it, will they come. Aah, they will come, they will come.

KNIGHTS OF THE REALM

After a few days, Albie was more like himself again. His normal weird-self and not this new weird-self. And instead of being in his head, he started to talk more again and be interested in stuff. Like if he was living in a flat all depressed and then suddenly started looking out the window at the world again, so I decided to organise a night out for us. Something more normal. Proper normal.

My nan used to take me to the fair when I was a kid. I can just about remember that, my dad used to do it when he come over but after he got bored of coming, my nan used to take us. I used to love it. All the noise and the colours and the lights and the smells. Crappy pop music rowing with itself, the pumping diesel engines, the screaming of the girls on the rides and the big pikeys with greeny-blue tattoos who used to run the place. It were great.

When I was up town, I saw the notices for one over the playing fields so I reckoned we ought to go. We didn't have much money but we could get a few cans and drink 'em up the back and then go over. If I was smart, there'd still be enough for a few rides and that.

I said it to Albie and he was well excited. You think he hadn't been to a fair or nothing before.

I said, 'Ain't you never been to a fair or nothing before?'

He didn't say anything and he kind of looked away and his hair fell over his face so I couldn't see it. Seemed a bit moody about that for some reason but it didn't bother me. I just shrugged and said, 'Well. We'll go down.'

So we went down. We bought a bottle of cheapo cider and a couple of Aftershocks 'cause Albie could get served in the super. We drank 'em in the rec 'cause there's always cops hanging round the arcade and I didn't want to get stopped and risk another evening in the old Hotel Plod.

The rec is alright. Sometimes, there's kids hanging about, but I knows most of them so there's no trouble. The worst they'll do is ponce drink and fags off you. No one else comes there after dark cause it's a bit of a shithole to be honest. And maybe 'cause they're scared of the kids. We call it the rec 'cause it's got some swings and used to have a football pitch before the goalposts rotted and fell over one day when one of the fat Sunday Leaguers crashed into it. Its proper name is Prince's Park, but there ain't much park or prince about it – just a scrappy piece of ground where people let their dogs crap everywhere, even though they're not supposed to, and a few manky bushes with litter stuck in 'em instead of flowers growing.

So me and Albie headed for one of the benches and we were just sitting there having a drink when this women walks across to us. She's pushing a pushchair with some kid hanging off her arm as well. You do get people round here who'll have a go at you or report you for drinking, though not many. Most of 'em keep themselves to themselves and I could see when she got closer, she was one of those. Looking at her and her kids, she didn't care much about herself, let alone be bothered about us. She gets closer and you can see the baby in the pushchair's all kind of dirty. He's got crap all round his mouth and his clothes don't look none too clean neither. The little kid walking must be about three and he's just kinda chatting to himself, like kids do. Talking nonsense in his little high voice. Then she stops and drags his little arm so hard you'd think she'd yank it out the socket and he spins off his balance, toppling against the pushchair.

She goes, 'Shut up you fuckin' little shit! I've told you. Shut the fuck up or you'll get my fuckin' fist again.'

I thought that was bang out of order. I mean, you can't talk to kids like that and he was only doing what kids do. He can't help it. It's like you can say to someone, 'Don't be such a fuckin' kid.' But not to a kid.' Cause that's what he is, isn't he? And he can't help it.

And she's his *mum*. She should be nicer to him, even if she's a bitch to everyone else. I kind of looked at them again at the kid's face... I thought he was gonna cry for a minute, but he didn't. He looked like he might. But then he just looked angry, dead angry. And I looked at the baby when they went past and the baby looked angry, too. You wouldn'a thought a baby could look angry, would yer? I mean they just kind of cry and shite, but this one did, and then I looked at the mum and she looked angry. Angry at everything.

I looked at Albie and jerked my head at the woman. 'Not right, is it, that?'

'No' he said. But that's all he said. He watched her as she walked out the rec, the kid kicking and stumbling beside her.

We was silent for a while. But then I got a bit fed up with that. I don't like it silent.

'Come on, mate,' I says, getting up. And we headed over towards the fair.

It was all I wanted. The big fuck off scary rides – *The Terminator* where they just drop you from a great height real sudden like and you leave your guts in the sky, and another one called *The Gyro*, where they strap you in this big cushiony seat and spin you round 'til you throw up. Or near enough anyways. Danny Sears went on there pissed last year and puked everywhere, and I tell you, it was a near thing for me this time. It were great though, all these colours and lights and sounds and faces spinning in front of your eyes and your poor old mashed little brain trying to work it out. Like some mega acid trip. Quality.

Then there were the little kids' rides – the teacup things and that the nans would sometimes go on – and the ones that always sounded cool but were a big piece of shite like the Ghost Train which is just like driving a pedal car through a dirty old garage with someone wiping old bits of curtain on your hair. Or the House of Horrors – which is just taking the fuckin' piss 'cause there's nothing horror about it at all.

There were also the ones that the blokes always took take their birds to, to try and show off doing the man thing and win them some shite cuddly teddy. You know the gun ones and the bow and arrow ones, and the chucking stuff ones that are always fuckin' fixed but the guy who runs is it some huge pikey with forearms like a JCB and a mug on him that says 'I hit myself in the face with a shovel for fun every morning so don't even think about trying anything with me.'

Albie loved all of it. He was like a little kid running here and there. His eyes were all bright and excited like they are when he's got some mad new idea. He wanted to go on everything, even the fuckin' merry-go-round. I said, 'I ain't going on that, it's for fuckin' babies.' He shrugged. 'So what?'

'It's embarrassing,' I told him. But he didn't care. He never cared about stuff like that. And up on one of the fuckin' painted horses he gets. Him in his big black boots and hat, all arms and legs and flowing black coat streaming everywhere with all these mums and dads with their little thumb-sucking toddlers staring at him like he's a mental case. And off he goes round and round and up and down and round and round and up and down. I was pissing myself looking at him, I was.

Then, when it stops, he grabs me and drags me up and all; makes me get on the one next to him.

'Get off!' I'm going but he's like,

'No, no. You've got to.'

And I said, 'What do you think I am? A kid?' and he goes, 'Yes.' And laughs.

And then, when he laughs, it's like a dare so I decide to show him and get on this fuckin' stupid little horse. And the bloke comes to take the money off me and I go,

'Two please,' all posh like and when he looks at me funny like I'm taking the piss, I look at Albie and we both start laughing. And off we go. I realise I'm actually a bit pissed. Actually, a lot pissed 'cause even this ride's making me feel a bit sick. But I stick a fag in my gob and light it, which is harder than I thought it would be and I look at Albie and hold me hand up in the air, all clenched fist like I'm fuckin' Maximus or one of King Arthur's knights or something. There's me riding around on my horse, my fag in my gob and all with the music going all tinkly-tinkly in the background and all these little kids staring at me and their dads giving us the evils and the pikeys just screwing me out and taking me for a total twat.

But it just makes me laugh and I say to Albie – well, I yell actually – standing up in my stirrups 'cept they ain't stirrups they're little pedal things. 'Look at me! Look at you! You're King fuckin' Arthur. We're fuckin' legends! Legends we are. The legends of fuckin' Albion!'

And then the ride stops and I fall off my horse.

The mums and dads are none too impressed and neither are the pikeys. I'm lying on my back on the deck pissing myself laughing and Albie's trying to drag me upright by the hood of my top and my trouser leg before the pikeys get over. He manages to get me up and tries to drag me away. But I'm looking for my fag – Fuck knows where that went - and trying to shake him off. But there's three pikeys heading over so I scramble up and we leg it before they can do us, running off, pissing ourselves while they're yelling at us to fuck off forever and not bother coming back.

We run off up the bank so we can look down on the fair and light another fag. I throw myself down on my back Albie flops beside me and sparks up. I'm worn out with all that laughing and running. It's not good for me at my age and I can hardly smoke but I do it anyway.

So, Albie and me are just lying there, smoking, and then something amazing happens. There's this big bang like a bomb's gone off and I open my eyes to see all these lights pinging round my head. For a minute I think it's the drink and someone spiked the Aftershocks or something then I realise, 'Fireworks!'

Fuckin' ace, some and Albie just lay there on the grass, pissed and looking up, watching the sky explode in all these colours over our heads, just smoking. You know, sometimes, life is just good, ain't it?

But then, on the way home, it started to rain innit. The good stuff never lasts, do it? Just little bits in an otherwise big pile of crap, so we got the fireworks .... and then we got the rain. .

The rain suddenly turned into hail. Like bullets it were, pinging off the ground and if they hit you, they stung something horrible. We dived for shelter in an alley way, which stank of piss but there was an overhanging bit and we huddled under there waiting for it to stop. Albie was alright in his coat and his mad frigging hats but I was fuckin' soaked.

'State of me,' I moaned at him holding out my dripping

top and looking down at my wet and filthy trainers. 'My socks are soaking. And my trainers are ruined.'

There was a bin bag beside me spewing out a bit of old blanket that someone had dumped. I thought about sitting on it to take off my socks but it looked too dirty.

Then it moved

'Fuck,' I yelled, jumping back.

A shock of blonde hair come out the top. Little white face, blue eyes. He rubbed his hand across his nose all kind of nervous. His eyes were a bit mad and starey and I could see he thought we were gonna do him over. His hand was up in front of his face in case we went for him, kicked him in the head.

He was even weedier looking than Albie and was saying something. He was so thin it was like his skin was stretched over his bones and you could see his blue veins underneath like a road map. He was really scared and all. By the stink of him, I reckoned the last fellas up this alley must have used his bed as a urinal, which wouldn't surprise me the sort of scum you get round here. S'pose he expected us to do the same.

We all stared at each other for a minute.

Then Albie did his usual, 'Allo.' It worked the same way it done on me. The fella just didn't know what to do with that. He weren't a fighter like me, this one. He were dead scared. I'd say he was older than me, nearer Albie's age but he had that look of a dog that had been kicked too hard, once too often. You know the kind, the strays that'll never come to you, even if they're rattling starving and you've got a McDonalds in yer hand.

Then Albie said, 'Do you mind if we stay here? 'til the rain stops.' All polite. Like we're in this bloke's fuckin' prize-winning front garden instead of up some shit-hole back alley.

The bloke shakes his head. He's still looks nervy but he's got his hands down from his face now. Albie starts chatting away at him. I just lean against the wall and stare out at the rain. It's a bit boring 'cause the bloke's not even answering, just staring, so I try and light a fag, which takes ages cause my matches are all wet. I think the bloke might use one so I wave one at him. He nods.

'Thanks.' It's the first thing I've heard him says. He's not from round here. I can tell by his voice, his accent, even with one word it sounds funny, so what's he doing here, up a back alley, wrapped in a blanket and a bin bag, stinking of piss? And Albie asks him – though not quite like how I said it.

He tells us he's come down from up north. Been in a couple of children's homes, he said. But he kept getting beaten up – didn't surprise me looking at him. He was one of them kids that have got, 'Beat me' written all over them - so he ran away. Bunked the train and came down here and had been living rough for a couple of months. Looked like it and all.

After the smoke, he relaxes a bit, although he's still watching us both trying to work us out and what we're gonna do to him. He was worse than I am for that. All I gotta do is move my hand up to wipe some water out my eyes and he's flinching back into the wall like I'm gonna crack him one. Fuckin' 'ell; he were a bit of a loser, alright but sound enough kid though, prob'ly, under it all. Albie looked at me and I looked at Albie.

'If you need a roof over your head, you can come back with us,' said Albie.

Fair enough. This weren't like stealing a baby, like the other day could'a been. At least this one was old enough to make his mind up and if no one had been after him so far, they weren't gonna bother at all were they?

He started looking worried again, so I butted in, 'It's my gaff; and it's sound. Nothing posh. But you can come if you want.'

He screwed his eyes up, thinking what to do. I could see he was desperate to get out of the hole he was in but he didn't trust us one fuckin' bit. You wouldn't blame him neither. He looked like he'd been through some shite.

So I said then, 'Nuffin funny, neither.' I nodded at Albie, 'He might look like a twat, but he's alright really.' And I grinned at him.

For a second, he almost smiled back. He didn't but he did start wriggling out of the bag. Then he started packing it up like he was gonna bring it with him.

I said, 'You having a laugh or what? You ain't bringing that stinking pile with you; we've got better stuff and I ain't having that in our gaff. Smells like someone's pissed all over it.'

He looked at me then, in the eyes for the first time. Ah, right, they had. I suppose that's what comes of sleeping up a back alley. I 'spect the drunks round here think it's a laugh to come and piss all over some kid who can't do nothing back unless he wants to get kicked up the road, which of course is what they want. Bit of fun to end the night off perfectly. Few beers, a curry and a shag – or a ruck if you can't get a bird to sort you out. You know how it is.

He dropped it then and stood up in front of us. Fuckin' 'ell, the state of him. He looked like something out of one of them zombie films. He was a walking skeleton with his clothes hanging off him like rags. Anorexic or what?

'Come on, then,' I said, wearily.

He didn't wanna tell us his name, so I called him

Homeless 'cause that's what he was. Albie thought it was a bit mean even though he called him Homeless too after a while. Homeless didn't mind, didn't take it personal or nothing. In fact, he found me easier to deal with than Albie.

Albie's just straight up and kind and open. That's just how he is. But if you're someone like this skinny runt who don't know anything about being treated like that, it's a bit scary. You dunno where you are. I was like that first with Albie 'til I got used to him and realised he wasn't taking the piss or trying some kind of funny business to turn me over, so he didn't mind me giving him a bit of lip, being a bit gobby, like, and taking the piss out of him. That's what he was used to. Poor old Homeless.

So Homeless moved in and then there were three.

The first thing Homeless did when he got there was get a bath. Thank God! We didn't say too much to him 'cause we thought he might be a bit sensitive. But it weren't just that bed of his that stank, you know. We lobbed in a load of the baby bubblebath, just to make him feel better. When he was in the bath, me and Albie got his clothes and took them out the back and burnt 'em. We carried them out on a piece of wood cause, to be honest, I reckoned they was crawling and didn't wanna touch 'em.

We gave him some of our clothes instead and I just hoped anything that mighta been living on him had drowned in the bath. He just about got into my trackies although they were short on him and looked really naff. And Albie gave him a sweatshirt, which hung off his shoulders and over his hands, so he looked pretty gimpy and we pissed ourselves when we saw him. But at least he didn't smell no more.

Homeless fitted in alright with us. He used to stay for a

bit and then go off and come back though we never knew where and never asked. He weren't no trouble and it was quite nice having him around.

THE CHRONICLES OF ALBION

In his vagabondage, he laid his head down on what he thought was a green and pleasant land for solace and found only concrete and brick and other men's kicks and other men's spit and other men's piss, so there he lay, in the sick of the night, watching the walls and the shadows.

THE WANDERING MAN

Sometimes, Homeless bought his mates in and we let them sleep here too. They weren't much fun to hang out with cause most of the time, they slept. But it was better for 'em than being out on the pavements, lying there to be pissed on by any fat, bald wanker who comes out the pub in a bad mood wanting a fight. It's funny how being fat and old seems to turn you into a bit of twat isn't it? They're all like that round here. Even if they're not bald, they shave their head so it looks like they are. And they're twats.

The odd times Homeless and his mates bought booze it was great 'cause for some reason – maybe 'cause of being all skinny and homeless – they couldn't take their drink and would crash out after about five minutes so me and Albie would finish it off. It was one of them nights that Albie started telling me about his big plan. We was on the whisky that evening, sitting in the room, Homeless and his mates all wrapped up in blankets sleeping round the place.

Albie was getting a bit overexcited. He does that sometimes, when he's been drinking. Funny how the drink sends Homeless and his lot to sleep and turns Albie into a mentalist. Spinning around in his coat, he was, and waving the bottle at them dozy lumps that were the homeless kids

'My knights awaken!' he goes in that funny way he talks sometimes.

Homeless does. Well he kind of shifts under his blanket and opens an eye, muttering 'Eh?' but when he sees it's just Albie playing the arse, he rolls over the other way and goes back to sleep.

Albie just laughs. Then he comes to me. And sits down

on front of me. Looking at me. 'I've been thinking,' he goes.

'What?'

'We could do something here. Build something. Create something magical.'

I screwed up my face and puffed on my fag. 'You drink too much.'

'No. no. Listen.' He jumps up. 'What we've done already. What we've created. It's beautiful. It's something wonderful.'

I look round at the shithole with the snoring homeless round the walls and screwed up my face. 'You mental?'

He's back to me again then, twisting round and dropping to his knees in front of where I'm sitting on the floor. One big movement, his coat swirling round him as he does it. And he fixes me with his eyes, staring right into mine. He can fix you like that sometimes, when he's telling you something and it's like you can't move. When I was a kid, I used to watch this Disney film round my nan's about this kid who lived in the jungle with bears and tigers and that, and it had this big snake in it that could just stare you down and like hypnotise you – and it was like that.

'But, listen,' he goes. 'It is. It is'

He got up then and went for his book and holds it out in front of him.

'You see.'

Not really, I thinks.

'Well, see what we did? We made something here.' He waves his book at me. 'You see there's something in this. There is.

'Where would they be? Where would they be if we hadn't given them somewhere to go? Or that little boy the other night? What about him? What if we had done nothing? What then? Someone has to do something… something to make something better... something to sort it out... something to start from.'

'What you on about?' I ask.

'Listen, Robbie, listen. Listen to me. What do you need?'

'What do I need?'

'Yes. Need. What do you need?'

'I dunno'. He was wrecking my head again. 'I need a fag.'

'No, no you don't. Basic human stuff. Basic, What do you need to live? If you were on your own in the world. What do you have to have?'

'What, if I was like a caveman?'

'Yes. If you like. But no cave.'

'Well I'd need a cave. Gotta have somewhere to sleep.'

'Yes, yes, yes,' he was getting excited.

'Somewhere to sleep, then. With a roof. In case it rains.'

'Yes, yes.'

'Umm. Food?'

'Yes. Food. That's good, Keep going'

'Umm, blankets. In case it's cold. Something to kill dinosaurs if they come and get me.'

'Okay, but no dinosaurs. Say it was like today. No dinosaurs.'

'Dunno, then. Some mates?'

'Yes. Friends. People caring about you. What else would make it really nice? Really, really okay? Happy.'

I thought. People caring about you. That would be good. I know I should have said my mum, but I didn't. I guess cause she doesn't care much about my really. My nan did.

I felt a bit weird saying it but I said, 'It would be good if my nan could be there but she can't cause she's dead.'

He stopped being excited then and was a bit sad for me. Stopped agitating me.

He said, then, 'Yes. But she cared, didn't she? She cared about you and helped you, didn't she?'

'Yes,' I said, a bit quiet. It makes me feel quiet when I think about her.

'So,' he goes, sitting up. 'We got a roof, blankets, food, people who care. Right?'

'I don't get it.'

'Wait, wait. I haven't finished. And what do children need? Kids? What do they need?'

'Kids? We're kids.'

'Yes.Okay. But kids, little kids?'

I thought for a minute, then ticked it off on my fingers. It ain't that hard to work out. 'Home, food, drinks – like bottles and that for babies – someone to look after 'em, someone to tell 'em off when they're naughty – but not in a bad way like that woman in the rec, not like that... Dunno. Toys?'

Then I said, 'Someone to look after 'em and bring 'em up proper.'

'Exactly. Someone to look after them and bring them up properly.'

He spread his arms as if what he was saying was obvious, which it weren't. Then he waves his book in my face, all excited like. 'You see, we could build something here. Something like this.'

Then I just burst out. 'What? A fuckin' castle? You're a nutter.'

'Well, no, but yes, in a way. You see King Arthur's Camelot wasn't about walls and wars, it was about a brotherhood, a way of behaving. Listen....'

He reads a bit: '*"Gentle to the weak, courageous to the strong, terrible to the wicked, merciful to all men, gentle of deed, true in friendship and faithful in love."*' What's wrong with that?'

I shrugged. 'Don't see what it's got to do with us.'

'Well.... we bring everyone here. Everyone. The kids on the streets, the little ones not being looked after, the ones like you having a tough time at home. And they stay here with us. For an hour, a day, forever, whatever. We make a home here and we help them, teach them to survive in the world. Teach them, like your grandmother taught you – heh, like I teach you sometimes – how to be, how to grow up right.'

'Eh? You're barmy.'

'No, no I'm not. We can give children what they don't get at home. In our home. Make them happy, make them good people, keep them away from the bad things in life. The things you've seen and I've seen. Do you understand? This will be amazing. Amazing. You know, Robbie, you and me, we can create a better world for The Children of Albion.'

I thought he was fuckin' mad. But I thought of that little kid out on the street at night and what would have happened has we left him. And I thought of how Albie had told me things and told me off when I was being a bit of an arse. And how it might be nice to have more kids around the place.

And so I said, 'Alright.'

He smiled at me and leapt up. 'We can build our own Camelot and fill it, fill it with the unhappy children of Albion.'

'Yeah, and then what? Take over the world, like?'

He spun again then and threw his hands up like he was chucking something into the air. 'Maybe. We could do anything.'

'Yeah, right. And who are you gonna be then? Fuckin' King Arthur?'

He stretched his arms out behind him like wings and bowed.

I snorted. 'You stupid twat!' But I was grinning when I said it.

We kinda slipped into a routine after that. Me and Albie. Though looking back, I'm not sure what we did half the time. I mean I got organised at getting the food in and did the cleaning most of the time while he ponced about and wrote in his little books and talked a lot of shite. Well, not shite. Just stuff. You know what I mean. Clever stuff. We'd play a bit of music, smoke fags, talk, get pissed. The usual. Sometimes, he'd go off somewhere for a bit… I never knew where. But he was always back by morning. I never asked him. And he never said. But that was cool.

Homeless was in and out. Sometimes, he brought mates with him. They'd stay for a bit and then drift off again. Like him. Mind you, it was cool when they were there. Sometimes, we could knock up a five-a-side and get a kick about together on the street.

I went to school from time to time. Put in the odd appearance like, to keep things ticking along and keep the welfare off mum's back. When I did go it was pretty fuckin' evident they didn't really care if I was there or not, but I had to keep tabs on it cause of Mum.

Danny Sears and Milo were pleased to see me. They'd been asking for me, so I told 'em where I was. I knew they wouldn't split or anything. They knew the score. Danny Sears would drop in round the gaff occasionally. It was the gaff in those days, I suppose, before it became the flophouse. Now there was the three of us, it wasn't just my place, like it used to be. And I didn't mind that. It was sorta more like my home, now, with Albie and Homeless and the others and that. And Danny was sound. He wouldn't say nothing about where I was. He said he'd cover for me in school and all if he had to. And it just meant he could call for me if he wanted. He always used to bring something when he did. Some fags or booze or some food he nicked out of his mum's cupboard. Like I say, he was sound. Milo dropped in sometimes but only with Danny. He bought food and all. It was good when he came over 'cause his family have got cash so he always bought really good stuff like posh pies and them little sausage rolls and big bottles of booze out his dad's drinks cupboard.

Paul, I suppose, was the next one who moved in permanent. One night, we were just sitting there downstairs, trying to get a fire lit and there was this little white face at the door, then it disappeared. I'd had a bit of puff that Danny Sears had left me when he dropped round earlier, so I weren't all there and nearly shit myself with fright. It were like that horror film I saw one Christmas when the ghosts were trying to get in the house. Scared the living crap outta me. Albie were a bit more on the ball than me and he went out to see what was going on.

He comes back in with this kid 'bout my age, I'd say. Bit shy. Pretty boy, with longish hair. Big blue eyes and big fat mouth like a girl. That was Paul.

Albie moved up so he could sit by the fire. And he did. And he never really went. I thought he was a friend of Homeless but I asked Homeless later and he said he weren't, so we never really knew where Paul came from. And he never said himself. Never said much at all. In fact, he never really said anything, but sometimes, he was more silent than others if you know what I mean. Sounds daft, but even though he said nothing anyway, you could tell the difference some days. You could sort of feel it off him, if you know what I'm saying.

It was Danny Sears who brought the first little kids here in a way. He saw Marty Malone down by the parade and his head was wrecked with trying to look after the kids and sort out his mum's social and get the shopping in and all as well as having fuckin' Education Welfare on his back so Danny said he'd take the little ones off his hands for a couple of hours 'til he got sorted. And he asked me if he could bring 'em over.

I didn't think Albie would mind and, nah, he didn't. Seemed delighted actually. He ran around the house with 'em playing chase, every so often stopping and saying to me things like, 'Exactly. Exactly it. These children.'

I hadn't got a fuckin' clue what he was on about. Quite a lot of the time I didn't when he was in one of his mad moods, so I just said, 'yeah,' and carried on watching him running around like a madhead.

Marty never stayed though. He always wanted to get the kids home. They had proper teatimes and everything. You had to hand it to him, he was a great mum. Milo brought Katie Hiller.

Katie Hiller. I wished she'd never come. I really do. Maybe things would've been different for us 'cause I kinda blame her for most of it. For what happened later. Might not be fair like, but I do. It's gotta be someone's fault. Ain't it?

Katie came with Milo one night. He dragged her with him 'cause the dickhead has been trying to get off with her for ages and thought it might swing it for him. Bit of privacy like. But it backfired big time. On all of us.

Katie lives up on the estate where Milo comes from. One of them houses with the garage and the patio and those funny puffy looped curtains with flowers on. Yeah, so she might be posh but she's a slut and there ain't no dressing it up neither.

She's a fuckin' saddo.

I wouldn't have much to do with her myself although most of the lads I know have had a go. She's pretty, alright, with big tits and she's got these long legs and she's always wearing really short skirts and that, flashing them off. But she's dirty. You see her often with bites on her neck which is really trampy, and she don't seem to care either. It's like she's proud of them. And the lads like to do it to her, mark her to prove they've been there, if you know what I mean. It's like dogs pissing on a lamp post.

I used to feel a bit sorry for her as well, although I didn't have no time for her. I mean no one really liked her. The lads just came on to her cause they wanted a shag and she gives them what they want, and the girls were real bitches to her in that way they are to girls who give it out for free, you know. Funny that. The way they gang up on the sluts as if it's saying something about all of them. They pick on 'em like zoo animals, like monkeys do to the weakest in the pack. I saw this thing once on the Discovery Channel. They all just beat shite out the runty ones and leave 'em for dead.

Mind you, these girls still hang out with her sometimes. Katie's parents - like Milo's are still together even though they hate each other's guts - buy her cool clothes and she'll lend 'em to the girls just to try and make friends. And they'll take 'em, alright 'cause although they don't like her they don't mind using her just as much as the lads in their own way. Sad, innit, really? I mean no one liked her. No one. Not really. 'cept Milo. He fancied her. Poor bastard 'cause she weren't gonna waste her time with a fella like him. He wasn't what she wanted. She was looking for something else.

That night he brought her along, he was delighted with himself 'cause she'd been hanging out with him. But she weren't interested in Milo. When I look back, I think maybe she was just using him and it was Albie she wanted right from the beginning. I dunno.

Poor Milo. He was so chuffed to have her agree to come anywhere with him, he was treating it like some date, the poor bastard. He was really like showing her off – to me and Albie and Danny and even Marty's kid brothers and sisters cause we were looking after them that day. Really proud of himself 'cause he thought he'd finally got her as his bird.

Only it weren't that long before the big shit-eating grin was wiped right off his face, poor sod. She fancied Albie. Big time. But instead of barging in like she normally would with her biggish tits and her even bigger mouth, she was kinda quiet. She sat on the floor in the corner with her legs all crumpled in front of her and let Albie feed her the alcopops, which Milo bought especially cause that's the kind of shite she likes. All those drinks that taste of sweets. Like girls do.

She was wearing one of her short skirts, some pleated thing, and long, stripy socks pulled up over her knees and you could almost see her knickers. Well you could every time she moved. If you wanted to. I didn't bother cause I weren't interested, and I didn't think it was right for her to be flashing the little kids. I had to slap 'em for staring but I'd rather have slapped her.

Milo was gobsmacked with her. I had to give him a slap and all for being a twat 'cause his mouth kept falling open and he was just looking at her like she was a fairy who just flown down off the Christmas tree. Staring with this stupid gummy look on his mug. He had it bad for that one. It was sad 'cause he was quite a nice bloke, to be honest with you. Even for a posh bloke.

Katie. She was just staring at Albie. Her eyes followed

him as he wandered around, talking to the little kids, handing out the food, writing his little notes and doing his little drawings in one of those little mad books of his. She just stared, all big-eyed and that. And even if Milo was talking to her she wouldn't look at him, she'd just keep her eyes on Albie. Even when she was answering him it was just 'Yeah', 'No', 'Sure,' 'Whatever', without paying him any attention at all. Rude, it was. If nothing else.

Sometimes, Albie felt her staring and he'd look up, catch her eye. There was no shame on her. She'd stare right back and give him that kind of porn star look, big, fat lips and finger in the mouth you know what I mean. It can give you a hard on like you get from reading the porn mags. That thing.

She knew that and all. And that's why she did it. Poor Milo was nearly wetting himself but I didn't like her behaving like that. In front of the little kids and all; it's not nice. But that's what she's like. Albie didn't seem to notice. I don't know how he didn't 'cause she was practically shoving her tits in his face. So, maybe he did but just didn't do nothing. He'd just look back at her. Give her that watching look. Like the one he gave me when we first met. Just kinda studying her, you know.

I thought it was funny. Drove her just as mad as it drove me at the time. She didn't know what to do 'cause she wanted him to fancy her, and he didn't. Or if he did, he didn't show it. She'd never had that before. She always got some reaction – but not from Albie.

So, anyways. That was us at the start. Just grew, it did. I thought it was just people telling their mates and wanting somewhere to hang out. But when I look back at Albie and his mad head, I wonder if he'd planned it all from the start.

Anyways. People brought people along 'til there were loads of us there. Some came, some went. But it was hardly ever just me and Albie any more. What was no one's home, became our home, and then everyone else's home. Danny brought Marty and the kids. Homeless bought his mates. Other kids, like Paul, must've heard something and then they told kids they knew. Me and Albie would bring back kids we thought were in trouble for a night, or longer if they needed it. Sometimes, there were so many little kids running around it was like a fuckin' nursery.

I thought about getting a telly but Albie was like, 'What do you want that for? Why do you always have to have noise going on?' I had to think about that and I didn't know the answer, even when I thought about it a lot and that worried me a bit 'cause I do like noise. That's why I like having my tunes. When there's no noise, there's a kinda noise in my head instead. Like the noise the telly makes when it's not tuned in. Fizzing. It's horrible, so I'd rather have the other noise. It's better.

The thing is, after Homeless and Paul, all these other zombie kids came. Homeless said he knew them from the Sally Army runs and that, when the do-gooders come out and dish out the soup on the cold nights. Paul never said nothing.

But word must've got around somehow 'cause that thing with Albie got even worse. It was mental. You'd be walking down the street with him and they'd see him, the kids. And then it were like the pavement or the alleyways or the railways arches would come to life. These little skinny figures would come out the shadows. All like him they were with raggedy clothes hanging off skinny bodies, little yellow faces with purple smudged eyes. It really was like a horror film where the zombies rise up out the graveyard and start limping towards you, so 'n dribs and drabs, they all came to the gaff. Homeless' mates usually just stayed for a while and then were off again; had a bath and a bit of food and a clean-up and a few nights' sleep without worrying about someone using 'em as a football or a toilet. But others stayed. Some for a few days like … and some for good.

One night, when it was just me and Homeless there, he told me it was worse than that what I'd thought. Living out like he had, he said it was tough to get by and if you were out at night, the sleazoids would come sniffing round. Sometimes, it would be hard to turn down the cash. Sometimes, there weren't no choice and they just made you anyway. He started saying something about Paul. Then he stopped. I didn't bother asking and I didn't bother asking if it had happened to him either. I kinda guessed it had 'cause he was so scared of us that first time when we met him. Nasty.

It's funny, I always thought the homeless were trampy or alkies or junkies. I didn't realise a lot of them were just kids like us. After I spoke to Homeless that night I didn't feel like myself for a few days. I mean you see nonces around but you can deal with 'em most of the time, but when you look at a kid like Homeless, he's not the kind of scrapper who can look after himself. I didn't like that so I was in a bad mood for a coupla days cause it made me feel a bit sick. These blokes going out and finding the weakest people they can to do their dirty stuff with. Twats. No wonder poor, pretty Paul never said much 'cause he knew, alright. We found that out later

THE CHRONICLES OF ALBION

So there we sit. Behind necessary battlements of our own building. Around a hearth of our own making. No still hearth and no idle king. Vagabonds, thieves, urchins, infants, victims and boy warriors, we. And we begin. The pathetic and the weak, the disenfranchised and the strong. Alone, our voice is quiet, nary a whisper. Together a chorus. Together we sing. A childhood conclave, and for once, we will be asked and we will be heard. A nursery of revolution while the parent flounders in a slime of his own making.

SiR JERRY

So there was quite a few of us hanging around the gaff now. Bit of a squash it were sometimes, depending on how many of Homeless's lot were looking for somewhere to crash out the cold. And it were a bit cold sometimes, at the time of year.

There was only one room which had a fire in it, a little lecky fire the old dear had left behind. We put that in the front room downstairs cause it were the biggest. And we let the littlest kids sleep in there. Seemed fair. Everyone bunked down on the floor in blankets there or in the other downstairs room, which was colder 'cause it had no fire. Sometimes though, there were enough body heat with everyone in there and it were okay.

Me and Albie had the front room upstairs, which we'd always had. Just me and him, unless any of the little ones staying were having nightmares and wanted to sleep in with us. Then there was a little back room, which we didn't use too often cause the window were broke and wouldn't close proper, and though we patched it up with cardboard it were always well chilly.

It was Albie who started calling it the flophouse and flophouse were a good word for it. We had places to sleep and Homeless and his lot used to get extra blankets off the hippies that used to dish out stuff to homeless kids. Other sound kids like Danny Sears and Milo used to nick a few bits and pieces from home so that helped, too.

It was hard keeping everyone in food, though. Danny Sears and Milo helped when they could and I was out robbing as much as I could get away with. That was bad enough. But

with Homeless' lot there, who had to be clothed as well 'cause
– I tell you, not being horrible or anything – we had to have a
lot of fuckin' fires out the back. And we couldn't keep giving
our clothes away, 'specially mine. I had some good stuff there.
All my labels, like.

I figured the best place to get some stuff was down the
market. The shops were all wised-up and they had their guards
and their cameras and electronic security and that. We'd be
wasting our time there. Nah, the market was a better bet.

It was a bigger job, so I recruited one of them from the
flophouse to give me a hand. A couple of them were well
sharp and all. I reckon that's what living in the streets does to
you. It either breaks you like it broke Homeless, or else it turns
you into a fighter, a real scally. And Jerry were a real smart
little scally, to be fair.

He was a weird-looking little kid. He was only tiny,
smaller 'n me and about nine years old, but he had this old,
old face on him. I mean, you look in his face and see this old
fella looking out. His face was set in a series of Vs. He was
always frowning and that, eyes and eyebrows pulled down
into a little pointy nose and a small, tight little mouth that he
squished up like a cat's arse. When he wasn't smoking that
was, and he chain-smoked terrible. I mean his fingers were
fuckin' yellow already, and he was only a nipper.

Like Paul, we never really knew his story. Homeless said
his parents were junkies so they didn't really care where he
was most of the time as long as he wasn't annoying them. That
kid. That kid in the flats – the first one that we found, well
Jerry were probably him in a few years' time.

Jerry turned up with his brother, Tim. His brother was a
quiet little kid, even younger. He was another of those like
Homeless and Paul, with that 'kick me' look about them. He

had big blue eyes and he always looked like he was just about to cry; whereas Jerry always looked like he'd stab you soon as look at you. He'd certainly stab you soon as look at you if you upset Tim. The only time you'd see him soft was when he was with Tim. Looking after him, looking out for him. If anyone had a problem with Tim – or Tim had a problem with anyone – they had a problem with Jerry. But Tim rarely had a problem with anyone. He just did his own thing, sucked his thumb a lot.

But he had a problem, alright. And as much as Jerry tried, I dunno if it were something he could do much about for all his trying, for all his lariness... See, Tim was fuckin' well nervous. When he came, he insisted on sleeping in the same room as Albie and me. And he had to have his brother there as well. He just didn't feel safe otherwise and he'd just lie there itching and twitching and driving everyone fuckin' mental. The other thing was the chair. That had to be there as well.

We'd found this old armchair, which was in the corner of the room, and he used to shove it against the door so no one could come in. Of course we knew that the stupid chair against the door wouldn't stop nothing at all, but we didn't say anything to him about it. We just let him do it. Dunno if he knew that really himself, but it made him feel better so every night he pushed that old chair into the door before he went off and lay down.

I thought it was burglars he was scared of but Homeless told me it was the same thing he'd told me about. Some bloke had come into his bed at night, know what I mean? Same as happened to Homeless. Homeless said once it's happened to you, you can see it in someone else. Even if they never tell you about it; just something in the eyes and the way they are with people. That give me the shivers that did. Poor little kid.

Homeless said he reckoned it had happened to Jerry as well, although Jerry was one of the hardest little nuts you'd ever see. Homeless said it affected people different ways – some kids went right into themselves thinking that's what they deserve but feeling bad anyways, others came out fighting, fists up, no-one's-ever-gonna-lay-a-fuckin'-finger-on-me-again attitude. I know plenty of kids like that. Yeah. Makes you think. Dunnit?

Anyways, Jerry was quite useful to me, to be fair. We'd go down the market, me and him, and just stay well out the way 'til the end of the day when everyone was packing their stuff up into their vans and trucks and that. The shoppers were gone then and the stall holders were all relaxed and that, having a chat, kicking back. Then it was easy to nip in when someone's back was turned and grab something out the back. Jerry was quick as lightening and got a real buzz out of doing it. I 'spose he thought for the first time in his life, he was getting something over someone.

I used to feel like that when I was his age. Nicking sweets and that. But I felt bad about stealing off the market 'cause these were prob'ly decent people trying to make a living and didn't have much. But we had nothing. Nothing at all, so what could you do? But I did feel bad so when I had a bit of cash on me I'd go and buy our spuds and stuff off the market instead of in the shops. I know it don't make it alright. Not exactly even-stevens, but that was the best I could do to square it up.

Like I said, we never knew where half of the kids came from. Someone who knew someone, you know. Friend of a friend, like. That's what started happening after a while. We'd have kids coming up to Albie in the street – he stood out a bit – or someone who'd been before would come back with some mates.

It made me laugh it did. I remember one of the stories Nan used to read to me when I was a real little kid. About this mad fella in fancy dress called the Pied Piper who took all these kids out of a town somewhere 'cause he thought the parents were crap or something. Albie was a bit like that, I reckoned when I thought about it. With his big long coat and those hats he wore and all these kids following him around.

Them hats. I nicked him one out the charity shop once. A big black top hat it was. I just saw it and I knew it were for him and I kinda wanted to get him something, you know. He loved it. You know what he did? He got some woman's scarf, a long black see-through thing and tied it round the hat band so the long ends were all streaming down the back and made him look even madder. Like an undertaker or something. I felt a bit bad about nicking out the charity shop though, so a few weeks later, I went back when it was closed and shoved some money through the door.

That Pied Piper story. Yeah he were like that bloke, Albie was. Mind you, it's a funny story to tell kids, innit? If you think about it. Lured away by some creepy-looking bloke. But when I remember hearing it, it didn't seem scary. Seemed kinda nice, alright. And the kids seemed quite happy to go off with him, so maybe he were okay, that piper man. To be honest with you, if their parents were anything like the shite we got, they'd be better off - even with a weirdo in a funny coat.

Anyway, Jerry was cool, he was a sharp little fucker and very quick. And there was another little kid, Liam. Those two became my crew. My little mates. Liam was a little hard nut. Me and Albie found him on the estate one day. I didn't know him. He weren't from the flats and he were a bit young for me to have come across him any other way.

We was walking on the estate. Albie liked going for walks and sometimes, he liked me to go with him. Sometimes, he talked. Sometimes, we just walked saying nothing. Either way it was always cool. We went down to the rec and back. As we walked down ,there was a dead cat on the side of the road. It had been there for days, someone had kicked it into the side and something had had a go at it so it was slowly rotting away there in the gutter. At first you couldn't tell what it was, then you could make out the leathery ear and the long tail.

On the way back, there were a couple of kids standing round it. They were poking it with sticks, not that there was much point 'cause it wasn't like it was gonna get up and start going 'miaow' was it? Then they started hitting it. Bringing the stick up and clubbing the thing like it had just insulted their mother. Stupid little bastards. Mind you, that was just the sort of stupid mindless thing I used to do when I were a kid.

One of them was really into it. His dirty little face all screwed up with rage.

Albie stopped. This kid, he just looked at him and then turned back and carried on with what he was doing. When he looked up I recognised him under his cap. I'd seen him round the flats, alright. Little hard nut.

Albie said, 'What are you doing?'

The kid goes, 'Nothing.' He says it like a cross between a question and a dare. 'What's it to fuckin' you?' it means.

It was just the stupid sort of answer I used to give and Albie came back with one of those questions that always used to get me.

'Why are you doing it?'

When he said stuff like that, it were never like he was telling you off, like a teacher or cop or something – just like he was really interested, and then when you thought about what he asked you, you realised you didn't have an answer and that made you feel weird and a bit of a prick.

I could see the kid thinking. It was like a little Countdown clock going round on his face. And when the time was up, he just looked confused, so he came up with the best answer he could. 'Fuck off!'

He went back to the cat again but he wasn't putting as much into it as he was before. Then he kind of followed us for a bit. Shouting stuff. Stupid stuff. Calling us wankers and shite and hitting the walls with his bit of stick. Albie put his hands up in an, *'Okay, okay, don't get mad'* kinda way and we carried on walking.

I wanted to go back and give him a belting but Albie said, 'Leave him. He's just trying for our attention.'

'He can have *my* fuckin' attention.'

'Leave him. He'll follow anyway. He's just lonely. He's just another one.'

'He's a fuckin' one alright.'

But I shut up and you know what? That little shite followed us all the way back, just like Albie said. And he became another one. Just like Albie said and all.

And that was Liam. Liam was a funny little sod. Reminded me a bit of me, you know, when I was little. Thought he was well hard, though he weren't really. Brutal little crew cut he had, a real skinhead. But he had a cute little baby's face underneath, though he always pulled funny expressions to try and make himself look tough. That kid'd take on anyone, and never give in. Never give in, never give in to no one. He'd never admit defeat, you know. I were quite proud of him for that. One day, I was coming back and he was getting a good going over from a couple of teenage pikeys over the back of the estate. I fuckin' ran in there soon as I saw it, clocked 'em both a good un and dragged him out. I might be little but I'm pretty mental hard when I get going and they legged it – but not 'til me and Liam had picked up some bits of wood and a couple of half bricks and chucked 'em after the pricks. Little fuckin' Liam's right there, tears running down his little face, cheeks all red with rage and crying, lobbing stuff good as the next man. Then, when they'd fucked off, he wipes his tears and snot out the way on his sleeve and goes to me, 'Didn't need your fuckin' 'elp or nothing. I was alright, I was'. Course we both know that's a lie. Those mugs were mashing him.

But I know how it is, so I just goes, 'Nah. I knows you didn't. They were just pissing me off is all.' And that's all we ever said about it.

Yeah. Jerry and Liam. My crew. My boys. And you know the best thing about them two? Below the age of criminal consent. With them, even if they did get picked up – and both two were smart and quick enough not to for some good while – there was nothing the cops could do anyway.

And I needed their help alright because kids just kept on coming to the gaff. More and more of them. And to be honest with you, it was starting to cause a bit of a worry for me 'cause Albie was the thinker and looked after the kids, but I looked after the practical stuff. The protector and provider. That was me. But it was getting harder and harder. Shopping for two was bad enough. Bulk buying was a fuckin' nightmare. And it was beginning to stress me out.

For Albie, it must have been a killer 'cause the practical stuff that I had to do, that was tough but I could handle it with a little help from my crew. But he had everyone looking to him for the answers. That's what they went to him for. And the thing was they really believed he could make everything okay. Just being in our gaff with him made some of the nightmares go away. For many of 'em, Albie was the first person who'd been good to them. Decent, like. For me, it was only the second, if you're counting, 'cause I'd had Nan. But at the end of the day, really, if you took away the funny clothes and the drawings and the books of writing and the stories and the weird way of talking sometimes, Albie was only a kid. Like the rest of us.

And some of those kids were well fucked up. They all had tales to tell. All different. Some of them made my life look like happy fuckin' Christmas.

THE BOGS OF DESPAIR

The rent boys were the ones that really used to get me and I'd thought Homeless was in a bad way 'til I heard about them. These kids used to have to go and get their money by selling themselves up the bogs. Not just 'cause they got attacked, but on purpose. That was bad. And most of 'em were doing it for drugs to block out the misery of what they had to do to at that moment to get the drugs they needed to block it out in the first place. Did my head in. It was like an evil circle, there was no way out of.

It used to make me feel a bit funny having 'em around sometimes. Not that there was anything wrong with 'em - apart from being a bit sad. I just kinda didn't want to think about all that going on. And it made me wanna get more cash, you know, 'cause I didn't want them doing all… that. And then having to get more food, that made me a bit stressed. And when I get a bit stressed, then I get a bit stroppy and that's the times when I lose it. Though I haven't lost it for a good few months now. Not since I been living with Albie.

Funny how they called 'em rent boys. I mean from what they were telling me, the price of giving some sad old perv a hand-shandy was something like the cost of two fuckin' Happy Meals. Makes you sick, dunnit? They told me that not all the guys that used to come up there were just sad old nonces, but some of 'em had flash cars and suits and wedding rings on. Stuffed shirts with briefcases and jobs. Missus and kids at home.

And that was Paul's story it turned out. We found out in the end.

Thing about Paul, he always brought money. You know like I said those kids who were still living at home always brought something like food or booze that they nicked for themselves. Everyone tried to give something, even those who'd nicked off the street would try and bring something back and not take it all for themselves. Though it was tough for me and sometimes I felt like I was just feeding, feeding, feeding everyone all the time, it was cool that a lot of them helped out in the way they could – though it was never enough.

But no one really bought money. Except Paul.

After what Homeless said about him, we followed him up one time when he went off. Me and Jerry and Liam did. Just to see what he did 'cause he was a real mystery that one. In some ways, I wish we hadn't. But also – at the same time – I was fuckin' glad we did. He wandered up to the dark end of the rec. By the car park. Where the junkies sometimes hung out round the back of the bogs. But he didn't do nothing when he got there. Just stood about outside the bogs and pulled out a fag. Just hanging about smoking, like he had nothing better to do.

We was looking at each other, bit confused like. Seemed a bit weird, unless he were waiting for someone. Then some car pulls up, parks right at the end of the carpark, which was odd 'cause there was loads of space. Posh car. Blue Beamer with some business-type guy in it, which was also weird cause there ain't no offices or anything round here but I s'posed he just wanted a slash. Anyways, he looks over at Paul and Paul looks back, looks down and stubs out his fag, and then looks up again. The man keeps looking. And then starts getting out the car.

This bloke heads for the bogs, pinstripe suit, briefcase and all. Paul follows him. And – after a bit – so do we.

The bogs stink. Filthy they are. There's no one at the urinals and only one cubicle with anyone in it. Two people in it. I look at Jerry and Liam and we goes up to it quietly. And then I smack the door as hard as I can with my foot and it flies open, banging back against the wall. I dunno what I'd expected to see. I mean it must have been this or something like it. But it was like a shock – that fat twat sat with his trousers round is ankles and Paul kneeling in front of him. Poor bastard. Like a smack in the head. And I lose it. Big time. Red mist comes down and all. I pick up the guy's case, which is on the floor, and and I smack him as hard as I can round the head with it calling him everything I can think of, the dirty, filthy little shit! His face, just before it hits is a fuckin' picture, gob hanging open, eyes like saucers then, 'Thwack!' I bet that got rid of his hard-on all-fuckin'-right. Jerry grabs Paul and drags him out. The little bastard's in a daze like he don't really know what's going on and his legs are all wobbly like he's stoned. Jerry shoves him in the corner, out the way, and he just kinda slides down the wall, his head in his hands.

Then Jerry and Liam are all over the bloke. He's still stuck on the bog there, dazed with blood coming out of a big gash on the side of his head where the case hit and he's trapped with his trousers all knotted round his ankles. Their little hands take watch, wallet, cash in seconds and we're off. I'm dragging Paul along behind us, dragging him by his arm cause his legs are still all over the place.

We run and run 'til we can't run no more. Though we know there's no way that bloke's coming after us. Not in a million. We run down a back alley out the way and stop to get

our breath back. I've still got the case, so we bust it open with
a brick but when we get inside there's only a shite load of
boring paper and some sandwiches. We eat the sandwiches
and chuck the rest away. Paul don't want none though.

'You alright?' I says to him.

'I wanna go home,' he said.

So we took him home.

Albie was back at the flophouse so we brought Paul to
him. He had started to cry by then. But even his crying was
silent. Just tears, coming out his eyes. He cried and cried and
cried. We didn't tell Albie what we'd done and he didn't ask.
I dunno if Paul told him. He never said. But after the crying,
Paul was a bit better. Sometimes, he spoke, even. But he kept
close to Albie all the time. And he never went out for money
again. I was quiet for a few days myself after that. Thinking it
through and that. But I knew we done the right thing.
Definitely.

And that's kinda how it went after that. I think after that
we became more like an army. It weren't just about having
somewhere to hang out and looking after ourselves. It were
more than that.

I dunno if Albie decided then or whether he knew what he
was about from the very beginning. You could never tell with
him. He must've had some of it planned, I reckon.

I remember it was after that thing with Paul, I asked him
about that name, Albion and what it meant. He said it was an
old name for England or something. He told me some story
about Troy – I'd heard of that. They made a film about it. He
told me Troy was one of the great powerful countries – like
America today – but it all went wrong and everyone left. One

of the great grandsons of one of these great boss princes came to England with some of the Trojans. No one lived there then apart from some giants and mythical creatures.

The island was called Albion, after one of the giants but when Brutus came they called Albion Britain after him and the people Britons. That's us. Anyway that's where Albion came from, he said. That's our ancestry. Our roots. The roots of Albion, he said. We were its children. Albion's children. The Children of Albion. It kinda fitted for all of us and all, I said. He didn't get that at first. Then I said, 'All of us flopping down in this house with you.'

He smiled then and his eyes went all dreamy. 'Children of Albion. In the flophouse. Yes. I like that.'

Then he started scribbling in his little book.

Albie showed me what he'd done later, after the others had gone to sleep. There was this drawing with one of the angel figures from his book that looked like him in it. I could see it was supposed to be him 'cause he was wearing that mad black top hat that I thieved for him. Then there were all these mad raggy kids, all skinny with big, big black eyes and dark smudges under them like they weren't feeling too good. In front was another little skinny one with a gappy little grin and dead short hair under a baseball cap and hoodie. He was all skinny too, with crazy black eyes and yelling – right out the picture with his hand up but you couldn't tell if he was trying to fight someone, or fight someone off. It was a bit creepy. But it was good. I'd give him that alright.

'What's that?' I said.

'That's us,' he said. 'All of us'.

And I could see, then. The yeller was me. And it looked like me and all.

The funniest thing, it looked more like I felt inside and

never said, than what I looked like in real life. But that was Albie. He always knew how you felt even if he didn't say nothing. I dint mind it being in a picture either. It was like he was talking for me, for things I couldn't say myself.

And then I got it. It wasn't just for me. It was for all of us. And I was proud.

There was Homeless in the background, all skinny with loads more skinny kids kinda coming out of the background behind him like zombies. There was Jerry and Liam in the front, little, grinning scallies fighting over something or the other like usual. There was pretty Paul, all big-eyed but with no real mouth to show he didn't speak, Marty's babies crawling on the floor. Even Milo and Katie were there, messing with each other off at the side...'cept I thought he'd drawn Katie prettier than she actually were in real life.

We kinda looked like those kids out of that Oliver film that's on telly at Christmas. And I s'pose we were in a way - though Albie was just one of us and dint make us do nothing. We did it 'cause we wanted to and 'cause we preferred our flophouse to anywhere else. And you know what, you couldn't fuckin' blame us could yer?

So that was us.

Yeah Yeah. Thing is, all of us in the flophouse were pissed off in one way or another, whether sad-pissed-off like Homeless, or angry-pissed-off like me. I dunno why. Albie said we all had shite parents and that's why we were pissed off.

I said to Albie, 'How do you know your parents are shite?' 'cause, like, Milo and Katie had parents with loads of cash who were buying them shite all the time like parents should do, but they still had the same pissed-off thing. He looked at me with those big old eyes of his and he said,

'You just know.'

I was gonna ask him more about his then, but I didn't for some reason. Wish I had now. Anyways, like I say, Albie stopped me. Stopped all of us. Even stopped that mad bitch Katie, in a way, I s'pose – for a while. Yeah, we all kind of stuck together instead of looking to our mums and dads – if we had 'em – we looked to each other – and to Albie. Albie called us The Children of Albion. That's us. And we were everywhere. Everywhere. Even if you can't see us, we're there alright.

THE CHRONICLES OF ALBION

Outside, the traffic wheezes and the sirens scream. The shadow men emerge and the people howl out into the darkest of dark voids, which orange light and bronzed liquor will not chase away. But my scream, it is the loudest and most silent of all.

THE CHILDREN OF ALBION

I didn't forget mum and Sam. Not altogether. I'd go by home from time to time. I could tell by the state of the place what was going on. I even popped in to see Mum now and then just to keep her sweet, like, and pick up a few things. Didn't want her calling the social on me or the cops, though I knew she wouldn't. Told her I was staying with a mate and she seemed okay. But there was a fella around. That much I could tell. And it seemed to be the same one 'cause his stuff was still there if I went and then went back again. That was prob'ly why she weren't winding herself up about me – busy with him, which was good. In a way.

On Sam's birthday, I bought her a card and snuck in the house to leave it in her room. I just put it where I knew only Sam would find it, in her drawer where her make up is. I figured for once, she wouldn't mind me going in her drawer since it was a birthday card and nothing rotten.

As I was nipping back out, I could hear the Thomas's downstairs rowing again. He was slapping her around and she was giving as good as she got. You should see her sometimes, with her head all pulped up and her lip out to here where he's been clocking her one. The scumbag! But you have to hand it to her for at least trying to have a go back, I s'pose.

Anyways, I was legging it down the stairs when I nearly fall over something. It's Lisa Marie Thomas. She's only little and she's come outside to get away, and she's crying. She's all huddled up, her teddy in her arms, with her head down on her knees and her arms over her head but she looks up quick when she hears my feet going past.

And I see her face.

She looks terrified and I see for a minute that it's 'cause she thinks I'm her old man. That fuckin' shocks me. I mean mine was a twat, but to be a little girl and to be that scared of your dad – that's sick, man.

I says, 'Hello, Lisa Marie. What you doing out here by yourself?' which we both know is a stupid question what with World War Three going on the other side of the door there. I sit down next to her and she looks at me, her eyelashes all stuck together and slicks like slug trails all over her cheeks where the tears have been.

'Look at the mess of you,' I says.

Poor little kid. I try to think of a way to clean her up and can't think of nothing but spitting on my shirt and using it like a cloth. It was my new one and all but there you go.

'There, now you're all pretty again.' She gives me this weedy smile but at least she stopped crying now, even though her mum and dad are still well at it. If I know them two, they'll be at it all night.

I think for a bit.

'Look, Lisa Marie, I gotta go, but if you want, you can come with me. I'll look after you. But only if you want. It won't be so nice as home but there won't be no shouting. D'you wanna come?'

She looks up at me. Big blue eyes. And she nods.

'Alright. I'll leave your mum a note so she knows you're okay. Just stay here for a minute and I'll be back.'

I run quickly back to mine for paper and a pen. Albie left a note that time we took that little kid the first time and I wanted to put that Lisa Marie was alright and I'd bring her back the next day. I didn't want to put my name, Robbie, in case there was any trouble. I thought of putting Albie's seeing as they didn't know him but that might be trouble for him and all, so I put that little Children of Albion symbol that he drew on his books the other day when he showed me the drawing and left that. I couldn't do it as well as him but it looked okay; sort of official.

I ran back to the Thomas's. Lisa Marie was whimpering a bit but she stopped when I got there. I put my hand out and she puts her little one inside it. I put the note through the door and we left. They never heard anything.

Lisa Marie was good as gold. I just took her back for a while. Played imagine with her for a few hours. Girls are funny, aren't they? She just had the teddy she was holding when I found her and she sat and played with him, like he was her little baby. I had to be the doctor.

It was kinda like family that night, as I looked around the flophouse. Our crew. The Children of Albion. Albie sitting by the fire with Lisa Marie on his lap. Katie and Milo sitting in the corner, him trying to get her attention as usual, her watching Albie. Homeless and his lot. Pretty boy, Paul, who had a bit more life in him after we did that bloke over. Jerry and Liam. And me.

It was funny me leaving that note 'cause that night – though I didn't know it 'til later, Jerry and Liam went out with a spray can and stuck our symbol up everywhere. All over town. I went out the next morning and there it were. On walls, on bridges, on the side of bus stops, on the pavement. Everywhere. It felt like we were taking the place back. I felt kinda proud.

'You know,' said Albie one morning, 'We should have a celebration.'

'What? Like a party?' I asked.

'Sort of. More of a pagan celebration thing.'

I thought of the fireworks and how Albie liked 'em that

night we went down the fair.

'On Fireworks Night. Bonfire Night?'

He thought about it. 'Yes, that fits. Remember, remember the fifth of November. Gunpowder, treason and plot. You know what fireworks night is about, don't you?'

'Yeah. Fireworks, innit?'

'No. Well, yes. But there's more to it than that. The fireworks are just symbolic. There was this man once who tried to blow up the Houses of Parliament with his friends. A protest against oppression and corrupt government. He was called Guy Fawkes. That's why you burn an effigy called a guy on the top of the bonfire. The funny thing is, though, that although it's supposed to be a celebration of the restoration of the monarchy and the parliament and everything, it's actually much more of a rebellious festival in the minds of the people. Much more pagan in its roots, I think. It's actually quite an anarchic night. Do you know what I mean?'

Hadn't got a fuckin' clue, so I said, 'It'll be a laugh. We could all do with a bit of a laugh. Let off steam like.'

Albie was off thinking again. 'We have to build a bonfire. We can't do it here.'

I shrugged. 'The rec?'

I could almost hear his brain whirring around in his head. 'Yes. The rec. A bonfire we must have. You know bonfires were very important to our ancestors, they chased away the darkness and were a form of rebirth. That's what we could do.'

'Yeah.'

He was off dreaming again so I started thinking how we could do it. Fireworks might be a problem. But maybe I could have word with Milo. He might be able to sort something off his old man and we still had all that cash off the pinstripe

137

bloke. Bonfire would be a cinch. I'd just tell the kids and get them to start stockpiling. There's always loads of crap being dumped at the rec, in the streets, and that.

'Best get cracking, then,' I said.

We went out into the streets like a little ant colony, finding crap and dragging it down to the rec. Bits of wood, old chairs and other stuff that people had left lying about and the binmen hadn't been arsed to take. Branches off trees, packing boxes, pallets, bits of plywood outside some of the derelict houses – anything we could get our hands on that would burn. Jerry even dragged over an old mattress and a sofa he found. We put the mattress on the fire but kept the sofa out for sitting on.

It was amazing to watch. All these little kids going out and the bonfire getting bigger and bigger. It was well good. By the time it started to get dark, it was about three times as big as me and you had to get about three people to lift stuff onto the top. I went over to get Milo. See what he could do. He was well good. His mum and dad were planning some kind of party in their garden and his dad had got a box of fireworks in the garage for it, so we took it. Milo said there'd be no trouble. His dad would just blame it on the window cleaner or the workmen doing their next door's roof. It was a huge box and all. We got it back between the two of us. I managed to blag a few bits by bullying the Asian guy in the super to sell them to me. Didn't like doing it really but you know how it is, so we had a pretty good haul by the end of the day.

Albie was delighted. He was getting well excited about the night. Running about here and there. All over the shop he was. He was even more het up than the little uns. I was looking forward to it now. It was gonna be a quality night.

Me and Jerry made up a stencil. Children of Albion. And sprayed it on a wall on the side of the rec. Like what they'd done before. Spreading the word, like. By the time it got dark, there were about twenty of us. Me, Albie, Homeless and his mates, Marty and his nippers, Pretty Paul and co, Jerry and Liam, Danny Sears had turned up and all with Milo and they'd bought that Katie.

Then the Hoodies turned up to see what was going on. I s'pose it were only a matter of time before they stuck their noses in.

The Hoodie boys. Their name comes from the fact they all wear baseball caps and hooded tops. They pull the cap down and the hood over the top of it, keeping their head down so it's not so easy for people to see who they are and if they're up to no good. And they always were. Actually, I was a Hoodie boy. Used to be, anyways. Before I met Albie. The Hoodie boys are basically all the kids on the estate that hang out at night. When I was younger, my nan used to look out the window when she saw 'em going past and say, *'Oh they're pulling their hoods up. There's going to be trouble somewhere.'*

It was a bit of a joke really 'cause everyone knew exactly who everyone was. I smashed this guy's car once and he came running out. We was playing bonnet, roof, bonnet, bonnet, roof - you know when you have to get down the street by running along the tops of the cars and not touching the road. Anyway, I was well pissed and I slipped on the last one and went crashing through the windscreen. Glass everywhere, me trapped half under the steering wheel and the crooklock with my legs in the air laughing my head off, and the fuckin' alarm going off and all. Anyways, the others yank me out – none too gentle, but I was so pissed I never feel it 'til the next day. Then the fella, whose car it was, comes running down the street, waving his arms.

'I know you boys,' he goes. 'And I'll be after you, Robbie Terry. You can be sure of that.' But he never did nothing. They never do.

People don't go to the cops round our way. It's just not done to grass. They'll go to your old man to give you a hiding but it's not like I had a dad who could beat seven shades of shit out of me anyway. There was no point in telling Mum on me. And also, they knew if they grassed us up, we'd be back. Then it's dog shit through the letter box, banging on the doors and windows late at night, phone calls, fireworks – it's just not fuckin' worth it, is it?

I can still be a bit of a Hoodie sometimes, but I do it for me now, or for us. I prefer what we do to the Hoodies 'cause at least we're trying to do something.

Being a Hoodie, now I think about it, was really just about smashing stuff up – people as well as things – until someone locked you away or you got some bird pregnant. Bit pointless, I think now I've grown up a bit. The Amery boys were Hoodies. They kicked shite out of this boy once. He weren't doing nothing, just walking home, but he was a Paki. They kicked him up the road so hard he was in hospital for weeks. His family called the cops and we started our own little war over it. But no one said nothing. I reckon the cops knew who it was, or at least had a pretty good idea. But the fella was too scared to say nothing so they couldn't press charges. I don't fuckin' blame him though. As it was, we monstered the family for weeks. Usual stuff. Fireworks through the letter box, dog shit on the windows. Luke Amery used to get a football and play against the side wall of their house 'til about one in the morning. Duwff, duuwff, duwff, thumping against the wall. Must've driven them mad. You'd see their little sad faces looking out sometimes, but they were smart enough not to come out and challenge him. He was waiting for that, see. Then he'd go ape. I felt sorry for the family cause there were kids in there, but I suppose you have to learn the rules if you live round here and they shouldn't have called the fuzz.

Anyways, The Hoodies. I looks up from moving this log for the bonfire and there they are in the shadows under the trees. Luke weren't there but Gavin and the others were.

Must've been the fire that did it. Gavin Amery loves a bit of the old fire. He was that kid at school who liked matches too much, know what I mean? He used to be always flicking them at people and things, trying to set stuff alight. Even now, he'll always be standing there, thumbing his lighter. Set fire to some girl's ponytail once, and it was on purpose. I said he burnt his granny's house down, didn't I?

That was what I was worried about, with the Hoodies being there. Nut jobs, they were. The Hoodies came out the shadows like Homeless and his mates. Except, instead of coming out like ghosts, they came out like wolves. It was a different vibe altogether. They come and stood in a line, caps on, hoods up, hands in pockets or arms folded in front. Watching.

There they were, watching. I was pretending I couldn't see 'em 'cause I didn't want to make eye contact. Gavin Amery knows me. He's not too bad to me after that thing with the copper and the cola can when his brother started calling me the Cop Killer. But I wouldn't call him a mate or nothing. No one would. Not even his mates, so there I was waiting for it all to kick off.

But then, you'll never guess what – Albie goes over, right up to Gavin and says,

'Do you want to come and join us?'

141

I was expecting it to all kick off big time then but, you know what, the next minute there they were, yanking bits of wood out the undergrowth and helping. Believe.

Of course, being Gavin Amery, he was ordering everyone about and threatening them if they didn't do what he said. But bottom line was – he was helping. And because he was, his little team of knuckle grazers were as well. I looked at Albie, my face all screwed up like. Uh? He just put his forefinger up, tipped the brim of his hat up and winked at me.

I shrugged. If he thought it was okay s'pose it was okay. You had to hand it to Albie, he could get respect off of anyone. Even Gavin Amery.

So there you go.

Then Albie called us all together. Gavin Amery and his goons hung back a bit, but they were still listening on the edges, like they wanted to be a part of it, too. Albie said it was time to light the fire. He pulled out a big piece of wood – a fencing post I think it was – and wedged a bit of rag in the top of it. He put his hand in the pocket and pulled out a lighter and some lighter fuel. Dripping the fuel on the rag, like making a petrol bomb, he wedged it in a fork at the top of the post and then set fire to it. It flamed like a torch. He held it up. All the little nippers had their eyes glued to him. Don't blame 'em. He looked like the God of Hellfire. He leant over and lit the bottom of the bonfire. It smouldered for a while and then went up in big blue and orange flames.

He turns round to us them and holds the stake up in the air, getting all excited like. Crazy bastard. Albie starts bouncing around then, his long coat and the streamers off his hat swirling and swirling around behind him as he's bending and lighting bits of the bonfire with the flaming stake. He's laughing and singing away – yelling more like.

I joined in the chorus, 'Heh, heh, heh.' Punching my arm into the air.

The kids looked at me then copied, joining in with their little high voices, 'heh, heh, heh.' Hands waving in the air, fists clenched, arms swinging over their heads. Whatever they wanted.

The flames had really taken hold now. The bonfire's massive. Big orange ball of flame and black smoke curling up to the sky. The little kids run to it, the warmth of the flames turning their cheeks red, the smell of smoke. Bonfire smoke. Different from fag smoke. The fags come out though, the bottles and cans. Kids are dancing and singing. Drinking and shouting and laughing. Homeless and his mates – I've never seen them so lively – are trying to jump over the flames without getting their arses burnt. Albie's just standing there in front of the blaze. He looks like some big black moth with all this mad orange light off the fire behind him.

Then he says. 'Stop!' Just like that. 'Stop!'

And you know what? Everyone does.

He started telling us then about this bird. Feenicks, it was. But it weren't spelt like that. He said it was a bird that flew into the fire. I said it sounded like a bit of a dumb type of bird but he said it wasn't 'cause all the bad stuff got burned up by the flames and afterwards the bird was better. Brand new again, like. He said we should do our own feenickses. The shite that we really hate, the worst thing in our life we should write on a bit of paper and then chuck it in the fire to burn up. The fire would eat it away, he said.

Albie had some paper and a pen. He always had a pen in his pocket. Even if he had no paper when he thought of something he would write it on his skin, on the inside of his arm or on his belly sometimes, if he run out of arm. Then he'd put it in one of his books later. Mentalist.

Some of the kids couldn't write, so he said they could ask one of the older kids who could to do it for them, or they could ask him. They all asked him, of course. He was the only one they trusted not to take the piss.

Well I thought it was a bit mad but I went along with it. And no I ain't saying what I put. That's for me to know. Albie knows of course, but he knew without me even telling him. That's what he's like. I told you. Strange thing was, I did feel a bit better watching the fire take a bite out the paper, then turn it black and then eat it up and spit it out as little black flakes into the sky. I'm just standing there, thinking about what he said, chilling out and watching when someone comes over and stands beside me. It's Gavin Amery. He pulls a packet of fags out of his pocket. I've just put one out myself.

Gavin opens the packet carefully and picks inside the top with his thumbnail. Inside the top is a wrap. He looks at me, the flames making his face flicker.

'Whizz,' he says. 'D'you want some?'

Did I? I sure as fuck did. Just to round the night off.

Gavin opened the wrap carefully, stretched out his hand, palm downwards and tipped a little into the hollow at the base of his thumb. Then he held it up to his nose and sniffed. He licked his finger and dabbed it in what was left so it stuck to the tip and then rubbed it on his gums. He sniffed again and grinned at me, baring his teeth. Then he offered the packet to me. I did the same, feeling the old familiar bitter burn in the back of my throat. I grinned back at him.

'Cheers, mate.'

'You're alright, you are,' he said, frowning at me at the same time. Not to be too friendly-like. You know how it is?

I grunt. We both stand there watching Albie, waiting for

the stuff to hit the system. By the look of *him*, you'd think he'd been mainlining the stuff since dawn. He was running about everywhere.

Gavin even offered me some blow. I thought about having a bit of a puff with him. But I said no and stuck with the whizz. I kinda felt I needed to keep my wits about me. Milo was scouting for some so I sent him over that way to get some sales. Poor old Milo. Still sniffing round that silly cow Katie, he was. Trying to get blow for her and all. To impress her.

Knowing her, she'd be off with Gavin Amery just 'cause she knew he had stuff. And he's fuckin' ugly.

I just sit there on a bank watching it all. Though I've got the whizz buzzing round my system and it's starting to argue with the drink, I feel kind of relaxed. You know like things are okay. Every so often, I see Albie in the distance leaping about – wherever he is, he's always being followed by a little line of kids. That feeling. It was the same feeling like the other night. Like family. I can see the spray-painted symbol on the side of the scout hut. The Children of Albion.

Things get a bit mad after that. Some of the kids get up on the scout hut. Gavin and his mates are buzzing. They disappear for a while. Suddenly, there's this huge roar of a car and big yellow lights blinding me. At first, I think it's the cops rolling up to put the mockers on everything. I put my arm up over my eyes to try and make it out. One of the fellas is standing up, hanging out the door. Don't seem exactly like the cops, and it ain't. It's Gavin. They've only gone off and nicked a car, ain't they. Stereo and all. To be fair to the geeks, that was pretty handy.

They drive it right up to the fire and start messing with the stereo, tuning it into that blinding indie station they do on Saturday nights and pumping it up real loud. The kids start dancing around, round and round the flames. Albie comes over and grabs my arm, spinning me round and round. Some of the kids have crawled up on the scout hut and are dancing around up there, waving their bottles of beer and cider in the air.

I'm looking for Milo 'cause I haven't seen him for a while and there he is, with Katie. He's got her backed up against the scout hut wall and he's going for it. Snogging the face off her and a hand up her skirt, so he's happy enough. Gavin and the geeks have climbed onto the roof of the car and are jumping around up there, holding onto each other to try and stop from slipping off. One of the geeks misses his footing and goes tumbling down onto the grass but he's so off his head he don't hurt hisself and the next minute he's up on the bonnet trying to drop kick the windscreen. The kids are round the car then and the fire. A huge jumping seething mass. One of Homeless's mates has pulled the chrome bumper off the car and is using it like some huge drumstick, banging it off the metal drainpipes on the scout hut. Some other kids have got a couple of bin lids and are banging them on the ground. Some girl I've never seen before, with her hair all twisted up funny, is dancing to the beat, just on her own, minding no one.

It's beautiful. It really is. Fuckin' beautiful!

Then I feel Albie standing beside me. 'We did this. Us,' he goes.

I looked around then. All these kids. Dancing. Laughing. Dancing and laughing like never before.

Nah. You know what they was doing? What they'd never done before? They was playing.

THE CHRONICLES OF ALBION

One seekest forever what one has lost. Freed from one's nuclear tribe but tribal nonetheless. Forging perhaps within one's own soul. And some angel or vagabond placed a sceptre in my hand, so I lead and I call.

At the witching hour, the churchyard yawns and the living dead awaken and dance like dervishes on the graveyard they have made of my once great land. My father sleeps on....oh, awaken! Awaken! Still he slumbers and only the prince and his pint-sized knights answer the call. The phoenix blazes and expires. And we build our Neverland, foreverland, foreverengerland. Forever-England.

A PYRE FOR THE GODS

But you know, it couldn't last. Some fuckin' old one from the houses by the rec must've called 999. The fire engine; you know the big old red Dennis like the little kids' toys, comes rolling up dunnit? With all the little Fireman Sams jumping out in their big fat farmers' wellies and their placky trousers and jackets.

To be fair, I can see they're pretty impressed by what we've managed to do 'cause that bonfire is something else now. The flames are bigger than the scout hut. The firemen go round the back to get the hose sorted but there's kids all over them. It's piss funny. Every time they try and get the hose connected, one of the nippers goes round and messes with it so they're standing there with this big fuckin' hose and nothing coming out the end of it. And then they have to start all over again. The kids on the roof start pulling up the tiles and chucking 'em down and all, trying to stop the firemen from putting out the flames. The firemen can't do nothing either. They're not like the Old Bill. They've got nothing on them and all they can do is pull the face shields down over their face helmets and keep moving forward. They're worried about the car, I suppose, more 'n anything 'cause if that goes up there's gonna be some wicked bang. But Gavin and the geeks ain't letting them get anywhere near it. They're still on the roof of the car and chucking rocks at the firemen. Little Jerry and Liam are collecting the ammo for them so as soon as they run out they've got a fresh supply. Told you them kids are well smart.

The Fireman Sams must've radioed the cops 'cause the next thing, there's the old blue lights flashing over the orange as a panda car swerves up, pulling a huge doughnut on the gravel as they do. You know, I don't mind firemen as it goes, but cops have such a big fuckin' attitude. There's no need for it. Always makes it worse 'specially the young ones, giving it the big 'un. I reckon it's 'cause they make 'em wear those crappy uniforms with the tit-head helmets. If they had cool sorta Robo-cop, superhero-cop gear like them ones who kick the shite out of England fans in Europe, maybe they'd be better. On the other hand, maybe they'd be worse.

I've sidled off backwards now so I'm watching out the way where they can't spot me. I don't fancy another evening at the Hotel Old Bill, thanks. I can see Albie – fair play to him – gathering up the kids and trying to get them out round the back of the fire without the cops seeing. Soon as the Old Bill steam in, everyone scatters, 'cept old Homeless, whose monging around, trying to work out what's happening.

'Oi!' I yell at him. He certainly doesn't want to get lifted. Or any of the rest of them. They'll be back in those shitty homes before they know where they are. Gavin and the geeks have legged it and I'm glad to see Jerry and Liam are out of sight in the shadows, too.

The cops are running here and there but the kids are too fast and within seconds everyone's gone. Out of sight. Like they were never even there at all. All that's left is a big smouldering heap of ash and a beaten up old car with the music still blaring out of it. One of the cops leans in and turns it off and then they hang around for a bit chatting to the firemen and having a fag before they pack up and go.

The panda car pulls out onto the road and then stops and reverses up. There's a couple snogging in the bushes. Copper gets out his flashlight and there they are. It's Milo and Katie. They make him turn out his pockets. They've found something. Puff. Only fuckin' puff. And it's Milo. *Milo*, for fuck's sake – the poor fuckin' bastard. It's not exactly one of us. You know. The *troublemakers.* The ASBO lads. And there's a few of us down here. The ones they're trying to build up a collection of behind locked doors at the secure units and YOIs – well they would if they had enough room in there.

But they can't get us. And they're pissed off they were just made to look like a bunch of mugs by a load of kids. And Milo's better than nothing, so he gets it for all of us. Poor bastard.

They took him down the station and did him for possession. He's not even been in trouble before so you'd expect a slapped wrist and a, *'naughty boy, don't do it again.'* You'd think they'd just let him go with a fuckin' caution, but no. I reckon that bitch of a mum of his pushed it to give him a fright. And they've got that new super down there who's always banging on the telly about juvenile crime and the scourge of drugs, so he was fuckin' well unlucky there.

Yeah, they pushed the whole thing and made him go to court and all. The juvie court. And they shoved it through real fast so it only took few weeks. Dunno how they did it. Anytime I've had to go up there, it's been months so by the time you're up there you've already done a whole bunch of other stuff and it's old fuckin' news, and everyone's bored of it.

It's horrible, the juvie court. Always stinks of fags even though you're not allowed to smoke. There's always loads of cross, skinny kids hanging round outside. And the parents. They're worse. There's the ones that care – all dressed up and scared more 'n the kids. And the ones that couldn't give a shit, who turn up in tracksuits and baseball caps with their bellies showing – if they turn up at all.

The court itself always reminds me of some old sci-fi programs you get on Freeview. Dunno what it is. I 'spose it's like you're in this other world that's just totally away from reality. All the ones I've been in – and I've been in a few – they're all the same. Funny kind of panelling everywhere, kind of gingery colour and everything looks like it's made out of cardboard and you could just pack it up, put it in back the box, take it off and build it somewhere else. Then there's the juvie mags – magistrates. Three types – old buffer, token woman, token Black or Asian. The buffers are usually bad news and the women can go either way. There's the 'poor you' brigade who will usually give you probation or some of their mental new community schemes, or the miserable old bitch who can be worse than the buffers. You know the kind I mean? You wouldn't even dare burgle their house. The rest just fall in between. It's all bollocks though. Bit like being in a play or something, 'specially when the cops have to get up and read their lines. Makes me laugh, it does 'cause half the time, no one knows what anyone's talking about. I think they do it like to make it seem important. But if you dunno what they're on about, it's just confusing. I've seen kids come out and not even know if they've got off or not. But I like it when they give you the big speech at the end though. That's funny. The telling off one. The 'naughty boy' one. Always cracks me up. Every time.

Me and Albie went up there for Milo. Bit of support like. I got us a couple of suits out a bag left up the scout hut for the jumble, and Albie sorted our hair. Couldn't do much with mine so he gave me a cap to wear. Not a baseball cap but some dumb, checked, grandad cap. He said it would make me look different. Did that okay. Made me look like an idiot. Albie slicked his hair back and to be fair, he looked quite cool – like a businessman. We weren't going in and that. You can't. Not when it's kids. We wanted to lurk so he knew we was there, but we didn't wanna be picked up by anyone else so we tried to look a bit respectable like. I certainly didn't want the cops asking me funny questions. They all know me like. They've got nothing on me and everything is pretty tied up out their way but I could do without the hassle, you know?

Juvie court's normal for me but I reckoned Albie'd never been there before 'cause he kept looking round at everything and I had to stop him walking into the courts a couple of times.

'This is weird,' he kept saying. 'Weird.'

I saw a few kids I knew and who knew me but I managed to keep my head down so they didn't see me. But Milo saw us and give us a grin. Bit of a lame grin. He looked shit scared to be honest wivya. But at least he knew we done the business for him 'cause he was our mate. But then Milo's mum saw us alright and we had to leg it. I saw Danny Sears down the parade the next day and he told me Milo got a fine which was grand 'cause his old man just paid that off, but that his mum went ballistic and he weren't allowed out in case he came across the likes of us, so we didn't see him no more.

That was why Katie started coming on her own. And I really wish she hadn't. I wish she'd just stayed away. Found some other mug to go after.

THE SIREN

I think it was about that time I started noticing things going wrong with Albie. Didn't realise it at the time but that's when it started. I 'spose looking back again, I can see why. It was tough on him alright. All that pressure. They all wanted him. Like a God. Or a footballer. Or a pop star or something. Must've been hard. Once I thought I heard him crying at night. But he said he was just sniffing cause his sinuses were all fucked up. I said he smoked too much, but he said he didn't smoke nearly enough – and then he laughed, so I reckoned he was okay.

Couple of days later, I was in the offy, down the parade, trying to lever a can of Strongbow into the pocket of my hoodie while the dumb tart at the desk was on her mobile having a row with her fella or something. And just as I did it, this hand come down on mine and grabbed my wrist. I tried to jerk away but the hand had me. I whizzed about trying to think how I could escape.

'What you up to?' a voice said. It was Sam.

I weren't quite sure what to do. Me and Sam used to get on okay and I kinda love her like I love mum. We used to be alright together a while back; we used to play together a lot as nippers. She used to invent all these games and we'd hang out on the Patch – the grassy bit by our flats where Mum could see us out the window – or in Nan's garden.

Sam's real smart. Once, she organised a sports day on the estate and all the kids from round here came along. And she did it just for me. I'd just got kicked out the school sports day for decking Dave Barrett 'cause he said our Mum was a slut, which was a shame 'cause I was fast on my feet and I woulda won stuff. Sam knew I'd been looking forward to it and all, and that Mrs Andrews had said I'd probably get a prize and that. Quick on my toes like, I am. Always have been. Could always get away from mum when I were naughty. Leave her clutching at air and me already out the door and down the street.

Yeah. Sam was nice then. She started going funny after dad left. I don't really remember him living with us but Sam does 'cause she's a bit older. She said it was like being in a real family, like off the telly like. I don't remember but I know he used to come and take us out sometimes and ring us on our birthdays and stuff, and come over and give us presents. Christmas presents we got. Then it stopped. Nothing. Not a dickie.

I knew he weren't dead or nothing 'cause one day, when we were up town, we saw him with some woman, his arm round her and that. She had a baby in a pushchair. Then, just in case there might have been any doubt about it, he kissed her. Big full-on snog, like. I just stared. I was young like and a bit confused. Sam was upset and ran off down the road. Me and mum had to go and find her. Asking in shops and that. Mum was spare. She was nearly calling the cops, but we found her in Millers'. She was crying in the nineties.

After that, she went moody, like. She used to scream a lot, especially at Mum. Like it was all her fault. But I suppose he weren't there to scream at were he? He'd gone and fucked off. Then she'd go up to her room and slam the door nearly off its hinges. She just used to ignore me. I used to sit on the floor outside her door, trying to be friends again like it was before but she used to step over me when she came out. I gave up and just got on with things myself.

When I think about it, maybe that was when mum got the

depression. I kind of remember her being like a proper mum, cuddles and that, but it's not a proper memory, more like a feeling. And...yeah... like a smell. But that's all I can remember.

I remember her looking out the window a lot. And crying a lot. Yeah, lots of crying and lots of looking. Looking fer 'im to come back, I suppose, thinking about it. Well that was a fuckin' waste of time, so she went a bit soft. She wanted Nan to look after her, then Sam, then me. Nightmare. I do it when I can. She's my mum after all, but I can't look after her all the time. And I dunno why she just couldn't work out you have to look after yourself. I mean, I'm only a kid and I worked that one out a long time ago.

Her best plan, the best she could come up with, was getting the depression so she weren't working no more, then getting the drink to look after her instead, which it didn't. Not really.

Anyways. That's just that, innit? Life, innit?

This, 'What you up to?' is the first thing Sam's said to me in years I reckon, apart from, 'Tttt' and, 'Fuck off!' so I'm a bit taken aback, like.

'So?' she asks, still waiting for an answer.

It's pretty fuckin' obvious what I'm doing with a can of Strongbow half way to my pocket so I decide to say nothing. Dumb bird's still on the phone arguing so she ain't noticed.

Sam sighs. 'Look, I'll get it for you, if you like. Give it here.' She takes the can off me. Then she pauses, puts it back and takes another. Not just one can but a pack of four.

'Don't drink 'em all at once.'

She goes to the counter. 'And twenty blue.' The bird don't even get off the phone while she's putting it through the 'til –

still whingeing away while she's taking the money and handing back the change. Sam takes the bag and I follow her outside. She takes the fags out, opens the packet, takes one and lights it and then puts the fags back. She gives the bag to me.

'There yer go.'

'Cheers! Thanks, Sam,' I say.

We stand together outside the offy, leaning against the wall. Smoking. The two of us. It's nice.

Then she says. 'You're not at home anymore.'

'Not much,' I say.

'Where you staying?'

I don't look at her. I just look at the ground. 'A mate's.'

There's a bit of a silence and then she says, 'I know where you're staying.'

I don't say, 'Why d'you fuckin' ask then?' 'cause I know this is one of them things where it ain't really what you say that's important but something else going on between the two of us.

And then she says again, 'I know where you're staying.'

You see? And that's why she'd be so annoying sometimes, Sam, because she's smart like that. And something about the way she says it makes me know it's not a wind up. She's not lying to me. She knows alright. She takes a big draw on her fag and blows the smoke out into the sky.

'I won't tell,' she says. And something about the way she says that makes me know she's not lying to me about that neither.

A car drives past. It's Ginger-in-our-flats' big brother. Kevin. He's alright.

He does this big fuck-off doughnut, gravel spinning everywhere. I think he's just acting the bollocks at me but then

I realise it's not for me. It's for Sam. He's showing off for her.

She pretends she ain't noticed but I can see she's watching him out the corner of her eye. Kevin's a bit of a one with the birds and he ain't used to being ignored like that, so he leans out the window and goes

'Oi! Legs! Gotta license for that skirt?'

I look at Sam. She flicks her ash on the ground and without looking up goes, 'What's it to you?'

He laughs. 'I'm the inspector, see. The skirts inspector.'

She snorts. She still don't look up though. He frowns. It don't usually take this long. He waves a packet of Marlboro at her.

'Wanna fag?'

'Got one, innit.' But this time she looks up.

He grins. Then he says to her, 'You coming over, then?'

'Might do.' There's a long pause. She levers herself off the wall and walks slowly over like she's walking to her own execution and like he's the judge who sentenced her, dragging her feet like it's the worst fuckin' thing that could ever happen. She's not even looking at him, she's kinda staring down the road.

But it's all all part of the act. The next minute she's over there and is sticking her head in the driver's window, her arse all stuck in the air and starts flirting back. Big time. I feel a bit of a mong just standing there. But I don't mind Kevin, as it goes. At least he remembers me and bothers to say, 'Hi'. He looks round Sam at one point and says to me, 'Alright?' so's I don't feel too much of a mug just standing there by the wall by myself.

I grunt, but not in a moody way. I suppose it could be worse. I mean there's plenty of scumbags round here she could have gone for and at least he's got normal hair. Not carrot like the rest of Ginger-in-our-flat's lot. And he's got a car. And his tattoos are cool. And he wears proper clothes, not just chavvy trackies like some of the blokes round here. Proper nice. Label jeans and shirts and that.

A lot of girls round our way fancy Kevin. He's always got someone on the go and at least one kid somewhere, or so the story goes. He's a bit of an old charmer and I didn't think Sam would fall for that but it looks like she has. I leave them to it.

'I gotta go,' I say.

Sam looks round. 'You be okay?'

'Sure.'

'Take care, alright.'

'Yeah.'

She turns and watches me go, and Kevin looks down to check out her arse as she does. I wonder if she's going to wander off and all. Make him work a bit harder for it. That'd be just like her. But the next minute, she's walking slowly round in front of the car and she's in the passenger seat. And off they go, snogging away like mad. There you go. Romance, Sned's style.

There must be something in the air 'cause it's all going off back at the flophouse and all. Homeless has found a couple of homeless birds. They're a bit grubby and quiet looking but ideal for him, and he's delighted with himself, sitting there sharing a bottle of voddy with them; them all flirting with him under their dirty hair all hanging down. Kids like him don't usually get the girls, so I'm kind of happy for him. And Milo's there. It's good to see him.

I knock fists with him. 'Alright, man. How d'you get a pass out?'

His old man and his old lady have gone off to their villa in Spain and got his nan to babysit for him to make sure he don't go out. But she's a bit of a gin monster and tends to get a bit pissed by eight and sits watching soap re-runs on Milo's dad's big screen, eating chocolates, so he sneaked out his bedroom window and off the garage roof. Katie saw him go from next door so he brought her along with him and all, so there's not much sense out of him cause he's just trying to get pissed and get in her knickers. She's taking all the booze he's offering but it's Albie she's after; her eyes are following him every time he moves and she's hanging on every word that comes out his gob – even when Milo's trying to whisper sexy stuff in her ear.

Poor Albie's wandering about with all the kids hanging off him. Looks like Marty Malone's dropped his crew off and all 'cause there's some real little ones running about, and Albie's got a couple of thumb-suckers gripping onto his coat and he's carrying another one on his hip.

'You look like the fuckin' Old Woman Who Lived in the Shoe, you muppet!' I says to him and he laughs and raises his eyebrows.

'It's just for a couple of hours.'

I nod, so there you go. Homeless is trying to get laid, Katie's eyeing up Albie, and Milo's eyeing up her. Albie's trying to cope with all the little 'uns and it's all wrecking me head – 'specially when they start asking me for the cider and moaning 'cause there's nothing to eat. Jesus, what more do they want? And not so much as a thanks for any of it.

It's getting to be a bit of a big worry to me now. There's more and more of 'em coming like nearly every day now. And they all wanna eat. And they wanna drink and all. And I'm beginning to wonder where the fuck I'm gonna get everything from. Plus, I didn't like being round there much when Katie was doing her thing and trying to get off with Albie all the time. I dunno why, but there was something about that I really didn't like, so I told 'em, 'I'm going out. Shopping.'

I went down the arcade. I weren't really shopping. At least not down there anymore. There weren't no point. They all knew me so you pretty much got a pat down every time before they let you out the door. And I got bored of doing the Pakis over and over. Seemed a bit mean, especially as they never got cross or nothing. Just looked really sad, with the big brown eyes they have on them.

So I was hanging around, wondering what to do and waiting to see if anyone would turn up when Gavin Amery comes down from the flats. He kinda grunts at me as he goes past and I kinda grunt back in a friendly way, not wanting to upset him now. He stands beside me, against the wall as if he's going to talk deep like. Then I'm aware of this big car kerbing us up the road. I spin round quickly. Pervs or cops. Neither. It's a massive four by four. Big black pimp mobile with blacked out windows and ace alloy wheels. Pulls up beside us. Gavin looks up and nods at me .

The passenger window opens slightly. Electric. Slow. A hand beckons us over. I figure it's just Gavin they want so I stay where I am.

'Cash?' says the voice in the car. It's low but I can still hear.

Gavin fumbles in his pocket. I can see he's dead nervous. I've never seen him like that before. If *he's* scared of someone you know that someone is a fuckin' headcase. Serious shit, like. He hands the money over, like it's the post office. Gets a packet back. There's a bit of chat I can't hear. The window goes up and the car moves forward. I can see Gavin relax.

Then it stops. Reverses. Comes back.

The window goes down again. Me and Gavin look back. The hand beckons.

'Here, you,' a voice orders.

Gavin shuffles over. I can see he don't want to go. He walks like something's dragging him back even though he's walking forwards, like. I'm hanging around waiting even though I'm feeling a bit uneasy. Then Gavin calls me over.

'He wants to talk to you.'

'Me?'

'Get over.'

I do. You don't argue with that family. Gavin's standing by the car. I can't see in the front cause he's standing in the way but I can see a big shoulder in a leather jacket and a big hairy hand with them heavy gold rings on and a dragon tattoo on the wrist. Dean Amery. I reckoned before it was him. I can't see properly in the back except I can see the shape of a couple of fat fucks. Back up. Figures. I'm still standing back a bit. Gavin says. 'He's doing a job. Cash and carry. Needs a little 'un.'

Dean Amery's hand comes out the window and gives Gavin a cracking backhander round the ear, which sends him reeling back off his balance. Serious skill that. It's all in the wrist action.

'Don't tell him, you stupid little twat.'

He beckons me over and tells me to drop my hood.

'Ah,' he says, grinning and showing a gold tooth. Mum said there's nothing wrong with his teeth he just had them taken out and a gold one put into make him look all hard.

'It's the cop killer.' He looks round at the fat fucks and they laugh like it's the funniest thing they've ever heard.

I looked back at him. Said nothing. Dean Amery's pretty

cool like. I mean he's boss round here. Respect. That's what he's got. And he wants to talk to me.

'Kid, I need a little help with something, and I've decided you're the man for the job.'

He stops, that's just the way he talks, and then goes on. 'Bit of climbing through small places, see. There'll be something in it for you. Cash. I want you to meet me tomorrow night. Ten thirty. Down Richmond Alley. Know it?'

I nodded.

'Good lad. We'll see you there. Don't be late, kid.'

Am I likely to be? I look back at Gavin, all back in his box after that backhander. Dean's treating me alright and I'd like to keep it that way. No is not an option here. But the fact that someone like him wants someone like me is making me feel the business again 'cause, like I say, he's boss. I feel like I've grown taller all of a sudden. I feel...well...*cool.*

I nod and the car drives off

There's a bit of quiet. I wonder if Gavin's gonna take all this out on me but he's just fishing in his pocket for his Rizlas.

'Comin'?'

I think about asking him about Dean but then I thought not. I'd be pretty pissed off if I'd been backhanded in front of someone. I thought he might act nasty over it to make himself feel better for being made to look an idiot in front of the likes of me, so I just said, 'Yeah'. We spend the rest of the afternoon smoking blow and finding trouble. I've not had fun like it in ages. No responsibility – not like at the flophouse with everyone wanting something from me. By the time I get back, I'm so knackered and doped I pass right out.

Albie's not about the next day, so me and Homeless take

over, cooking up the grub and organising a kick about to keep everyone occupied before they all start fussing about where he is. He came in later. Katie was with him. I heard her. She was spending a lot of time with him. I didn't like that. He was *my* mate after all.

The next evening sees me waiting down Richmond Alley for Dean Amery. It's not worth it not to. Like I said, you just don't say no to an Amery. And anyway, I need the cash. And I must admit I'm feeling a bit of the big 'un 'cause Dean Amery came up to me.

Richmond Alley's round the back of the cinema. It's well out the way of everywhere. Can't even drive down there, so t's a bit of a hangout for the alkies and sometimes gets used as a bit of a shooting gallery by the junkies, too. But there's no one hanging there tonight. 'Cept me.

I been waiting for a while when this big red van pulls up. It's not Dean's. He always has something flash, like the pimp wagon of the other day. If it's for some job, he's probably half-inched it somewhere. Looks like a piece of shite to me anyway.

Front door slides back and there he is. Dean. With a couple of his fellas. 'Get in,' he says.

They're having a laugh, aren't they? There's hardly any room with those fat fucks sitting there.

'Get a fuckin' move on!' One of 'em reaches down a big hairy arm, grabs the top of my arm and pulls me up by it.

'Agh. Fuck off. You fat –' I start.

He ignores me and just yanks me into the cab and slams the door shut. 'In,' he says to Dean. And they drive off.

I'm having to sit almost in this bloke's lap, which I don't like and I don't think he does either 'cause I keep moving to try and get the door handle from sticking in me leg and each time I do, he gets an elbow in the ribs.

'Oi,' He goes, pulling my ear 'til I yell. 'Sit still, you little prick.'

Dean looks over crossly. 'Stop messing about. Drivin' aren't I?'

He leans over, rummages under the dash and throws something over at me. 'Take these.'

It's a pair of leather gloves. Wee ones. They fit me great. 'Thanks'.

'They're not a gift.' he says, as we stop at the traffic lights by the kebab shop. He fixes me with his eyes. What they call a hard stare.

I look him back dead in the eyes. 'I know.' He has these weird eyes. Cold and silvery, like they're made out of metal. They make you shiver. They're not like Gavin's. His are all mental, jumping over the place and mad, like he's taken something, which he usually has. No, these are totally still. Fixed on you. Dead. It's not nice when he looks at you like that. He keeps staring at me for a bit, checking me out. Then he leaves it. It's clever, what he does. I'm not feeling quite as sure of myself as I was.

I'm glad when the lights change and we move off again, him with them evil eyes back on the road. He takes the car out onto the motorway and we go a few miles in silence, me trying not to wriggle too much 'cause I don't want to piss Dean off in any way. He pulls into this big industrial estate near the service station off the slip road. At the back, away from the other units, is a big warehouse for the cheapo supermarket down Station Road. It's all in darkness, and although there's a sign warning of security, Dean ignores it, drives through and round the back to the deliveries yard. I suppose he knows what he's doing.

He pulls up and gets out. Fat fuck gets out and all, but not before he shoved me out on the ground. It's a big drop if you're not expecting it and I turn my ankle. It hurts alright but it's okay so I decide not to make a fuss and keep quiet.

'Right,' Dean says to me. 'You're going in. Up there.' He points up to a window, a little one, up under the guttering.

'It's sorted. You'll be able to open it. It's been left undone for us. Then I need you to get the stuff out to us. Fags and booze. That's all. Got it?'

I nod.

'Good. Off you go, then.' He jerks his head to the side and my mate from the cab comes forward. 'Get him up there.'

The fat fuck walks up to the wall below the small transom window. He makes a step by knitting the fingers of both hands together, leaning forward slightly for leverage. 'Come on then.'

I come forward and get close enough to climb up, my hands grabbing the sleeves of his jacket for something to hold onto. I can smell his breath and a thick animal stink off his skin. I put my left foot on his hands for him to heave me up. Only my toe hits soft flesh and in seconds, I'm on my back in the dirt as the bastard chucks me on the floor. 'Mind my bollocks, you little prick.'

Dean blows smoke out his mouth, slowly. 'Will you two get on with it?'

The fella cups his hands again but he's watching me the whole time so I go careful. He pushes me up 'til I can get a foot on his shoulder and then shoves me, none too gentle like through the transom.

There's a fuckin' ten foot drop the other side and the way that fat idiot has me I'm looking at head butting the floor. But

I manage to swing my legs through and back under me by gripping onto the window latch, and then I hang full length before dropping to the floor. Hurts my ankle a bit but I'm okay.

It's a warehouse alright. Pallets stacked with stuff. Boxes of washing powder, trays of tin cans and big squashy piles of loo rolls all piled high. But of course, they ain't interested in that. Booze and cigarettes. The lot. Total clear out.

'Come on. What you doin' in there?' It's the twat I got in the bollocks. Bollock brain.

I head over to the booze corner. It ain't gonna be easy getting the drink through that little window although the cartons'll be okay. There's one slightly bigger window over in the corner so I pad over there and make myself a ladder of heavy boxes so I can climb up and down. Piling them up like a little baby's tower of toy bricks – five, then four, then three, then two, then one – so I can use them as steps. The window opens easy and I stick my head out. They're all standing like muppets outside the one they shoved me through. Dean's just standing away from them, leaning against the van, smoking, with this careful look on his face. Watching everyone.

'Here,' I call, urgent but quiet and they come over. I hurl a box of fags out the window and keep going – they've got the lot here. Fag heaven. I open one and take a few out for myself, stuffing them in the pockets of my jacket. Then the booze. This is harder 'cause they're quite heavy and I have to lump 'em up to the window, which ain't easy on your own. Bollock Brain is right underneath me and he keeps moaning and whingeing. I feel like dropping one on his head but I daren't 'cause I know the bottles would probably break and Dean would be after me. Be funny though. I imagine Bollock Brain's yell when a big heavy carton of booze clocks him on the nut. It's a nice thought and it keeps me going as I hump the stuff backwards and forwards, backwards and forwards. Up and down, up and down 'til my head's dizzy with it and my arms and legs are aching. But I keep going, all the time listening in the back of my brain for any noise.

Noise. Security or something. And some of them in these places have dogs. Dean said it was all taken care of tonight but you can't be too careful. Ever. Don't fancy some big Alsatian devil dog taking a bite out of my arse. Up and down up and down, I keeps going 'til it's all done and one corner of the warehouse is empty.

'Come on. You nearly done?' Bollock Brain hisses from outside.

'Yeah. Just a couple more,' I hiss back. I see what I want and lug 'em up to the window. He starts moaning again – he's really got it in for me – and I shove 'em through as hard as I can. These won't break. There's a really satisfying howl of pain. They must have got him one on the head.

'What the fuck!! Is he fuckin' mad? That's it. Let's leave the little bollocks here. Just leave the little prick inside.'

I needed them to get me out else I'm trapped like a kid in the well.

'Do that,' I yelled, 'and I'll grass you all up and say you made me do it. They'll believe me 'cause I'm a kid. I know who you all are.' I didn't but I figured it was as good a bluff as any.

Then I heard Dean's voice, sounding bored. 'Oh, just get him out. Get on with it.'

I climbed up onto the window ledge and slowly lowered myself 'til I was hanging by my elbows. It was too far to jump safely with the ground all uneven and hard like. Bollock Brain helped me none too gently down. At one point, he gripped my thigh so hard I swear his fingers touched bone through the flesh. But I kept quiet; didn't want to give him the satisfaction.

Dean was standing in front of me when I got down. 'Well done nipper. You did okay. Just one thing....' He lifts his hand and cracks me on the side of the head sending me flying onto my arse. I sit up, blinking; my ears ringing and my head banging and all these little tiny fireworks going off round my eyes. That's what they call seeing stars I suppose. It was just like in the cartoons. Made me almost wanna laugh but I figured that wouldn't be a wise move. And my brain hurt with this funny cold feeling. To be honest, I was shitting it a bit, and that's the truth, I don't mind telling you.

He kneels down to me, his faggy breath in my face and fixes me with them little sharky eyes. He don't say nothing for a bit. Enough for me to wonder what the hell he's gonna do. Then he goes, 'There's just one guy who calls the shots round here, little fella, and that's me. You just remember that and you and me is gonna get on fine. Forget and we falls out. And I wouldn't like that. And neither would you, I can promise you. Savvy?'

Loud and fuckin' clear, mate. I nod my head, which make me feel like puking, so I stop quickly. 'Yeah,' I say. What else is there to say really?

'Good. Then you and me will be fine.' He throws a carton of fags at me. They hit me on the ankle. 'You can have them cigarettes on me. A gift.' A gift? I thinks. If it weren't for me you wouldn't have none at all, you shitbag. But I don't say it.

I struggle back to my feet and as I do so one of the packets of cigarettes that I lifted myself falls out my pocket. Shit.

'Here, look,' yells Bollock Brain, happy to get me in the shite with the big boss. 'e's thieving off us. Little piece of crap. Let me do 'im.'

Dean stops. He comes back towards me. I'm half on my feet and I'm wondering shall I just get back down in the dirt on my back again? Save him the trouble of banging me there again. He leans over and looks me in the face, with something that could be called a grin but looks more like the face a dog pulls just before it's going to go crazy bollocks and bite yer. Don't care what mum says about them gold teeth, they work for me. Makes him scarier. Dunno why, I'm thinking. It's not as if they're fangs. Now that would be scary. Then I remember, I'm in a bit of a shitty situation here and I try and zone myself back in.

Dean Amery flicks me on the side of my face with his fingernail, which hurts. But not as much as the lamping, which I can still feel all over my head and the backs of my eyes.

'So you dipped your fingers in the 'til did yer? Well I don't blame you really. I like that. Would have done the same myself. Shows initiative. And a bit of guts. Yeah... I like that.' He looks round at the others for approval, which of course he gets. Even from Bollock Brain, who I know is dying to give me a good kicking if Dean 'll let him off the leash. Bunch of lick-arses.

Then Dean comes back to me. He's so close I can count all the individual black dots of hair on his chin where the razor's been over them. 'But there's a valuable lesson for you to learn here, young man. What you took for yourself – what is it? Six measly packets of fags? That cannot match the generosity extended to you by my good-self uninvited, can it?' He pauses as if he's waiting for a round of applause or something. 'Think on it, my little friend. And of course, I said you can take something for yourself for the job along with the readies. And I stand by that. Man of my word. Whatever you want. Another carton of fags, lager?' He waves his arm towards the back of the truck.

'No, I want them,' I points to the heavy trays that clonked Bollock Brain in the head. He recognises them alright and starts up.

'Tins of beans? What you want them for, you nutter? You weren't s'posed to get them anyways.'

'Nothing. Just do.'

Dean shrugs. 'Please yourself, Nutboy. Put them in the front of the van then. We'll drop you where we found you. Go on. Get in.' He cuffs me on the back of the head, to encourage me like, but it's not hard. I put the beans on the floor, which means Bollock Brain puts his feet all over 'em just to annoy me. But they're in tins, silly fucker, so there ain't much he can do to wreck 'em and piss me off.

They chucked me out at Richmond Alley with my fags and my beans and a big roll up of notes, which I pack into my sock. And this was a *big* rollup. This is a much better way of doing things than trying to shoplift all the time. Much better.

To be honest, looking back, getting involved with the Amerys wasn't the best decision I ever made. But the thing was, I was having a bit of trouble dealing with life at the flophouse. The kids were vexing me. I was beginning to feel a bit like a mum. You know having to go to work and provide everything and look after everyone and that? 'cept Albie of course, but then he was different. He had his own thing to do. And although I didn't realise it at the time, it was screwing with his head as much as it was screwing with mine.

So now I'm on the way back to the flophouse, lumping my beans. Yeah *'This'll shut 'em up for a bit,'* I thinks to myself. They can stick this lot in their gobs for a while and shut the fuck up. But I'm not cross about it like I was this morning 'cause I'm pretty proud of myself for handling the evening the way I did. Getting in with someone like Dean Amery, and even getting a bit of respect off him. 'Initiative,' he said. 'Bit of guts,' he said. And he said he thought I was, 'alright', which gives me that feeling you get when things are going good; the one that makes you feel you're bigger than you are. Like you're a bit taller suddenly and your chest is a bit bigger. Like a man.

Now this is better all round. I'm wondering if Dean'll need me again for something and hope he will. There's a few weeks of dinners here *and* the cash. Not bad, even if I say it myself.

I head for the back door, which we managed to unlock and open after finding a rusty key when we cleared out the kitchen cupboards. It's unlocked and I crash it open, dropping the tray on the ground and standing there, panting. There they all are like a bunch of baby birds with their gobs open, yelling. Homeless and his mates, the nippers, Jerry and Liam rushing forward as proud as if they done it as well just 'cause they were my crew, and wanting some of the attention.

Albie comes into the kitchen then. Behind him, I can see Katie, which don't please me much but as far as him and me go, we're still mates. I know 'cause he laughs. Not at me but just 'cause he's pleased. Even though Katie's there, I grin back at him standing there towering over the rest of 'em in his long black coat and that mad undertaker's hat. He even had a pair of woolly gloves; them ones like old men wear with only half the fingers in.

'You look like that bloke in the film. Whatsit? Oliver. The old bloke. Fagin, that's it Fagin. Fagin, that's you.'

'Fagin!' he laughed again then. 'That makes you the Artful Dodger then.'

Artful Dodger. I liked that. Yeah, the Artful Dodger,

that's me! Then I didn't mind so much about anything 'cause it was back to normal. I was still his best mate, girls or no. I'd do anything for him, and I knew it was the same with him 'cause we were mates. And that's how it is with mates.

THE CHRONICLES OF ALBION

My apprentice, my boy, my fighting fish. He fights for all of us with the heart of a lion. My little warrior boy. I said to him, 'You are like the fighting fish. Always fighting everyone and always alone.' 'No,' he says and looks at me with breaking eye, cracking his broken grin, 'I have you.'

LA BELLE DAME SANS MERCI

It was still a lot harder with Katie around though, even after the night of the beans, to get time to talk to him, like it used to be. He was getting quieter. More in himself. She and him would disappear off, 'specially at night. She started staying over and I began to feel a bit left out. And I didn't like the way he was changing much, 'cause he was. I noticed. He never told stories any more like he used to and he was looking even thinner and paler than he was before. And that was saying something.

One day, I went in to our room and I could see he was crying. He was kind of lying down on the bed, all his clothes on, even his coat and boots, with his arms over his head. I was scared then. I dunno why. I'd kind of felt safe for a while round here and I didn't like the feeling it was slipping away. I mean, I might be the one who got the food and that but Albie had to hold it all together. We needed him.

'Albie?' I said it quietly.

He moved, rolled over a bit and dragged his coat sleeve across his eyes. But he left his long hand on his forehead, trying to hide his face from me. But I could tell. It was bad.

'You alright?'

'Yes,' he said. 'Fine.... Thanks.'

But he weren't. He weren't at all. I could tell. I wanted to do something. But I didn't know what. 'Listen mate, I'll get you a drink. I've a bottle of whisky in the chimney. Hid. We'll have a drink, okay?'

But before he could even say a thing, Katie came barging in. I dunno where she even came from.

'Albie,' she goes and pushes me put of the way to get to

him. 'What is it?'

She throws herself on the floor beside him and gathers him up in her skinny little arms, rocking him against her chest like as if he was a baby. She put her head down and kissed his hair. Then she looked up over his head at me. And she threw me a look that I didn't like. I didn't like at all.

So I went and found the whisky bottle. But I drank it all myself. I drank 'til I passed out on the floor downstairs. And the next day, I felt like shite.

I got up early and fucked off out of there. Just went walking around. Down the rec, passed the hospital, the flats, the parade, the cop shop. On and on, 'til I ended up by the swimming pool.

Now I haven't been there for years. Not since my dad was around, and to be honest, I can't really swim neither. But for some reason, that's what I wanted to do now, so I paid my money to get in, through the clicky turnstile and into the building.

It's a shit pool. Most places now days have them big leisure centres or aqua world things going on, with slides and flumes and waves and all that shite. But, like I say, no one bothers with nowt round here so we've still got the same old concrete shithole with big cold glass windows we always had. Mum said she came here when she was a kid and all and it hasn't changed since then.

It smells of that swimming pool smell. Clean chemicals. Like some drug you'd fancy snorting if you were hard up. But as it's round here, it also smells of damp and sweat and dirty old men – 'specially the changing room.

And there's often funny little insect things running round the floor. Danny Sears said they were cockroaches and one fell on his back when he was swimming 'cause there were colonies of them up in the roof and it fell through the glass. But sometimes, with Danny, you never know whether to believe him or not.

I don't like the men's changing rooms. They stink of sweat and piss and you wonder about the pervs. Especially in the day with all the old weirdos about, so I stripped myself quickly down to me kecks and stuffed my gear in a locker by the door so the lifeguard could see if anyone started trying to rip it off. You can see where they do on some of the lockers round the corner 'cause the sides of them are all bent up. But I reckoned here would be safe enough.

It was freezing. I caught sight of myself shivering in the long mirror. State of me. Purple black bruise on my thigh where that twat got me the other day and my body looked really milky and skinny. Skinnier than before, and I was always a bit of a runt. As well as my ribs, I could see all the dips and grooves of my chest and my shoulder blades stuck out like wings. Even my belly looked bony. I frowned and went up close to the mirror to look in my face. Do you know that one? If you look at yourself in the mirror for long enough. Really stare into your eyes. You can see yourself as really old. It's like an old fella staring back. Weird. And that day I looked fuckin' old.

Shivering again, I tiptoed round the shite they call the footbath with its bits of hair and tissue and dead insects, and fuck knows what else floating in it, and lowered myself down into the pool. It's cold when you get in, but it's cool 'cause it gives yer old heart a big, old bump start. Then I held my nose and ducked under.

Down there, I could hear nothing. See nothing, really. Even when I opened my eyes, just blues and blurs. I surfaced with a gasp and started swimming, as best I can. It's better if you try and float rather than thrashing and it's nice with the water kinda holding you up. I caught some old geezer looking at me, so I gave him the finger and he fucked off to the other side of the pool. I duck-dived. I'm quite good at that, swimming underwater. It's nice down there. All that noise, shouts, yells, screams are all muffled and it gets further away the deeper you go 'til it becomes something you don't have to worry about any more. Bit like going to sleep.

I stayed down as long as I could. And then came up and went down again. And again. And again. 'til the lifeguard shouted at me. But when he weren't looking, I did it again.

It was fuckin' freezing coming out, me kecks hanging off me and dripping. But I felt clean in my body, but also in my head. Ready to go back. It was like the chemical water that I swallowed cleaned me on the inside, like it probably bleached away me skin on the outside. Felt better anyway, whatever.

I dried myself a bit on my socks and then stood under the hand drier 'til I thought it was okay to put my clothes back on, wringing out my kecks and socks and putting them in my pocket. Outside it was already dark, so I went home the quicker way.

I was hoping Dean would come after me again for something 'cause we were really fuckin' skint, but though I kept hanging around the parade and went to skin up with Gavin a couple of times up the rec, I didn't hear anything more about it, which was a bit of a bummer.

To be fair to that Katie though, much as I didn't like her, she helped out and she got well good at the thieving, too. She came up with the idea of doing the ladies for handbags. She said it would be a piece of piss and it were. She said these dozy women would sit down on the bog and put their bags on the floor and you could easy get your hand in under the door and drag it out. She used to check the bogs for us; wait 'til all the cubicles were occupied and there was no one hanging inside waiting or washing their hands and then in we'd pile. Took seconds. Course the women couldn't do nothing, they're just trapped there with their knickers round their ankles, watching their handbags disappear under the door. By the time they've got themselves sorted, we're well gone. It was a great one, you had to hand it to her. After a while, they introduced a charge to get into the toilets. A barrier like at the railway stations. You had to put coins in to get through the turnstile. They did it to keep the scumbags out, the junkies and that. And us. But it didn't keep us out did it? Hah! We regarded the payment as a business investment like. It wasn't like we didn't get it back thousand-fold.

At first, we used to just take the cash and the mobiles but after a while, we found we could get money off the cards as well. Katie used to borrow some of her mum's clothes and dress up like an office girl, you know the sort of one who'd have credit cards and that. When she did her make up different she could look about twenty. Then she'd fix the card so it wouldn't fit the machines and it had to be signed off the old way, go straight from the bogs into the market, fill trolleys with as much food as she could and then get maximum cashback on the card before the owner had managed to block it. It was fuckin' ace. She even got booze and fags as well. Like I say, I had to hand it to her. A credit card would keep us going for weeks, even though we only ever used 'em one time before chucking 'em. It weren't worth getting rumbled even though it were a bit of a waste. But you have to do these things properly.

After that night, I went out with Dean Amery, Katie started staying over a lot. I slept downstairs those nights. I'd hear 'em together sometimes. Albie would always make sure everyone was asleep. She never cared, but he always worried about the little kids hearing. Maybe he worried about me hearing and all.

I hated it. I could always tell however quiet they were. It wasn't like I didn't hear it enough times through the wall and that at home with Mum. The rustling and the whispering and the way the breathing changes – heavy and then little gasps and groans. I hated listening to it. Really hated it. There was something about it I really didn't like. It was just....well, it's not that I'm a virgin or nothing. Well not a *virgin* virgin. I've done stuff with girls and that. Just ain't done *it* yet. Thing is, I think you should do it with a nice girl. But the nice girls don't do it, so it's all a bit of a bother really.

Anyways, I could always hear 'em. It was like being at home again in a way and I came here to get away from that. It was just.... not.... right. Apart from that, I was worried for Albie. He seemed to be slipping away somewhere that I didn't understand. I wanted it back how it was. How it used to be.

THE CHRONICLES OF ALBION

Walking through the empty streets, I am getting tired. Is this of what I dreamed? Tired, sick and tired, and tired and sick. My heart's soul struggles and sickens, sickens and dies. My head is a tumble torture of tiresome thought and to lay it down gives it no relief. The lily white hand of my own artful nymph gives only temporary solace. But then how can the comforts of warm flesh alone suffice to soothe the nightmarish contortions of the soul?

THE KINGDOM OF DEAN

A couple of days later, I'm just hanging round the estate with Homeless, smoking fags and chilling out when I get the feeling someone's behind me. I'm being kerb crawled by Dean Amery's pimpmobile or something like it.

The window buzzes down.

'Here, Nutboy!'

It was one of Dean Amery's hoods. My old pal Bollock Brain, riding around like Johnny Big Potatoes in Dean's motor.

'Dean wants to see yer. Get in!'

I'm standing there, thinking. Homeless is looking at me a bit confused and anxious like.

The voice goes, 'I said. Get. In.'

Didn't seem to be much choice. Either I got in or one of those fat fucks was gonna get out and pick me up and throw me in the back. I'd rather travel in comfort so I walked over to the back passenger door, which someone inside had thrown open for me. Homeless is still staring so I said, 'Gotta go. Catch yer later,' but I say it all bright like so he won't stress about it. Then I got in the car. It was nice in there. New. Still smelled of leather. Big puffy cushion thing to put your arm on and leather lining on the door. My old friend Bollock Brain was inside in the front passenger seat and he snapped the door locks so it looked like I was staying if I wanted to or not. I didn't recognise the other two but they were the usual tattooed meatheads.

'Where're we going?' I ask.

'You'll see. Dean's invited you for tea. You lucky little boy.'

Meathead number one pulls the car round and we speed off towards the back of the estate where the big blocks are. This guy's chucking the thing around like an eleven-year-old joyrider. Bet Dean wouldn't be too impressed and I'm beginning to feel a bit carsick in the back. But I stay silent. He pulls up in the car park under the blocks. Bollock Brain turns round. 'Get out. Primrose House. Flat 114.'

I'm not sure what to do.

'Get out and go.' He spins round, opens the door and pushes me out. Then they drive off.

I don't have a lot of choice. I take the lift up to the tenth. It smells of fags and piss, so I have a fag myself to calm my nerves.

Number 114 is at the end of the corridor. Blue door with paint peeling off it. The doorbell don't seem to work so I rap the letterbox. I hear footsteps and the door is opened. A woman, skinny, bleached blonde, tight jeans and vest top. Too many earrings. Too much make up. Looks like any of a hundred women round here. It's hard to tell how old she is. Older 'n my mum at first look but somehow she seems younger. Friendly enough. She says,

'You must be Robbie. I'm Marlene. Come in.'

There's a voice I recognise calling down the corridor behind her. 'Is that Nutboy? Good. About time.'

Marlene nods, encouraging me to follow the voice, which I do. I find Dean sitting at the tiny kitchen table behind a large ashtray full up with butts. He's leaning back in this little chair, his legs all splayed out, taking up as much of the room as he can. Grinning. He's like a king sitting there. Well he is a king round here. Respect. That's what he's got and that's what you need. Yeah, I thought, I want some of that. Respect, for a fuckin' change.

'The name's Robbie,' I say. I mean you gotta stand up for yerself. Respect innit?

'Okaaay ……….. Robbie.' But the way he says it I knows he's taking the piss.

Marlene goes over to the cupboard. 'Would you like a cuppa, Robbie?' she says, trying to be all nicey, nicey, which is kind of her.

'Cheers.' I'm trying to be the man, conscious of him looking at me.

'Cigarette?' she asks.

I'm not sure if it's me she's trying to please or Dean. Him I 'spect but I might as well take advantage and I take the packet she throws on the table.

'Cheers.'

Dean watches her with his little shark eyes as she fills the kettle and gets out the teabags. 'And one for your man as well,' he says. It sounds a bit like a warning the way he says it. Sour.

She nods.

I hear this thin little whining noise from somewhere in the flat, like a sick kitten. Marlene disappears out the room for a minute and when she comes back, she's got a baby slung over her shoulder. It's a skinny little thing, 'specially for a baby and it's none too clean either. In fact, it's so thin, it don't even look like a proper baby, 'part from its big head.

Dean's annoyed. 'Marlene, don't bring that in here. Me and the little man here have business to discuss.'

Marlene looks up then, pushes some of her hair out of her face and looks at him for the first time. 'Business? 'Ow old is 'e Dean?'

Dean's more annoyed now. No one questions him. That's

how cool he is. He lifts his hand from the table and holds his forefinger out towards her. Warning like.

'No, Marlene. I've told you before. You keep your nose out. Now shut up and make this fuckin' tea before we die of thirst.'

He looks at me then. 'Women. Gotta keep 'em in line, son or they'll fuck everything up for you.'

I know what he means but somehow I don't like him talking to her like that. She looks like she's gonna cry.

She puts the tea on the table. And she even smiles at me. Or tries to. Seems like a nice lady really.

Dean stares at her and jerks his thumb towards the door. 'Out.'

'Excuse me, Robbie,' she says all polite. See what I mean about the lady bit.

Dean rolls his eyes at me. 'Women. Fuck 'em.... And if you do, Robbie mate, make sure you keep a hat on. Know what I mean?' He glances over to the tins of baby food and bottles in the corner and laughs. But it's the kind of laugh when something's not funny at all. A kinda hard laugh. It's all loud enough for her to hear and I kind of feel sorry for her. But I can see you have to be like that, if you want to be ...... Anyway, I stop thinking about it 'cause Dean's already started up with me.

'Right. I need someone to do some delivering for me. Not much. Little stuff. Local like. I need someone who won't be noticed, know what I mean? You up for it?'

I push my bottom lip out as if I'm considering. 'Maybe.'

He knows I'm acting the bollocks and just ignores it. He don't need to bother about a little shite like me.

'Like a bit of hash do you, son?' He grins, showing his glittery teeth. Well do the odd job for me and you can have what you want, special rates for staff. And you can make a bit of cash on the side.'

I nod. 'Fair enough.'

'Right.' He pulls out a drawer and slams a big block of hash on the table. Size of a brick it is. I've never seen so much. It hits the table with a bang and the table top wobbles on its little legs. 'This is what we're talking about. I have people who wanna buy round here. It's all set up. You don't have to deal with them, just deliver the stuff and collect the cash. Right?'

I nod.

'Good.' He leans back in the chair and puts his hand in the kitchen drawer behind him. He pulls out what looks like sweets but they're little lumps of hash wrapped up in silver foil and cling film. He chucks them down on the table top.

'That's to start. There's six there. I'll give you four addresses to drop off. You can keep two for yourself. You deliver the others and bring the cash back to Marlene, here. I'll know if they don't get delivered and I'll know if I don't get the right cash. If that happens you owe me. Twice over, which will not be a good situation for you to be in, my little friend. Gottit?'

I nod again. He names the price. It's a bit more than I've ever paid for a lump but I suppose if Dean's involved in it, it must be pretty good shite.

'Can you write?'

I'm a bit pissed off then. 'Course.' I mean my writing's not good and my spelling's shite but I can write stuff alright. I'm not a total div. He throws me a pen and a bit of paper.

'Write these down.' He gives a list of names and addresses. Three of them are in my flats, one on another part of the estate. I know a couple of the names, too. Seems easy enough.

'Okay, there you go. We'll see how you get on. Do it right and there'll be more of this for you. And I'll look after you alright. Fuck it up and you don't even want to think about what might happen.'

I nod, gather up the packets and put them in my pocket.

'Burn that paper, after.'

I look at him. Does he think I'm stupid or what?

He nods. 'You seem a smart enough kid. If anyone stops you…'

'Yeah, I'm on my own right?'

He grins. 'Right. We're gonna get on. I can see that. Now off you go. Be back here same time tomorrow. I'll be waiting for you.'

I ain't finished my tea, but I know it's time to go, so I do.

When I get down to the bottom again, I find those pricks have gone so I have to walk all the way back myself. Don't mind really, though 'cause I've got a lot to think about. Me and Dean Amery. That's pretty cool. Getting rid of this shit 'll be a cinch and I'm feeling pretty good about being in with him alright. Pretty sound. And the dosh. The dosh will be great and sort out one of my other little problems. Sound. Things beginning to go my way for once.

I end up doing the drops on the way home. It's easy enough. Funny thing is, they seem to be expecting me and I know some of them so it's sound. By the end of the day, I've got a roll of notes in my sock and a couple of lumps for myself. I stop in the shop and get some Rizlas and head over the back of the rec for a smoke for myself before I go home.

In the old days, I would have gone back to Albie and maybe we would have had a bit of a smoke together, but for some reason, I don't fancy it. It wouldn't be like the old days. Not with everyone about and all.

The next day, I'm back at Marlene's with the cash. Dean's there, waiting in the kitchen again like before. I hand over the money from my sock and he counts it out in front of me. He grins up at me.

'Not bad son,' he tells me. 'You'n'me are gonna be working together more.'

He's got another list and a bigger handful of stuff. Again, there's a load to sell and a couple of lumps for myself. I decide to flog these on anyway. Split 'em up smaller and sell 'em on for a bit more maybe. Have to be careful 'bout that though. Can't have him finding out. Dunno if I dare but if I do it round the flophouse and Gavin don't find out should be okay.

Some of the addresses are right on the other side of town and Dean goes to me, 'Gotta bike?'

I shake my head

'You get one?'

I nod.

'Right.' He goes on, 'And you can deal with Marlene from now on. Just give her the cash and she'll sort you out. Any problems you can come to me, but there won't be. She's good girl if you keep her in line. Aren't you, my princess?' He grins at her and slaps her arse. She giggles. It's the first time I've seen 'em together – sort of happy. But I dunno if he's happy with her, or if he's just trying to keep her happy, if you know what I mean.

I start looking for transport on the way back, and I'm lucky. Round the back of the new houses, some divvies left their back gate open. Kids' bikes piled up. Three sorts. Mountain bike, a knackered old thing and a little girl's bike with a basket. I'm thinking about the knackered one but the mountain bike's just too tempting. It's pretty smart and I'm flying along on it. Back at the flophouse, I pull out one of the old cans of paint we found out the back and splash some paint over it so it's not so noticeable and don't look like the sort of thing someone would want to nick off me and all. I scrape the ID off with a penknife.

Jerry comes out to see what I'm doing. 'Wossat?'

'Bike, innit? And don't you fuckin' touch it alright?'

He shrugs. 'What you wanna bike for?'

'Just do. Alright?'

He shrugs again and goes back in.

Shouldn't have yelled at him. Although to kids like him, it's water off a duck's. But I'm getting a bit pissed with the flophouse just now. Albie off with Katie, hungry kids all the time wanting something. It's nice to get away and do something myself. And it's pretty cool to get a bit of respect from someone like Dean Amery. Yeah, they can think about that when they're all moaning about their fuckin' dinner. Didn't tell Albie neither. I'm not sure how he'd be about me and Dean Amery.

I keep myself to myself for the evening and then sneak off and do my drops. Jerry's dying to know what I'm up to and barely lets me out of his sight but I give him the slip when he's troughing. Job's easy enough and I fly through it on the bike.

Jerry's waiting for me when I get back, pissed at me. But I just leave him to sulk and go to bed. Downstairs.

The next day, when I take the cash over to the flats, it's just Marlene, like Dean said. Marlene is known as Dean's bird but I don't think she's the only one, and I think she knows that. But if you're Dean's bird, you're Dean's bird and that's it. You don't go messing with anyone else – whatever *he* does. Poor tart. Can't be much fun. And he treats her like shite.

She looks quite pleased to see me. Guess she gets a bit lonely maybe. Stuck up there in that shithole with the baby. And it's not like you can go out much. Those blocks are really disgusting now. The front door's broken so the dossers come in and sleep there at night and sometimes, during the day as well. They do their dirty business there and all, which can't be nice if you're trying to bring up a kid. Sometimes, the prossies use it, too – since someone pulled down all the security cameras the council put up to try and stop what was going on. Now, like with most things round here, they've just given up. You'd think Dean might get her something better wouldn't yer? For her and the kid, like. But that's not really Dean's style, I suppose.

She takes the money off me. Don't count it but she does go out the room and puts it somewhere, where I can't see. I'm about to go when she comes back and says, 'Fancy a cuppa?'

Well, I don't really but I've got nothing on and it's quite warm in her place. Much warmer than the flophouse, which is pretty fuckin' freezing most of the time.

'Alright. Why not?' I say.

'Go through,' she says. 'But mind the baby. He's asleep.'

I head into her front room. There's this massive window and you can see all over the city. The TV's on quietly and the baby's sleeping in a cot in the middle of the room. That poor kid worries me. Even though he's only tiny, like *really* little, his face is all screwed up all the time. Even when he's not crying, which he looks like he does most of the time anyway. Poor little nipper. He's too young to know the half of it. Fuck knows what he'll be like when he gets to my age.

And there in the corner is an old lady. I don't see her at first and when she moves, it makes me jump out my skin. 'Fuck!'

Marlene's voice calls from the kitchen, 'And don't mind Nan. Just ignore her. She just sits there cursing all day at nothing. She's a bit touched and don't know what she's saying.'

The old lady looks at me with eyes like a little bird and says, 'What do you want?' Then she starts muttering under her breath, staring at me all the time. Muttering about me too by the sound of it and don't sound too polite. Her fuckin' language is worse than mine. Whatever Marlene says, I reckon the old dear's as sound as a pound in there. Her little eyes are sharp as you like. And if I was some old lady who'd just been dumped on someone like Marlene, someone who didn't even want her and thought she was a moron, I'd be cursing away all day and all. You see that's the thing with the old ones... no one wants 'em and they just get dumped on the scrap heap. And they know no one wants them and all.

But even though I feel sorry for her, the old lady's still giving me the creeps so I go to the window. It's a boss view. You can see down to the town hall and then everything out from there. The shopping streets and the big mall, the posh houses and then the estates and then the scumbag estates like ours, the hospital, the cemetery, the schools, the roads, the railway lines, all running off into the distance.

Marlene comes back in with the tea so I go back over and sit down on the sofa, stretching out my legs and putting my feet on the table.

'You men. Dean's always putting his feet on the table and all. I'm always on at him not to. But he don't listen to me.'

'Sorry,' I say and take my feet down. But I like the idea of being like Dean. Even if it's just over my feet.

Nan's watching one of the MTV channels.

'You got Sky? Cool. What channels you got?'

'All of them. I think. Dean shocked the box. I only watch the music channels, and those American shows. The ones in California, with the kids all having great lives. I love them.' She looks all sad then. 'I wish our school had been like that.'

'Where did you go?' I ask.

'Same as you. Same as everyone round here. I remember you there, actually.'

Eh? I think. 'How come?'

'You was always running away weren't you? There was a big fuss about you.'

'You were there? How old are you then?'

'Seventeen. I was quite smart and all. Doing my exams. But I met Dean. It all went a bit wrong after that.'

Then I remember who she is. The girl who was always sneaking out to meet Dean Amery round the back. Jesus Christ! I thought she was loads older. Like my mum's age. But I don't wanna upset her so I say, 'You caused a bit of a fuss and all.'

'Yeah.' She laughs one of them not funny laughs. And right on cue comes the reason there was such a fuss. A little nipper, just out of sleep comes through the door, rubbing his face. He's skinny, too, like the baby, and his pyjamas are dirty. He goes over to Marlene, who picks him up and puts him on her lap.

'This is Rooney. He's not been well.'

The nipper looks at me with little eyes just like Dean's. Shark eyes. Full of suspicion and hate.

'I'd better go,' I say.

'You want your stuff, don't you? Hang on.'

She went over to the baby's cot by the window and put her hand in very gently. She pulled out the bag for me. 'There you go.'

Putting the drugs under the baby. Smart. The cops ain't gonna go near, even if they bust the place. Very smart. Still, somehow it don't seem quite right.... Boss idea though. You had to hand it to her, or Dean or whoever's idea it was. That and the old dear – Psycho Granny – the cops are fucked.

'Cheers,' I say. 'Marlene.'

She smiled at me. Jeez, her teeth were worse than mine.

'See yer, kid,' she says as she opens the door to let me out.

THE WEIGHT OF THE CROWN

Well, it were all going not too bad for me actually. It was cool working for Dean and it sorted out the cashflow, especially as Katie was still doing her stuff when we needed it – to be fair to her. Got everyone off my back for a bit. And I reckoned we could flog on the credit cards and stuff to make things easier, just take some cash in hand and let someone else do all the scamming. The only worry I had left was Albie. And he weren't hisself, I tell you.

Like I say, he always looked shite. But he was starting to look *really* shite. His skin was always white but now it looked kinda yellow with big stains the colour of tea all round his eyes. Sometimes, he was all sweaty in the night, and other times he was really cold. And when I saw him changing his shirt one day, I could see all his bones sticking out his back. Not just his ribs, like, but all the lumpy bits up his spine. Really sticking out they were. It looked a bit disgusting to be honest.

But the worst thing was there was something I saw different in his eyes. They were kinda... I can't explain it properly... sorta ... dull? They used to be all bright and... like dancing? Kinda lively, like. I dunno.

But now, it was like someone put the light out. I didn't like it. I suppose he was getting vexed a lot. By everything. Even though it was good, like, what we done, it was hard. He's walking around all the time now as if his body's too hard to drag along, like he's got a big weight hanging round his neck. And if you think about it, he has. Everyone's after him. I mean when it was him and me it was fine. And maybe when it was just a few – like when it was Homeless and that 'cause they had a bit of brains in 'em and could look after 'emselves, and also they didn't stay round all the time but just came for a few days at a time, but now, the flophouse is bursting and it's 'Albie this' and 'Albie fuckin' that.' You'd think half of them couldn't wipe their arses theirself. At least I can just get out and do my stuff and get on with it, and that's all anyone wants from me – just to come up with some dinner or a bit of cash now and then. And that was bad enough before I started working for Dean and getting some proper money.

I don't get much chance alone with Albie any more. There's always someone about. Not even at night now what with Katie dripping all over him. Well, I s'pose he's getting laid and that but she's one messed up little girl if you ask me, and I reckon we'd be better off without her.

But Albie was really sick and I was worried. But we couldn't go to the doctor's or nothing could we? And if I ever asked him, he said he was fine, which was an obvious lie. You could see that just by looking.

When I was a bit down, my nan used to take me down the sea, so that's what I decided to do. She said it was good for you. All that healthy sea air and that. *'Good for you when you're sick. Chases all the germs away.'* That's what she said anyway. I loved the sea. It weren't that far but you have to get the train. It's no bother to jump it if you go to the next station along the line 'cause there's never anyone there and you can just get over the turnstiles. I decided to take him along on the Sunday when it's even easier. There's no staff at all 'cause they got rid of them ages ago and not many passengers either 'cause it's only a commuter line now. Once you're on the platform, you're fine. The only danger is the ticket inspector on the train, like, but if you look out to see where he gets on you can bunk in the toilet 'til he gets off again. You just need to work out how long the train is and how long it'll take him to get down it.

So that's what we did. The two of us squashed in this stinking, filthy toilet which stank of smoke because everyone always goes in there for a fag now you can't smoke on the train anywhere. Albie thought it were all a laugh and it was good to see him giggling again, so I knew I was doing the right thing for him.

I love going down the sea. It smells different. I mean you can still smell all the town shite and that – buses and cars and dirt and dog shit, and the general stink of too many people and everything they bring with 'em. But still, over the top of it, there's a clean windy smell and a smell of salt. You wouldn't think you can smell salt would you? I mean if you went in the cafe and tipped it in your hand and sniffed it wouldn't really smell of nothing. But down the sea, it does smell. Weird, innit? And the seagulls. Running round in the sky, screaming and screeching and laughing over the rooftops. Mental they are. I like 'em.

Vicious little fuckers, too. You need to give respect to them birds. They'll have your food off yer soon as look at yer. Right out your hand, and all, and take yer fingers with 'em if they could.

Nan used to bring me to this place when I was a nipper. Me and Sam. In the days when Sam was a laugh. We used to play at jumping the waves and making these big canal ways and castles and channels trying to beat the sea. The sea always won though. When it got fed up with us, it just totalled everything.

I tried to race Albie across the sand. He couldn't really run. He had a kind of loping run, like a dog with three legs.

All over the place. I beat him easy and I felt a bit mean like I was trying to show off and be the big man so I slowed down and went back to him, where he was, staggering on the sand.

'You hurt?'

'No.'

'Your leg. You're limping?'

He sat down in the sand.

'You trip? Twist it?' I press.

'No. I'm fine. It was a long time ago.'

I grinned. 'Ah. Playing football? Like that?'

He smiled, weird kind of smile. Like when you're sad really. The not funny smile. That one. 'You could say that.' He picked up a pebble and threw it into the distance. It hit the edge of the water. His eyes stayed where it landed rather than look at me.

'My father,' he says, 'I think he thought I *was* a football sometimes... ironic really – all the time I was in boarding, I just wanted to go home – and then on the rare times I was home...' He stretched out his long leg with its sore ankle in its big old boot and looked at it. He didn't say nothing for a while. And then he said, 'He stamped on it. It's never been the same since.'

'On purpose, like?' I ask.

'On purpose.' He laughed in that way people do when something really ain't funny.

He didn't say nothing else so I asked, 'Couldn't the doctor fix it then?'

He looked at me, very slowly. 'We never went to the hospital in our house. None of us. We just didn't go'

I got the picture. He threw another stone and then started drawing circles in the sand with his finger.

I shrugged. 'Dads are shite ain't they? Mums ain't much

better, neither.'

He looked sad again so I pulled his hair. 'Come on. Let's go and spend that train fare we just saved. There's an ice cream place up on the Esplanade. It's boss.'

He brightened up a bit but he still seemed sick. It took him a long time to get up. I thought it was his ankle but it weren't that entirely. He was just knackered and he didn't eat all the ice cream but gave half to me. He fell asleep all the way home and went to bed soon after we got back. Before he went up, he turned to me though and give me a big smile.

'Thanks, Robbie. You are a good friend.'

Katie didn't come round that night and I slept upstairs again. It was just like the old days. Almost.

'cause of that, I was in a right good mood for a few days. Albie seemed a bit brighter and the flophouse was pretty calm. I was bringing the money in. Expanding like. Dean always used to give me a couple of extras for myself, but I didn't really want 'em. I mean I like a puff now and then but not as much as I was getting. He said he'd get me what else I wanted as well – pills and coke and crack.

'Only a little bit of the hard stuff, mate, 'til I know you can handle it,' he goes.

But, to be honest, I weren't that interested. I'd drop the odd pill now and again for a laugh but I always got into fights on coke. And I had too much on my plate to risk fuckin' my head up. I said thanks and I'd let him know. I was thinking about taking some and flogging it on but I was a bit worried he might find out through Gavin or something and burst me for it. The odd bit of puff to kids in the flophouse I could probably get away with but that was my limit, I reckoned.

To be honest, I reckon drugs are a mug's game. You've only got to look at some of the sights round the estate –

limping and whining and selling their own kids for a two-bit high. Pathetic losers. Still, I took the puff. I thought I'd take some round to Milo. We hadn't seen him for ages since he got grounded by his old dear. He came out sometimes, when he could swing it, if they went out or something. I thought he might end up getting me a bit of extra business and all. He and his mates were a good bet. Milo goes to the snotty school up the hill, where they have to wear uniforms and play rugby and cricket and stuff – and there's no girls. But if I could drum up a bit more business there, I could rake in a bit more cash. Everyone wins, as far as I can see.

Then something else happened which changed things even more.

I was just on my way over and I got another kidnapping. You see, Dean, whenever he wanted me, he'd just send someone out to get me. I'd be walking along the road, minding my own and suddenly, Dean's pimpmobile or some other car would be behind me. A couple of Dean's meatheads would get out and pick me up and chuck me in the back and take me to wherever it was he wanted to see me. It was mad. Somehow, he always knew where I was, even if I didn't really even know myself. I 'spose everyone round here knows me and everyone round here knows to tell Dean what he wants to know. It was weird though, just like being kidnapped all the time. Smart though. On his part. Making sure I knew who was boss and there weren't no getting away from him even if I wanted to.

So I'm just heading up to Milo's with the puff when the pimpmobile pulls up. Bollock Brain gets out. I can't even leg it 'cause I know it means Dean wants me. Anyway, he chucks me in the back and drives me to *The Moderation*. But we head in the back, not through the bar. There's a door by where the toilets are and we go through it and up some stairs into a back room. And there's Dean Amery sitting round a table with a bunch of his Hoods. It reminds me of them war films, you know with the Gestapo and that, or the Mafia. Behind him, on either side are two big Hoods the size of brick shithouses. Bollock Brain clumps into the corner behind them where he can watch the door.

'Get him a drink,' he says.

'What d'you want?' says one of the pricks, none too nice.

It's worth trying it on. 'Lager.'

Dean snorts. 'Alright, Nutboy.' He looks at the pricks. 'Somebody get him a fuckin' drink.' He holds up a finger on his gold plated hand. 'A half mind.... you cheeky fucker!'

I shrug. Prick shuffles off and comes back with my lager.

Then Dean goes, 'I've got another job for you.'

Thought as much. I swig my drink, knocking it down like it was orange juice in case they change their mind.

'Bit harder, but it'll pay a bit more.'

Bollock Brain's shifting about. Seems none too happy. 'Dean...'

'Shut up,' Dean says to him without even turning round.

Then he throws this package about the size of a bag of sugar and wrapped up in cling film down on the table. It lands in front of me with a thwack.

'Know what this is?'

I do. Of course. 'Yeah. Brown, innit.'

'Yup. You're right there, smart lad. Interested?'

I'm a bit windy about it, to be honest. A bit of puff is alright but heroin? Helping someone along a junkie path. You know where it ends and it don't end good. This is a whole different ball game. I felt a bit sick, but I can't see I have much of a choice. The way Dean's looking at me, and the way he said 'interested' it's a statement. Not a question.

'I haven't sorted it with Marlene yet, but she'll be alright once I've had a few words,' he goes on. 'So, you be there. Thursday night. Right?'

'Okay,' I says.

'Alright,' he nods at the pricks. 'Now fuck off.'

I fucked off.

I went over the rec. I was gonna need some help with this one. And I needed to think what to do, so I sat on the swings and had a few fags and then headed over to Milo's. Get that bit sorted anyway. I rang the doorbell and this funny tune came out. Then Milo's mum came sashaying to the door.

'Yes?' She looked at me like I was something the cat had just puked up.

'Milo in?'

She gave a little shake of her head, as if there was some annoying fly or wasp round her head – which wouldn't have been surprising, the stink of flowery perfume and hairspray off her. Then she puts her head on one side and frowns like she doesn't have a clue what I'm talking about, her mouth all pulled together like a cat's arsehole.

'Oh.' She gives some stupid tinkly laugh. 'You mean *Miles*?'

'Yeah,' I said. Then I says just to annoy her. 'Mil-*o*.'

She shudders and then calls up the stairs to Milo. She's still holding the door like a barricade, like she don't wanna let me in the house, which, of course, she don't.

'*Miles!*' That's for my benefit. 'A little friend to see you here.' She looks down her nose at me. 'And you are?'

Fuckin' bitch. She knows damn well who I am. Weren't

that long ago her old man used to go drinking down our way with my mum and the rest of 'em.

'Robbie.'

She calls up again. 'It's Robert.' She really is *such* a bitch. But it's funny 'cause she thinks she's all posh now, she can't just say what she wants to say which is, 'Fuck off you chavvy little bastard and don't come near my son again.'

Milo leans over the banisters. 'Oh. Yeah. Right. Robbie. Come up.'

I push past her bleedin' Majesty and go up to Milo's room.

He's got a cool bedroom. It's big, like, and he has it to himself. His little brother's only four and he has his own room and all. It's painted blue and there's a desk in the corner with a computer and bunk beds for if he wants a mate to stay over. But the best bit is, he has his own telly and it's a big flat screen one with a gamestation, not just some piece of old crap or nothing.

'I got some puff for you,' I say.

'Excellent.' He goes to his drawer and pulls out a few notes. I hand him over a lump and he wraps it up in the sealed poly bag and then puts it inside the lining of his poncey little school cap.

He sees me watching. 'I have to be careful. She looks everywhere,' he goes.

'Right.'

'Skill. Sorted. Cheers mate. Boss one.' He's funny Milo. Sometimes, he talks all posh and then sometimes, he talks like us. But somehow it don't sound right. Still. He's alright.

'Listen,' I goes, 'I can get more. If you want. If your mates wanna buy it.'

'Yeah, sure. Sure thing, bro.' See what I mean about the

way he talks? 'How much?'

I give him a good price, but not a stupid one 'cause I know him and his mates have got cash. 'And you can have the odd freebie,' I said, cause I'm like that and Milo's alright.

'Cool… cool.' Then he goes, 'Want something to eat? I was gonna get something.'

I have to admit, I'm starving. I haven't eaten since that day me and Albie went down the sea. Not prop'ly anyway. Just chips and shite.

We go downstairs then, into the kitchen. Milo's kitchen is like something off those American soaps on the telly. It's massive. Big white units all around the room and a sort of table thing in the middle, but not one you could get chairs round and sit at prop'ly cause it's too high and there's no room for your legs to go. And then another table you can sit at, with chairs. The cupboards have got little windows on 'em so you can see what's inside and the fridge is like… taller'n *me*. And when Milo opens it, it's full.

He's staring in the fridge. 'D'you wanna sandwich or something?'

'Yeah, sure. Cheers.'

Then he starts dragging stuff out. Different kinds of bread, white and brown and brown with bits in, cheese, ham slices and some cold chicken – proper chicken like not just chicken roll – mayo and sauces and pickles, tomatoes, lettuce and a couple of cans of Coke.

'What d'you want?' he asks.

I'm looking at this feast. 'Fuckin' all of it.'

He grins, then gets a big knife out this wooden block with all knives sticking out of it and starts slicing these great big lumps of bread. He makes me the best fuckin' sandwich in the world. Three slices of bread and everything stuffed in there.

It's hard to get my gob round it but I manage somehow, sitting round the proper table.

Milo's mum comes in while we're eating, with Milo's little brother, Max. She obviously don't approve of feeding the poor. She starts crashing plates into the dishwasher and huffing and puffing a lot to show she's not happy. Then she finds some ironing to do in this kind of ironing room they have on the side of the kitchen. I reckon she's only doing it so she can keep half a beady on me.

Max comes toddling over to me on his chubby little legs. He's a cute little kid. Always smiling and I'll say it for the old bitch, she always dresses him nice. Today he's got a little stripy jumper with jeans and trainers. Just like his big brother actually, but all small. He comes over to me.

'Wobbie.' He's not so good at saying his Rs yet. 'Wobbie.'

He's got something in his hand he wants to show me.

'What you got there, mate?'

It's one of them Easter eggs they sell all year round. You know the ones. They advertise them on telly a lot. You get this nice chocolate egg. Not just normal chocolate, but the posh white stuff as well and then you get a toy inside. They're pretty crap. Bit like cracker toys and you have to make them up yourself from the bits inside. But kids love 'em. Must be that thing of thinking you're getting something for free even if it's a piece of shit.

He hands it out to me like it's made of gold. He's already had a go at taking the paper off and the chocolate on the outside is a bit smudged from the warmth of his hand.

'Open it, open it, open it.'

'Please,' prompts Milo.

'Pwease.'

I take it from him and unwrap it. I try and prise the two halves of the egg apart.

'Don't bweak it, Wobbie.' His breath is coming in heavy pants, like a dog, he's so excited about this thing. It's big deal for him. I remember being like that, too.

When bitch face ain't looking, I put my hand in my pocket and take out my knife. I know, I know. Albie would go mad and all. He don't approve. But you gotta look after yourself in this game and he don't really understand that. I mean he's smart and all but sometimes, he's really naive you know. A total innocent. You'd look at him sometimes and think he's just a kid. That's why I have to look out for him.

Anyway, the knife does its job and the egg spilts in two unbroken halves. Max is delighted with himself and immediately stuffs one in his mouth – which kinda makes you wonder why he needed them unbroken but that's kids for you. Inside is the little plastic egg thing.

'Open, open,' he splutters through the chocolate. Inside that is little bits of plastic to make up some toy or another. I look at the picture. It's a motorbike. Or s'posed to be.

'Want me to make it up for you?'

'Pwease.'

Me and Milo put our heads together with these crappy instructions and fiddly bits of shite and, within a few minutes, we've done it. Max is well chuffed and starts pushing it around the table top making stupid engine noises.

Milo's mum looks up. 'I'm not sure he should have that, Miles. He might break bits off and swallow them.'

'No mum, it's safe. He's not a baby and it says it's okay for his age.'

She tuts and watches Miles with this worried expression. Bleedin' hell lady, I'm thinking. If you're looking for danger in this world, love, there's better places to be looking than at some fuckin' Easter egg toy.

There's a scratch at the back door. It's all glass like a window so you can see into the garden and the dog's there scratching to come in. He's a little spaniel, like the police sniffer dogs and you know what – he comes in and heads straight for my pocket where the stuff is.

I try and push him away but he's having none of it. Milo's yelling at him and all and then gets out of his seat to drag him off by the collar.

Milo's mum looks up. 'Well if you boys will eat like that and drop food on yourselves, you can't blame him.'

Number one: there's no food on me and number two: we both know what he's after. They're sniffer dogs, spaniels. These ones with a super turbo nose that just cuts through all that plastic and foil I've wrapped the stuff up in. When his mum's not looking Milo bangs the dog hard on the nose and sends him off to his bed. I felt a bit bad 'cause it weren't the dog's fault but it were getting a bit bad you know, having him all over me like that. Bit of a wake-up call and all cause I don't need that happening all the time out and about when I've got the stuff on me. No way.

I'm rolling my fingers round while I'm thinking and I look down at my hand. There's the little plastic egg thing that Max's toy motorbike came in. He don't want it no more. He's off playing with the bike and sucking the other half of the chocolate.

And then I have the most brilliant idea...

THE BROWN DRAGON

On Thursday, I went over to Marlene's, like I said I would. Marlene looked worse than ever, and it seemed like Dean had had a few words with his fists 'cause she had a big mark by her eyebrow and she looked like she'd been crying. A lot. You know that all cried-out look? She wouldn't look me in the eye, either. Even when she was speaking to me. She just kept her head down, looking at the floor.

Felt a bit sorry for her actually, so I said, 'Thank you' extra nice when she give my my tea.

The stuff was on the kitchen table. Just a few again, like the very first time. But wraps of the brown stuff this time. And Dean sitting behind 'em. No, 'Hi' or nothing; he just starts into it. 'Well you can take these. And see how you go.' He chucks over a piece of paper with addresses on it. 'Same deal as before. You sell the stuff and bring the money back to me. Burn the list. If there's any fuckin' around, I'll know and I *will* break your legs, okay?'

He says it like he's offering to buy me a drink, which is why he's so scary 'cause I know he'd think as much of breaking my legs as buying me a drink. Less prob'ly.

I take the stuff and ram it down my sock and leg it out. I wanna offload this as soon as possible. Being caught with hash is one thing, being caught with this stuff on you is a whole other ball game. Quick look at the list, then on my bike and off to drop it all. I still felt bad but I reasoned these guys were going to get it anyway so's as long as I wasn't giving it to anyone who wasn't *already* a junkie, maybe it was okay.

I reckoned I had quite a sweet deal now. This stuff and the hash as well if I could, 'specially as I knew I could get a lot of sales through Milo. It wouldn't be bother, 'cept I couldn't be everywhere and I knew Dean's hard stuff would have to be the number one job. Even with the bike, I couldn't do it all. It would be too much and too risky. What I needed was a bit of help.

My first deliveries were over the back of the back. Not far from the flophouse. They're big old houses. Really big. Bigger than our one. And with gardens in the front and the back. Big scrappy overgrown gardens. I reckon once they would have been pretty posh but they're all pretty run down and knackered now. It's student land. All bedsits and flats now.

I pedal up the road, big wide road it is with trees on either side. Bet these houses were great when they were in good nick. Maybe we could find one, since the flophouse were beginning to burst at the seams these days. Move over here into one of these big gaffs. I decided to keep an eye out, but I couldn't see any empties. They all seemed to have someone in 'em by the look of it.

I find the house where my customer is, wheels my bike up the little path and knocks on the door. It were a total dump. The paint was all coming off the door and the doorbell was so gunked up with shite that if you pressed it, it didn't even move. The windows were filthy. Looked like no one had cleaned 'em in hundred years, and there weren't no proper curtains. Downstairs, a couple of blankets were pinned up but to be fair, the glass was so dirty that you wouldn't have been able to see much inside anyway. Upstairs, a couple of flags – not England ones – some stupid student revolutionary shite I reckoned. Dunno why they bothered getting excited about all these fuckin' stupid countries. There was enough going wrong round here if they wanted to bother their arses about stuff instead of sitting round getting monged out on puff and talking shit about poetry, and politics, and stuff or flying off their heads on the brown stuff.

Still, I had a job to do and it was that brown stuff that was gonna feed us so I hammered on the door. Nothing happened, but I could see one of the window blankets move so I knew they were there. I knelt down and opened the letter box. A disgusting musty smell came through. I looked at my fingers. There was all filthy shite all over them where I'd been touching the door... I wiped 'em on a bit of grass – didn't want that crap all over my tracky pants and I tried again. I could hear music inside so I yelled through the flap.

'Listen. I got some shit for you. D'you want it or not? 'cause if you don't, I'm gonna fuck off and flog it somewhere else.'

There was some shuffling on the other side of the door and the bolts were draw back. It opened a crack and this bloodshot eye looked round the corner. I don't have time for all this mysterious shite.

'D'you want it or not? I ain't hanging around, so either we get on with this or I'm fuckin' off. Okay?'

The door opens and I go in. The fella's a real muppet. All skinny with that feeble, dope-head scarecrow look on him. His hair's all lank – like his body – and he's wearing some yellowy T-shirt and loose girly trousers with patterns on 'em and flip flops. Flip flops! His chest's all hollow and his arms are hanging like his shoulders have been dislocated. His head's nodding like one of those stupid toy dogs. Them students. They just can't handle the shit can they?

'You got the stuff man?' He's got that stupid whiney junkie voice on him and all.

'Yeah, yeah. Readies first,' I tells him.

He puts his hand in his pocket and pulls out some grubby notes. They're a bit mankey but they're notes alright. I put my hand in my pocket and pull out the lump of shit, wrapped up in silver foil. He's delighted. He almost livens up for a minute. We do the deal and I'm out of there, just checking the road as I leave. What a dump. Makes our place look like a palace. And those mugs pay rent for that.

There were a coupla drops more down the shitty end of the flats. Didn't even see the fella but you could tell it was the right place because someone had painted 'junky fuck off' on the door. Spelt wrong and all. The door took ages to open and all I could see was a big yellowy eye and a dirty hand curling round the door.

'Cash first,' I goes and I can hear him shuffling off to get it and shuffling back and I could smell the inside through the door. Smelt of bodies, and sleeping, and old food cooked. You'd be hard pushed to get your breath in there. What a fuckin' way to live.

He comes back and we do the deal – still without laying eyes on each other. Then I'm off and I'm glad to be out of there and to have got rid of the stuff. It's not a great feeling to be walking around with a good few ounces of brown on you, even if it's hidden down in your sock. Makes you feel kind of vulnerable, like.

I walked my bike back most of the way to give me time to sort things through in my head, like. I had already worked out how to make things a bit safer for me. And once I felt things were a bit sorted that way, I could bring in someone else. I couldn't do it all and I needed to do Dean's big stuff and the hash and maybe a few pills or whiz as well. I knew he dealt it, and I knew he'd be happy to use me to get it about for him. That would really bring the cash in.

So all I needed was a partner, a Boy Wonder. And who else but Liam? He was hard enough, smart enough and he'd be up for it okay. Bit young but at least that meant he wouldn't get done if he got caught. And if I just let him do the dopey students and Milo's mates, they'd never do him over or anything. I'd be more worried about him doing for them, to be honest.

Seemed like a reasonable plan to me, so I allowed myself back on my bike and pedalled home.

When I get back to the flophouse, Albie's up and about and Katie's nowhere to be seen. He's in the kitchen filling a glass of water from the tap. He holds it out to me. 'Drink?'

I s'pose it's like a peace offering 'cause we haven't really seen each other for days. Not really. I don't want a drink, but I takes it anyway.

'Cheers.'

'So where've you been?' he goes to me, still standing at the sink and looking sideways at me out of his big grey eyes.

'About.' I was still a bit narky with him.

He raised his eyebrows at me and as he did so he put out a hand to block the flow of water coming out of the tap so it fizzed out sideways all over me.

'Oi, you cheeky fuck! Look at me.' I looked down. There was water running down off my trackies and the front of my T-shirt was soaked. I jerked my hand and the water shot out of the glass and into Albie's face.

He was shocked for a minute, then started to laugh. Jerry and Liam came into see what was going on and they started laughing, too.

Albie filled another glass and chucked the water in my

face as well and then Jerry and Liam rushed him and I bundled in as well, shoving him backwards across the room and into the bathroom until he overbalanced into the bath with me on top of him. Those two little fucks turned the shower on and there was just the two of us, a tangled, wet mass of bodies and legs but laughing fit to bust our guts. We hadn't laughed together like that since the old days – since that really cold night when we drank the whisky. It was nice to be like that again. Having a laugh, grinning into each other's faces. I think, if I look back, that was the last time we laughed together.

THE PRINCESS MARLENE

The following day, I start to put my business plan into action. I go off to the super where they have these bulk buy offers all packed up. The drivers always go off for a fag and a cup of tea about eleven so it's easy to nip in the back and run out with a carton. I get them toy eggs, like Milo's little Max had, and I take them with me over to Marlene's when I went to take the money for Dean.

She's on her own and gives me the stuff. I tell her my idea and we both sit down in front of the telly splitting up the eggs, pulling out the plastic capsules. We put the toys together. They're a bit crap actually but it's quite a laugh making up little motorbikes and cars and things. I told her she could have them for her nipper for when he got better.

Then we take the wraps and put them in the capsules, put the egg back round them and wrap them up in the foil. It's fuckin' perfect. Even if I get stopped no one's gonna cop on are they. And I get to eat the chocolate after every delivery. Excellent.

'You be careful, Robbie,' she says as I go.

'Ah. I'll be sound. Can't kill a bad thing, eh, Marlene?'

She smiles sadly and then comes over and gives me a hug. I can feel her thin bony body through her clothes. She's even thinner than Albie I reckon. One time, me and Danny Sears found a bird's nest with little dead baby birds. She feels just like they did when we picked them up. Like you have to hardly hug her at all or she'll break.

Now I'm sorted with my stash, I pedal off to go seek out Liam. He's mucking about on one of the bulldozers that have been left sitting by the builders who are knocking down the streets around the flophouse to build one of them shopping complexes and some new ring road or some shite like that.

He's trying to start the fucker. I was watching him for a while and to be fair to him, he nearly did it and all. Told you he was smart. I called him over.

'I need you to help me on something. Delivering stuff.'

He nods.

'We'll get you a bike and then I just need you to drop some stuff off where I tell you.'

He shrugs.

'You're not to fuck up. And you're not to say nothing to no one, neither.'

He frowns and looks at me with his little sharp eyes. He don't really like me talking to him like that, giving it the big I am. But he's only six and he has to do what I say.

'And whatever I give you, you don't look at it, you don't touch it, right.'

He looks back at me again, sulky now.

'You don't look at it, you don't touch it or I'll rip your fuckin' head off.'

I'm only gonna let him deliver the puff and maybe the speed and I'll sort the rest of it but still I don't want him messing about with any of that stuff. Even the puff. I mean six is just a little bit too young, innit?

'Alright?' I say a bit louder, clenching my fist a bit to show I mean it cause he still ain't replied. I don't wanna threaten him but that's how you have to deal with Liam. It's all he knows. I ain't really gonna club him but he don't know that and I've still got my cop killer rep hanging round, which, which can be quite useful in certain situations. Like this one, for example. See, I need him to be a bit scared of me. It's for his own good. I hold his gaze. I'm having to stare him down, the cheeky little fuck. Eventually, I win. He cracks and looks down, pouting a bit.

'I know what it is anyway,' he goes, all know-it-all smartarse like, but he says it a bit quiet like he's not sure if he's pushing me too far now.

So I jump on that. 'I don't fuckin' care,' I yell at him. 'You don't look at it. You don't *think* about fuckin' touching it.' I stop and think and carry on not quite so loud to make sure he gets it. 'And if anyone stops you – know what I mean, the cops like – you don't fuckin' know what it is. Alright?'

He grins then. ''Course. What d'you think I am. Fuckin' schhteeeewpit or somefink?'

I wanna laugh then. But I don't, to keep it up the hard man act I'm gonna have to do with him now, so I just keep staring at him, like I see Dean do. Then look away and then quickly back to check he's got it. And he's got it.

'Alright,' I say grudgingly. 'We'll get you a bike.'

We lift one up the park. Not our rec, the posh park. On Sunday: Divorced dads' day. That's when all the divorced dads from the posh families go and take their kids out. And they always buy them good stuff 'cause they feel guilty about not being at home no more. And the other thing is, being posh, they ain't clued up to us lot, so we can just wander over and hang about and when little Johnny's fallen over and is crying and bawling, or little Samantha wants to go on the swing, we just wander over to where the stupid fuckers have left their bikes and leg it.

So that's what we did. It weren't a nice day so there weren't many dads about. But there were one with a couple of girls and guess what – off they go to the swings and leave the bikes lying on the side.

We took the biggest, which was about right for Liam,

even though he's a bit little. It's a bit of a girls' fairy cycle actually and he was pissed 'cause he wanted a BMX or something, but I told him he had to have a shite bike or he'd attract attention. We took that one back to the flophouse and painted over it with some dark blue paint we nicked from up the building site. It looked fine and he'd be able to get about on that. Fast he was. Even faster on his wheels than he was on his feet. Billy Whiz I called him.

And he was in more ways than one. I did the brown and the heavy stuff and he took the hash and sometimes, a bit of speed. We was flying, the two of us and Dean was well pleased, which was good, so everything seemed to be going well. Me and Liam was smashing it. We had the business going, all under control. Jerry helped Liam out a bit if he needed it, if it was safe. Dean was in a good mood with me and sometimes used to bung the odd bit of extra my way. We were doing fine for cash.

PIRATE CODE

I was still worried about Albie. Quiet, in himself more than before and still looking a bit sick and skinny. But then other times he was alright. I came back one night and it was just like the old days. I could hear the noise of laughing when I came in the kitchen. He was holding court for the kids in the big room. There were loads of 'em in there and all. He was up there in the middle of the room, talking and waving his arms about. His eyes were all bright as well. Kinda like they used to be. Like some light was on inside him.

When he saw me come in, he came running over. 'Look, look what we've done! Isn't it beautiful?'

I looked. Katie was standing on one of the chairs, a paintbrush in her hand. Her eyes were all bright like his as well. And behind her, was this huge painting. Like a big film poster or something. And it was amazing.

There was a huge sun in the corner of the wall on the right. Big burning orange. It looked as if you would burn your fingers if you touched it, it was so real. In front of it was the outline of the cranes and offices and houses and flats of round here, all in darkness still. You could recognise some of the buildings like the school and the hospital and the flats. But what was weird is that you couldn't really tell if the sun was rising or setting, if it was early daylight or dusk. The sky was all lit up, the clouds all bluey orange at the edges and then disappearing into darkness. Behind it was the flag, like Albie's tattoo. The red cross. The cross of St George. Our flag. And it looked like the edge of that was burning up as well.

On the other wall, opposite there was the Children of Albion picture that Albie drew 'cept bigger. Well good it were, I had to give her that.

'Turn round,' said Albie.

I spun round, and on the wall behind me there was this big skull and crossbones. It was well good. Big and black and scary. I wish the one on my arm had turned out like that one and not all wonky.

Albie loved it. He was well pleased. 'Look at it. It's great! This is what it's all about!'

I grinned at him. Madhead, he is sometimes. 'What's the pirates for?' I asked.

He laughs, waving his hands in the air again and spinning round on his feet like a dancer as he tries to explain to me. 'Pirates! Freedom! Independence! The skull and crossbones is their symbol, their flag. You know they used to fly it when they were out on the sea. And it meant they bowed to no government or authority. To no one but themselves. But they weren't anarchists or nihilists...'

I were gonna ask him what that meant but he was in full flow so I just let him go on and hoped it would make sense at the end.

'They set up their own community that didn't recognise those who were supposed to be ruling them. They were true rebels.'

'Telling everyone to fuck off. They didn't give a shit like?' I said to him. I'd seen the movies. They were cool dudes those pirates.

'No. But they did have their own code of honour and set of rules amongst themselves. And though it was all a long time ago, the skull and crossbones still symbolises disassociation, disconnection, rejection. A place or state or being that is beyond the law of the land. The true spirit of rebellion, which is why it is here now. On our wall.'

I didn't know about that. I just thought it looked cool. That's one of the great things about Albie, he always came out with loads of cool stuff that you didn't know. And he was still going. Flying he was.

'Come here! Come here!' He grabbed me by the hand and dragged me to the stairs. There, climbing up the stairs were the knights, Arthur's knights. In their long robes and their armour and swords with their long faces, just like Albie'd drawn 'em in his books.

'What d'you think?'

'Well it's cool like. Having your heroes on the walls. From the stories. Like posters, I spose,' I said. He was so excited it was almost scaring me.

'No, no. These aren't heroes to us; we are our own heroes. We have written our own stories.'

He still had my hand and he was spinning me round with it, trying to dance with me.

'These are us. The spirit of these men are in you. Their lineage travels down.'

I was feeling a bit embarrassed 'cause he was still spinning me about, dancing round me, and everyone was looking. 'What you on about?'

'You have their qualities. You are their seventy-fifth generation – or whatever it is. The land we stand in is the land they stood on and now sleep on. You are they and they are you and ...'

I couldn't cope with this. He was really off on one. 'But they did all these great things.'

I frowned and shook my head but he carried on anyway. 'You asked me once about my name. Albion. Well, Albion was a giant. The giant. The last of the giants. And he lived here on this island. He was very, very old although he looked like a young man. And his memory went back to the beginning of time. He gave England its name.'

'Uh?'

'The old name for England was Albion. And this is why I chose it for my name. I chose it for its spirit. A spirit we have forgotten, but a spirit that is still there. In this land we walk upon. This was the island of the blessed and Albion ruled it. The people were happy for they were under his protection and that of his supernatural helpers. Many tribes tried to attack and take the island, but he fought back bravely. Eventually, the weak and the warmongers and the selfish and the greedy and those hungry for power and riches destroyed the community and enslaved its people. But not everything can be suppressed, and if you listen, you can still hear the spirit of Albion whispering to you and you can feel his soul within you.' He put his hand out then and touched my chest.

Fuck, I thought. He's finally lost it.

'Arthur, in a way, was one of his sons. A young king fighting his enemies on all sides and me, you and us — we are doing the same. For our lives must not be enslaved by those who corrupted this isle.'

Fuck.

His voice went quieter then. 'You have the choice, Robbie. You can live your life like a hero or you can follow the others down into the cave. It's up to you. All of it. Everything in your life. It's all up to you. Your choices, your decisions. Whatever you think or whatever they say or do.'

He grabbed my hand again then, quite hard. His hand was hot and dry and he gripped my fingers 'til they almost hurt. 'You know how important this is don't you?' he said.

I said, 'Yeah,' though I wasn't sure I did really know. I mean I thought it was cool what we were doing but I don't think I felt about it the way he did. But if he was happy….

And he was. He span away from me then, calling for music on the CD player and for drink. Now that, I could understand – and sort out.

We partied until the sun came up, drinking and talking and dancing and smoking and admiring our newly decorated flophouse all led by Albie on fine form. I thought then everything was alright.

Only I thought wrong, didn't I? 'cause I never looked right into his fuckin' eyes, did I?

ĊꞪꞓ ꞓꞪꞦꝊꞐІꞓꞍꞓꞩ Ꝋ꜡ ꜞꞮꞲꞮꝊꞐ

Ah, my belle dame sans merci, my comfort and my pain, my desire and destruction. She comes to me and touches me with one cool white hand and one that is warm and brown. Her nimble fingers spin a web, with skeins of her silken honeyed locks and wraps it round me. Weakly I struggle, for this is a trap I would wish upon myself. Delicious prison, sensuous incarceration. A shining guillotine slices through. Chase away the weariness the fever and the fret. I feed deep on those dark, dark eyes and feel the blood in my veins turn to gold.

You'll lose your mind in a caramelised mist. My desire and my destruction. The prince, his horse and his blade. And the beauteous mistress of his downfall.

FALL FROM GRACE

Next day, I was out on a fag run down the shops when Dean found me again. I was just crossing the road when some prick drives up and nearly hits me. Just stops in a squeal of brakes. I jump out my skin and I start yelling, 'Oi,' when I look up and see Dean's face grinning at me over the steering wheel. Very fuckin' funny.

He beckons me over to the window.

'Alright, Nutboy?'

'Yeah, Dean. Blinding.' Anyone with half a brain can see I'm lying. Dean's got more 'n half a brain but he don't care if I'm alright or not. As long as I'm coming up with the goods for him, that's as far as it goes.

'Pop round Marlene's in a minute, will you? I want you to deliver something for me.'

And he's off with a spin of tyres. Please would've been nice but you'd be daft to hold your breath and wait for that one from him. I turn round and start heading for Marlene's.

He's there when I get there and it occurs to me then... he could have given me a fuckin' lift couldn't he?

Marlene's making tea as usual. 'You want one, Robbie?'

'He ain't got time,' Dean snaps. Then to me, 'I need you to run this over to Shaggy for a test drive. You know where he is.'

He puts a wrap on the table.

Everyone knew Shaggy. He was your friendly neighbourhood junkie. Nobody knew how old he was. He looked about a hundred and fifty and he's been around forever. It was a fuckin' miracle the amount of shit he stuck up his nose or in his veins or down his neck that he's still here at all. The geezer must be fuckin' indestructible. Captain Scarlet's got nowt on him. Actually, I reckon it's only the shit in his veins that keeps him standing. If he cleaned up, he'd just collapse like a suit of clothes with no one inside.

Shaggy was Dean's taster. Any new stuff Dean gets in goes through Shaggy first. He knows his stuff and he knows what tastes good, if you know what I mean. I just pick up the wrap and head out the door. There's no point in going back for my bike so I just head straight over.

Shaggy lives in one of those council bedsits over by the station, where they dump all the people no one wants to think about. Some of 'em are for the old uns and the rest are for people like Shaggy, for the asylums and immigrants, for the old alchies and for single mums who've run away from some bloke and his fists of fury.

'cause Shaggy's been there so long, he gets a bigger bedsit than some of the others and he's got no one else on his floor. Just the loo.

The door is open when I go up and Shaggy seems to know who I am and what I'm there for. He just holds his hand out and then disappears into the bog across the landing. Funny, everyone knows he's a fuckin' smackhead but he still likes his privacy, going to the bog to jack up.

I hang about outside. Didn't offer me a tea or nothing but looking at the state of the place, I don't think I'd wanna drink out of any of his mugs. Filthy shithole it is. And there's nowhere to sit except his bed and that looks like it's never had the sheets changed since he moved in. There's a packet of biscuits on the table but I don't really feel like taking one, even though I quite fancy one. You just never know what you might catch in these places. Junkies are so fuckin' *dirty*.

Then the lock on the bog clicks and he comes out, a big fat

grin on his mug, rubbing his arm.

'Tell 'im it's the dog's bollocks, mate. The dog's fuckin' bollocks.'

So that's it. And a couple of days later, I'm lifted by Dean's gimps again and off delivering what I s'pose is 'the dog's bollocks'

Funny, this being the shit hot stuff according to Shaggy and way more dear, that the places I deliver to are real shitholes. None of these shabby student houses but real scary holes round the back of the station, past Shaggy's. Desperate. Shooting galleries and the sort of street that even the stray dogs don't bother going. I take my bike and never even get off it, if I can avoid it. Just in case. This area is *nasty*.

Seems like the premiership of drug taking works in reverse. All the places were holes but it was the last one I remember most, for another reason. It's the same story. Some dump, door hanging off, 'Junkie fuck off' painted on the side, smashed windows boarded up with cardboard, stink of body and shit and old food and other such crap. Usual shambling wreck comes to the door with bloodshot eyes and desperate claw-like fingers to do the deal. As we're working it out, the door falls a bit open behind him and I can see inside.

There's a guy in there and he's on his knees by the side of this girl with a big spike in his hand. She's got a tie round her arm. He taps the barrel. They're both fixed on that little metal tip. Knocking out the air he sticks it into the skin of her arm, the blue veins in the elbow. I can see her shiver as he pushes it in and the stuff hits her.

I can't see her face. Just her arm and her legs crumpled in front of her. Long legs. Stripy over the knee socks, little pleated skirt, so short you can see her knickers, if you wanted to.

Yeah, I'd know it anywhere.

The stupid cow. Fancy getting mixed up with someone like that. And then I see his hand creeping over her thighs and in between them. Christ.

The guy at the door cops onto the fact I'm looking round him. 'Hey,' he says. 'Whachoo looking at?'

And he pulls the door closer to behind him.

'Nuffin,' I say, looking at him all big eyed and innocent. And I go.

Stupid bitch, I thought as I pedalled back to the flophouse after the last drop. Mug's game. And what's to become of her? Flogging herself like that for a bit of brown. I thought I'd better tell Albie soon as. It's not good having a junkie about. And with Albie and her knocking each other off there's AIDS and shite and all. It really is a dirty mug's game. Not fuckin' funny.

When I get there, Albie's out but the lads are out the front having a game of footie so I drop the bike and join in. It's nice to have a bit of a run around sometimes. Let off a bit of steam, innit. It's like being a kid again.

I'm not bad at the old footie, to be fair. Fast, quick. Midfielder really. Homeless is good, too, for such a skinny and sick looking streak of piss. Bit of a showboater though. Damian, one of Homeless's lot, is pretty shit-hot, too. Any position. But he's a big fucker so he gets to do defence most of the time. It's seven-a-side. We could easily have a proper team. Children of Albion Rovers. Something like that. I'm thinking of that and not what I'm doing and get nutmegged and shoved in the dirt. Story of my life.

When it starts getting dark, we go in and get some tea. And I hear Albie come in the front and go upstairs. You can always tell it's him 'cause of them big boots he wears and the shambling way he walks.

That means he's in one of his weird quiet moods again. Or he's sick. The fact he don't come and say 'hi' or nothing. I start to get worried again 'cause I'd thought we was back to normal after the other night and he was better. 'I mean, he was always pale but his skin had this kind of waxy look now and he had these big dark smudges under his eyes all the time, like bruises they were, real black eyes. And often he got in these moods where he weren't so much fun. He'd used to spend a lot of time just rolled up in his coat looking at the window. Sometimes, he couldn't even raise himself when the little kids wanted him. That weren't like him at all.

With all he's got going on and feeling rough and all that, the last thing he needs is Katie's junkie shit. I'm thinking about not telling him, but the way I see it, I have to. Not to would be worse.

I go up to what was our room but is now more often his and Katie's. The door's shut, which is unusual so I open it a bit in case he's trying to sleep. He's lying there on the floor under the blankets – his fuckin' coat and boots on as usual – but I can tell he's not asleep. He's twitching and itching and his eyes are open. Only there's a look in then like he can't see anything. Anything at all.

'Albie…' I start. I'm really panicking now. He looks like he needs an ambulance. Or he's just too late for one. And I wouldn't admit it to no one but, yeah, I'm frightened. And for some reason, I feel bad in my guts as well, even though there's nothing wrong with me.

As I'm standing there – for the second time that day looking into a room and wondering what to do – guess who comes up behind me? Katie. Brimming with junk, looking at her.

She ignores me and she says to Albie, 'I've got something that will help you feel better, Alb. It's okay.'

And she goes in and shuts the door on me. And I'm not sure what to do and I start feeling a bit sick. I dunno what she's talking about but I know it's one or the other. I hope it's the one where she takes her knickers off. Not that I'm keen her on doing that 'cause I think she's trouble and I don't want her anywhere near him, 'specially now. But it's better than the alternative.

But, if I'm honest, I know exactly what it is. I fuckin'' know.

And now I understand.

And I know what that sick feeling inside me is.

I lean against the wall and slide down.

I feel like crying but I find a fag instead. I smoke one. Then another and another and another. And I sit there 'til I fall asleep.

I wake up stiff and sore sometime before four. I heard the clock strike. I don't go to bed though. I can't go in there, so I just go out for a walk and wait for the sun to come up.

It's beautiful when it does. Really fuckin' beautiful. The sky's all streaked pink like women's lipstick and blue grey like those uniforms them American Yankees wore in the old films. And then there's the yellowy, bluey light of daylight trying to get through. And then the sun picks up the buildings, splashing on the windows so they look like they're made of gold. Even the shittiest blocks.

Funny that. Even when the world is shite, sometimes when you look, when there's no one there, it's really fuckin' incredible.

But I'm just not in the mood.

Not today.

CHE CHRONICLES OF ALBION

Up on those hills, covered now in concrete and river, rivers of streets running up and down like tributaries rich in iron. Ironmen maybe. Or iron corroding, disused. But still they run, running somewhere.

Running, running always running. Running forward, running away, running to only stand still. Who knows?

Sometimes my head hurts and then it is time. Time to take in the brown, take it in and exhale it all as it runs runs runs through my veins like the houses, the iron men running up and down those hills. Running, running, always running.

INTO THE WOODS

Things was alright then for a while. Well actually I don't think they were at all, I think I kind of blocked it out. I kind of kept in myself for a bit. Carried on like everything was normal. Normal. That's a laugh. But Albie was sound again. Blinding form. Obviously, I s'pose, now she was providing a regular supply of everything. But I kind of kidded myself that it wasn't that and there was nothing wrong.

In the end, I never told him about Katie. I didn't have to, did I? He obviously knew right? – some of it at least. But I just shoved all that to the back of my head. Blocked it out. Bit like cats crossing the road with their eyes shut – cause if you can't see it, it ain't there.

And that worked for a while. I was able to do it quite easy. But it didn't last. And then I started noticing the pattern with Albie and I couldn't work out how I never noticed it before.

He got really sick again. Really, really sick. Worse than ever before. Not coming out of the room. Lying in his clothes all day or looking out the window. Sometimes, he was sweating but at the same time when he was sweating he was really cold. At night he twitched and itched and thrashed about like he was fighting someone or something. And he'd cry out in his sleep with terrible nightmares. It scared me but I still didn't know what to do.

I used to go out and walk around a lot; smoking, thinking. Thinking if I smoked enough things would come clear in my head. And it was on one of those walks I met the last person I wanted to see, pulling up behind me with a gravel-spitting broadside in Dean's immobile. Bollock Brain.

'Alright, Nutboy?'

'Yeah. Fuckin' great.' Dickhead.

'Get in. Dean's after yer.'

Brilliant. That's all I need just now. But, when the boss calls...Ten minutes and a puke-making drive later, I'm back in Dean's Gestapo room at the pub. Same set up: Dean and the pricks, Bollock Brain standing guard.

'We need you to do something else for us,' says Dean.

I'm not sure if I like this or not. I mean what I'm doing is cool alright, but..

'We need a kid to help us with a job.'

Bollock Brain's itching and twitching about it again. He ain't happy but it seems like he never is when it involves me. Knee him in the balls once – by fuckin' *accident* – and he'd never forgive you. Not that I care. Thick, fat prick.

Dean goes on, 'We have to pick something up. I need Gary here' – he nods towards Bollock Brain – 'to go with a kid. Looks better if there's a kid. Father and son. Respectable.'

'Him? My old man?'

'You look young enough,' says Dean, fixing me with his old shark eyes. 'How old are you?'

'Eleven?'

'Yeah. Well you look younger.'

Bollock Brain starts whispering in his ear. Dean nods.

Then he goes on, 'What about that little nipper I see you with? On the bike. The cheeky little one.'

Liam? Fuck.

'What kid?' I go.

'Don't be fuckin' funny with me. We've seen you alright. You and those kids. That one and there's another one. They'll be younger than you.'

I know what he's thinking. But it was alright for me using Jerry and Liam – them being underage and that and not criminally liable or whatever it was – 'cause I looked out for 'em, looked after them and only got 'em involved in stuff after I checked it out. Nothing nasty. But I knew Dean and his lot wouldn't give a shit. They'd cut your arm off soon as look at you for a laugh. Even a kid.

I think fast. 'Nah. They'd panic. No good to you. Bit of a liability to be honest. Big gobs on 'em, know what I mean. I'll do it,' I said. 'I look young. You said.'

Dean narrows his little eyes even more as he runs it by himself. He looks at me sharp one more time to check I'm not pulling something funny and then he goes, 'Okay. You, then, Nutboy.'

'Okay,' I says to Dean and then over to my new old man, 'Okay….Dad.'

I can tell that right now he just wants to pick me up and shove me head through the window but the big boss has spoken.

'Right.' Dean looks at both of us. 'No squabbling and no fuck ups. Alright?'

Now to be honest, I don't wanna do this it all. Whatever it is. But I can't see like I've got a choice. Dean Amery ain't someone you say 'No' to and I've heard of quite a few people who found that out the hard way. Still, I'm not down yet so I go quickly, before they turf me back out,

'I want sorting properly for this. If this is a big one, you have to sort me. I'm not so young I ain't going down.'

Dean puts his hand in the pocket of his leather coat and pulls out a bundle of notes. 'That now. Same again after. That enough?'

Jeeez. Half that'd do but I know to keep cool and act like I'm considering. Bollock Brain's looking annoyed but I know Dean's not daft enough not to know I'm seriously bought this time.

'Alright.'

'Good. Oh..' Dean taps his fingers on the table. 'And there's just one other thing....'

Yeah.

I walked back to the flophouse, wheeling my bike. I tend to do a lot of that these days, when I ain't got deliveries of course. Gives me time to think. Though thinking this one over is a bit of a waste of time 'cause it's already decided. There ain't really no choice. Whether I wanna do it or not, I'm doing it. I would've preferred not really 'cause I preferred working the way it was with just me and Dean and Marlene without being drawn into the gang. But looked like I was in the gang, anyways.

Albie always talked about choices and about how you could make your own choices in your life. I hoped he was right but I'm not so sure he was. Not now 'cause there weren't really no choice. a) I needed the cash more and more. Despite my extra business we always seemed to be running low, b) like I said, I was in the gang now, with all that – good and bad, and c) once you were in that gang the only way out was something involving a wooden box and a church service and I didn't fancy that.

Like I said, bollocks to choices. Choices are supposed to be about a good thing versus a bad thing, not two options just as fuckin' shite as each other. But maybe people like us don't get the normal choices – just the shite ones.

True enough, the same went for what happened later between me and Albie. No fuckin' choice at all, did I have? Fuckin' none. I ask you, what would you have done?

When I got back, the flophouse was quiet. Not quiet as in there was no one there; there was never no one there. It was just quiet. Albie weren't nowhere to be seen. Katie weren't there either – out whoring for smack probably – and most of the little kids were kipping in their room. Homeless and some of the others were sitting around a fire, drinking cans of lager and listening to miserable CDs. Some moany cow whingeing on about how some bloke had left her. Who would've fuckin' blamed him, if you ask me.

'Where's Albie?'

Homeless jerked his head towards the stairs. I went up.

He was on the bed again. Curled up, his arms wrapped round his belly. He was sweating like a wrestler but his skin looked waxy and icy cold and he was shivering at the same time. His eyes were staring at the wall and they looked black, not grey at all like they should be, and with that horrible tea stain colour around them. He was staring but not looking, if you see what I mean, and all the time holding his belly and moaning and roaring like a woman having a baby. Real pain. Real fuckin' agony.

I didn't know what to do. There was no point saying: 'Albie? You alright?' 'cause it was fuckin' obvious he weren't, so I just stood there like a muppet, sort of thinking if I did nothing, said nothing, somehow it would all be like it weren't happening. But I knew it wouldn't, I knew it wouldn't.

I just knew it wouldn't.

And he saw me then. Not saw me as in looked at me, but saw me as in knew I was there. Without even looking 'cause he couldn't, the state he was in.

And he goes to me, 'I know you can help me. I know you can. Liam told me.'

And then he looks at me with those eyes in that face; that face now yellowy and waxy looking, those eyes all black with big stains round 'em.

'I know you can, Robbie,' he goes. And he sighs. And then he starts to cry. Not proper crying, but big tears come out his eyes and run down his face, like he's all filled up with water and it's just spilling over out of him.

What could I do? I mean, I know what that shit does to you. I know more than I wanna know. But what could I do? See what I mean about fuckin' choices? I thought of the only thing I could do to help him. The dog's bollocks. It had to be. Maybe that would help him. It's got to be better than the stuff Katie gets given as payment by those shitbags she lets screw her. Shaggy said it was the best. And it cost enough.

I go over to Marlene's. The lift's fucked as usual so I have to take the stairs. Filthy they are. And I thought the lift was bad. You'd get a better smell in a fuckin' phone box. For a minute I think she's out. I'm banging on the door like mad and nothing's happening. Then eventually, she comes. She looks like she's just woken up or something and she has the baby in her arms.

'Robbie! What's the matter with you? I thought you were the fuckin' cops.'

I'm still puffed from running up them stairs. 'Shaggy wants some more. Of that stuff. The new stuff. The dog's.'

'Alright.' She moves back into the corridor a bit.

'He paid upfront.'

I hold out some notes. They're mine. From the Albion fund. I figure it's fair enough. This is for Albion after all. In a way.

'That's unlike him,' she says. She looks at me funny, then.

She's no mug, even if she is stupid enough to take Dean's shit. 'It is for Shaggy, ain't it... Not you?' Then she says quieter, 'Not you, Robbie....?'

I open my eyes as wide as I can, to look innocent. 'Me? You having a laugh intya? I wouldn't touch that shit. You know that, Marlene.'

'Mmmm.' She stopped and looked at me for a while. That schoolteacher look. I kept my face as it was, not blinking, looking her right back straight in the eyes.

'Alright,' she goes finally and I breathe again. It's okay. And there'll be no bother with Shaggy, cause he's so out of it most of the time he won't remember and Dean won't care, as long as he gets his cash. 'Hold on.'

She disappears into the back yelling, 'Wait there, but shut the fuckin' door, will you?' She comes back with the wrap and even smiles as I pull out one of my eggs to put it in.

'Oh, you. You're such a kid really, aren't you, love?'

I give her a grin but I need to head off.

'See yer, Marls.'

I pedal my arse off all the way back to the flophouse and up the stairs. Albie's still on the bed where I left him. He looks fuckin' awful. Worse, which I didn't think was possible.

But maybe this stuff will make him feel better. It's so much more expensive than Dean's normal shit and Shaggy give it the thumbs up, plus, so it must be real good, real pure. Maybe it won't make him so sick as that stuff Katie was bringing him.

I know what to do. We had a baby sitter who used smack when I was a kid and I seen her do it often enough. I've got a lighter. It's just a case of finding Albie's stuff, which ain't that hard cause there ain't that many places to look. His bag. High up on the built in cupboard where the kids can't reach it.

I climb up using the shelves as a ladder. Bingo. A spoon, a spike. The works.

So I cook up for him.

He's rolled over now. Looking at me. Pleading.

Lying there, whimpering like a weak, hungry baby; tearing at his skin like he's trying to climb out of his own body; jack-knifing as if some invisible man is booting him in the belly; jerking his neck back as if the same invisible thug has yanked him back by the hair; sweat pouring off him and his hair all stuck to his head with it but at the same time his grey white skin looking cold as death. I look in his face and eyes looked old, older than a thousand, million years. A thousand, million years or more.

 I don't have no choice. Do I?

It's like this film I saw once, where this guy finds a dying fox and he has to shoot it. Them fox's big eyes. Pleading to be put out his misery with a bullet and the fella ripping his heart out and doing it. I cried at the film and I felt like crying now. Only I ain't a cryer, so I never cried.

I just did it.

I know what to do. Cook up on the spoon, let the syringe suck it up and then tap the barrel for air. Making it right. Checking for air bubbles and that. Everything I can do, I do, to try and make it okay. But it's not okay. It's not okay at all. And every second of it kills me.

He's already freed his arm out of that big coat, pulled his belt off and yanked it tight around his arm to plump out the veins. And he don't take his eyes off the syringe neither. He's looking at it like a starving dog staring at a lump of poisoned meat. Only the thing is, the dog don't know it's poisoned and somewhere in his head, he does, Albie. He does. I know he does.

But still, he's all excited. I can see it glimmering at the back of those grey, old eyes.

But I'm not excited at all.

I feel sick.

I take a deep breath and I dig the needle in. As I push the plunger he looks at me. His face is like an angel. No one ever looked at me like that before. It's hope and it's love, real love. Real, real love. It's beautiful.

But it's sickening, too.

Love?

For me? For what I did? For that shit?

His head rolls back and his eyes close. For the first time in a long, long time he looks peaceful.

But I go outside and I throw up 'til I think my guts are gonna end up on the ground between my feet.

ĊꙐꙐ ꙐꙐꙐꙐꙐꙐꙐꙐꙐ ꙐꙐ ꙐꙐꙐꙐꙐꙐ

And they carried him away, the nymphs and dryads clad in golden brown, and he floated away on the rivers of Lethe to where falls not hell, or pain, or any snow nor ever screams crow loudly, and he resteth crowned with golden summer warmth and heal me of my grieving, grievous wounds. Think of me and I shall return.

THE VALLEY OF PLENTY

I dunno what to do then. I can't go back to the flophouse and I've nowhere else to go. I don't wanna go down the rec. I don't wanna bump into people that I have to be hard with. You know 'cause I don't feel very hard just now.

It's funny, even though I know this old gaff like the back of my hand, I feel a bit... lost. Like everywhere's big and strange. Even though I know it's not.

I end up just wandering. Tennyson Way, Galahad Drive, Churchill Gardens, Longfellow Avenue. Round and round and round. And round. Going nowhere, really. Shakespeare Drive, Albion Way. Funny how I never noticed that before. And I must've been down here hundreds of times. Albion. I thought back to the time when I first met him. And the time when he told me about his name.

Albion. Albion the proud. The island of the giant. The giant who protected us. Who fought off enemies, who stood for what was right, who protected the weak and afraid. Well, just like old Arthur, he was well and truly sleeping now.

And I wasn't sure if he was ever going to wake up.

I ended up outside *The Moderation.* I didn't in my head think of going there but when I got there I knew that that's where I wanted to be, and there was someone I wanted to see. Dean and his mates were inside. I could see through the window. He was up at the bar. I waited there, outside in the cold, just peering over the ledge for him to leave. Dean. He always knew how to handle things. He could handle anything. Anything.

I see him stub out his fag and neck the last of his pint. He slaps a few hands and backs goodbye and heads for the door.

He sees me hanging around as soon as he gets out the door. He's with some of his pack but he stops and frowns at me. 'Waddya want?'

He says it all stroppy like. And I know there's nothing for me there.

'Nothing,' I say, more to myself than him. And I lean back against the wall and watch him go off, laughing, with his mates.

I dunno how long I've been standing there when I think, 'Sam.' And I start heading back to the flats. When I look up, I can see the lights are on so I know there's someone in. I dunno if it's mum or if it's Sam. I'm thinking about going in when the door at the bottom opens and Sam comes out. I'm just taking a breath to call her and then I see Kevin coming out behind her. He grabs her as he comes through the door and pulls her over closer to him. And they're both laughing and joking and then he's snogging her. Right up against the wall and that, so anyone can see, his hands all over her and that.

So I don't say nothing. I just watch them from where I'm standing. Then they head off, his arm round her waist, leaning into each other and giggling together like kids.

The lights are still on upstairs so mum must be in. I decide to risk it and I go up, using my key to open the door. She's crossing the passage as I do so, and she stops, a bit surprised. Like pausing a DVD.

She's got a fuckin' glass in her hand. And it ain't full of water.

I went and picked the wrong time, didn't I? My heart sinks even further than it was before. If that's possible. It must be coming out the soles of my arseing trainers by now.

'Where have you been, my baby boy?' she croons.

I stand there against the wall, shifting a bit from side to side. Feel a bit uncomfortable 'cause I really don't know if she's pissed or not yet. 'Just out and about. Staying with friends, like.'

Ah, no. Hang on a minute. Her eyes look massive. She's got all this black stuff round them and it's smeared a bit where she's been crying. Makes 'em look bigger. Big black rings round 'em. Like a clown – especially with the big red mouth she has painted on herself. But somehow all twisted, not funny. The colours are all wrong for a start. And for something else, she ain't making me laugh. She puts her hands out towards me. She's wobbling.

'Why don't you come home, darling? You know I need you. My little man. My *little* man.'

Her mouth is a big red O and then her bottom lips starts wobbling and I know we're in for it. Oh FUCKIN' hell. Not this. Not this now.

And we're off.

She's started trying to come towards me now, trying to pull herself forward up the passage, using the wall as a support with one hand while balancing the glass in the other but she's too pissed. She's getting closer and I know any minute she's gonna grab me. I'm trying to shrink back into the wall and edge for the door but I don't reckon I can make it.

'Is it something I did? It is, isn't it? I'm a bad mother, I am, aren't I? Oh I feel so bad. You don't know what it's like for me and I need you, my little Robster. I need you to look after mummy. My little, little man.'

She overbalances then and ends up on her hands and knees on the floor. To tell you the truth, it's fuckin' pathetic. She's still looking up at me, trying to crawl across the carpet and grab my ankle to make me stay.

'Robbie, don't leave mummy. Mummy needs you and mummy loves you so much, so, so, very much.'

I feel like my head's just gonna explode. I don't fuckin' need *this*. Not at all. And finally, something does explode. And I yell at her. At my *mum*. Screaming at her. My voice gone all high like a girl.

'DON'T do this to me now. I can't DO this now. I CAN'T do this. PLEASE.'

But she's still there on her knees, pleading with me. Crying, with all this black stuff coming off her eyes and her lipstick all smeared over her face. And it just don't work anymore. It's not even sad. It's just disgusting.

This is not about me, I realise. It's about her. Some other prick has done her over and I'm supposed to step in until some new prick – the same prick, basically, with different tattoos – comes along to make her feel good for five minutes. And then after that, it's all down to me again. Sam had enough ages ago. Then it was down to me. Well, I can't do it anymore. Not with all the other shite going on for me. No. NO.

NO!

And suddenly I don't feel angry or sad for her any more. I just feel kind of cold. Nothing. Nothing. Nothing at all.

'I. Can't. Do. This. Any. More,' I say, dead slow. Icy cold. Cruel. It don't even sound like me. It sounds like someone else talking but I couldn't think who.

And it kills me but I leave her. I walk out that door and I leave her crying. I walk slowly out the flats. And as I go it comes to me who I sounded like back then. I sounded just like Dean Amery.

I'm feeling really pissed angry so I go over the back, right over the back to the waste ground where the bulldozers are. And I go beserk. Picking up concrete slabs, bricks, bits of wood. Anything I can find and chucking them all over the shop.

I lose it completely. I think I actually forget myself 'cause finally, I find myself right up against a wall, kicking it over and over again with no idea how I got there. Once I stop, I can feel my toes and they hurt so fuckin' much I think I might have actually broke 'em. But when I was doing it, I didn't feel nothing. There's tears on my face, tears I don't remember crying – 'cause I don't cry – but they're there all over my face somehow.

I sniff and wipe my nose on my sleeve and look around, coming back out of my head. I've totalled the place. There's smashed up bits of wood everywhere and a pile of shopping trolleys upside down in the middle of the grass and the windows on the bulldozer are all smashed in. I don't remember doing half of it but I do feel a bit better.

But I'm tired, really, really tired. There's nowhere to go but back to the flophouse, so even though I'm scared to go back, I start heading over that way.

I don't wanna go back 'cause I don't wanna see Albie just now. Not 'til I can work it all out in my head. And there's no room in there for working anything out just now. It's like every time I try and think of something, loads of other stuff comes piling on top of it 'til I can't see what I was thinking of and I can't work out what the new stuff is either.

Then something else happens that means I don't have no time to think of nothing.

A big fuckin' pimpmobile pulls up beside me and the window is buzzed down.

'You were s'posed to be in Richmond Alley fifteen fuckin' minutes ago.'

It's Dean and his merry crew and that 'just one other thing' he was on about, I'd forgotten all about it. Not only did they want me to give them cover for their big pick up of the brown stuff, they wanted me to nick them a car for it and all. A creeping job.

Not something I like to do, to be honest with you. I mean nicking's nicking and TWOCing's – that's what the charge is… taking without the owner's consent – TWOCing. But I don't like going into people's houses. But that's what Dean wants. And what Dean wants, Dean generally gets. Creeping's the easy way round posh cars with boss security systems. You just go in the owner's house and nick his keys and not bother with all that shite.

Like I say, I'm not a big fan of burglary but I weren't in the mood for a row or any more fuckin' hassle than I've already fuckin' had, so I just get in and take the clump round the head for not being in Richmond Alley when I said I would. Bollock Brain jeers at me,

'Oi, you been crying? Like a girl?'

I don't reply, just squash myself as far as possible to the edge of the seat and stare out the window. He prods and pokes me a few times but gives up when he can't get a rise out of me and I just sit there watching the tarmac disappear away underneath us.

We drive around looking for what they want. Something fast, flash but not too flash. Well-off bloke's car. The sort of bloke who don't need to do crime, the sort of bloke who never had to and don't draw attention to himself neither. That's what they want. We head out of town a bit, up to the big new houses over the back of the park. That's where the dosh is, so that's where the car will be.

It makes things much easier for people like Dean, people

like us. With security on motors so fuckin' good, trying to break in is a pain in the arse. I mean 'course you can if you wanna but it takes a lot longer and you're dealing with alarms and immobilisers and all that shite and it ain't worth it. Far easier to just get the keys. Common sense, innit?

There's two ways to do this. Mugging someone in the car – like parked up or at a junction, lights or jam – or mugging 'em before they get in or just after they get out. Not keen on either to be honest. The other way is creeping.

You go window shopping up some posh area where you're gonna get nice cars. You find the car you want parked up on a drive somewhere and then burgle the house for the keys. You'd be amazed how simple it is. Like this night. Cinch, which was good 'cause I weren't really sharp enough to be mucking about creeping. But I'd already been told, none too fuckin' gently either, that Dean weren't in no mood for moaning or backchat. It were just a case of fuckin' get on with it.

So we did. Bollock Brain's gonna be driving it and he's got his eye on something flash like, which of course is fuckin' dumb. Dean calls him a prick for pointing out a new Merc and a big flash Rangie with tinted windows. Dean spots a big Beamer. Saloon. Baby seat in the back and all.

'That'll do.' He sits back and waits for us to jump. We do.

Bollock Brain and his mate shove me out and Bollock Brain grabs me by the hoodie so I'm hanging off his fist like a kitten he's got by the neck.

The car's parked up on the drive in front of the garage. Bollock Brain nudges me. 'Check the garage.'

No security lights go off as I hurry up the drive to peer in the garage. It's empty. The lights are off in the house, too, 'cept one little one in the hallway, so it all seems good.

The two meatheads come up to join me while Dean sits back in the motor and waits, grabbing me by the hood again and dragging me round the side of the house with them. There's one of them plastic windows in the side. Part of the kitchen, looks like but you can't see properly 'cause the glass is all bobbly.

Bollock Brain's mate has a go with a screwdriver round the edges and a bit of leverage and it's out. All in one bit. He puts it down careful on the grass, propped up by the wall, as if he's moved some precious painting or something. Then he turns to me.

'In you go, you little twat.'

They heft me up, quite gentle actually. But only 'cause they are worried about me knocking off loads of shite on the window sill and waking up the house, in case there is someone in, though the house seems dead.

I'm sitting on the sill looking into what looks like some sort of shop cupboard. Shelves up both walls with tins and jars and packets and all sorts. Biscuits and tins of spaghetti with cartoon faces on 'em. And loads of packets of cereal, all the fancy stuff, not just Corn Flakes. There's about ten bars of chocolate so I take a couple and put them in my pocket. Then I try and untangle me legs without bringing the whole fuckin' lot crashing to the floor.

I look behind me at the other two who are hissing and flapping at me to hurry up. Their big fat faces white in the dark. Pissing me off.

I climb down and move to the door, opening it carefully.

It's a big fuck off kitchen. Like Milo's. Fuckin' hell. All that food then. That's just for them, innit.

Blimey.

Some rich ones these are, eh?

The house ain't dark 'cause the moon outside is well bright and there's no curtains in here. Also they've left a security light on for the burglars. The hall light so as it looks as there's someone in. But no one with half a brain falls for that one.

Funny really. It's supposed to keep thieving toe rags like me out but it's actually doing me a big favour. I can see what's going on perfect.

Now. Car keys. It's probably her car. The woman. I reckon. Kids' stuff in it and the driver's seat pulled well forward. Didn't seem like a bloke's car, so I'm looking for a handbag she's left out. Or maybe they're in a drawer somewhere. I start pulling open the top drawers. Keys is always in top drawers. Then… .bingo! Happy days. Right by the kitchen door. There it is. A big thing with hooks on and KEYS written on the top. There's door keys, house keys and – yes, thank you very much – a set for a Beamer. This must be them. Couldn't have been easier if I planned it. Rich folk. They aren't that bright are they, considering... like 'cause I found 'em so quick, I decided to have a look round the house 'fore I go. Not to take anything. Just to have a look. Just to see.

It's a nice enough house, alright. Yeah, I'd say. Carpet fuckin' everywhere, thick carpet that joins up properly with the walls and when you step on it it's all funny and bouncy. Like walking on grass, sorta. There's a few toys lying on the stairs. New ones by the look of it. Not broke or anything. *And* them new electronic games they were advertising on the telly and they're well fuckin' expensive.

I go up. You know, they even have carpets on the stairs and all. Everything's all painted. Brand new, like. And special, shiny paint on the wooden bits. All really *clean*.

There's a landing with six doors. All bedrooms and a bathroom. The bathroom even has carpet on and all and there's gold taps and a gold shower thing. It's like a palace.

Three of the rooms are kids' bedrooms and – you'd never guess – they're all made up special. Special for each kid. One's a baby's room with a little cot and everything all yellow like sunshine and blue like the sky with little stars and that painted on the ceiling so as the little baby can look up at them. That's sweet, that is.

There's one for a little girl all pink with Barbie stuff everywhere. There's even Barbie curtains and matching duvets and that on the bed. And there's white furniture with bits of gold painted on it as if it's for a real princess or something. Looks so comfy I could just get in it – even though it's all pink and that – and sleep for a hundred years.

And there's a boy's room with bunk beds all kitted out with football wallpaper and matching curtains and duvets on the beds. Don't think much of the team but it's still well good. He's got his own computer and stuff and all. And a TV and gamestation. All to himself, like. And some pretty boss games and DVDs and all. Fuck me.

Then I'm thinking, I'd better get out, so I leg it back down the stairs.

But before I go, I sneak one look in the front room. That's where the light's coming from. It's all warm in there, even though there's no one in the house. And there's the biggest Christmas tree. Touches the ceiling it does, the old fairy head-butting the roof. Lights all over it and pretty tinsel all different colours – reds and greens and blues and whites and purples. All them fireworks colours. It's so pretty. Real pretty.

There's loads of presents under the tree. More toys for the kids. Big boxes, funny shapes all wrapped up. I sit on the floor for a bit. Thinking. Just looking at it – that tree and them presents – 'til my eyes go funny and a bit watery from staring at the lights. Some fuckin' house. It's like the best of what you can see when you walk down the town at night, when people leave their lights on before they draw the curtains and you can see in and see them all having a laugh and being all cosy and nice. Yeah, like the best of that. But even better. They must be well happy.

I wonder though. You'd think they'd love their kids a lot looking at all this. The presents, the tree, them bedrooms all done up, all that food. But Milo's house is like this – maybe not quite as posh but almost – and his mum and dad are just as shite as the rest of ours. Even with all the dosh.

Maybe it's just people think kids are cute when they're babies and then when they get to be big and ugly like us they don't want 'em anymore? Maybe that's it. They just get bored of us. You know, I dunno these kids in this house – and I nicked their chocolate – but I kinda hope that don't happen to them.

I'd better go, I think, before them two start bellowing, so I find me way back to the kitchen, to the mad cupboard with the food and them two waiting to drag me outta there.

'Where the fuck've you been?' says Bollock Brain. 'You got 'em?'

I wave the keys at him.

'Right. Hurry up. Let's get out of here.'

In a couple of minutes, we've fired up the car, heading back to our side of town. Dean behind us. I look out the window on the way back and all. But for different reasons this time.

Bollock Brain pulls up at the end of Richmond Alley and turns round to me, sitting in the back.

'Right. Twelve-thirty lunchtime. Here. Tomorrow.' He waves a warning finger in my face. 'And you'd better fuckin' not be late.'

I'm just looking at him. Not moving. He frowns at me.

'Well, fuck off then.'

I still don't move though. Truth is, even though I don't wanna be where I am, I've got nowhere to go. Don't wanna go to the flophouse, can't go to mum's, Marlene's? Nah. Milo's? Forget it. And there ain't nowhere else. That's it.

'Oi. Stop mucking around. Are you fuckin' getting out or what?'

I shift in the seat and put my hand down beside me and feel something soft.

'Can I have this?'

It's a big rug blanket thing. Tartan.

'What?'

'This.' I holds up the corner so's he can see.

Bollock Brain looks at his mate and rolls his eyes then says to me, 'What the fuck you want that for?'

'Just do.'

Bollock brain turns to his mate and says. 'See. Told you he was nuts.' Then he shrugs. 'Sure. Take it if you want, Nutboy. Just get out the fuckin' car, fuck off and be there tomorrow.'

'Alright.' I gather up the rug and get out.

'Twelve thirty,' he warns me again.

They drive off, a squeal of tyres and flash of brake lights as they turn away.

THE WARRIOR CAPE

I scrape the shrapnel out of my pockets together and head over to the burger place to see what I can afford. I sits there for a bit with my burger and cola. I finish off with some of the chocolate I got earlier. Then I head back towards Richmond Alley. But I go past it and down to that place round the back of the cinema where we first met Homeless.

Fair play to him, it's not a bad spot. You can back yourself right in there up against the wall and no one can really see you're there. Like we didn't that night we first fell over him. And we had to fall over him to find him, so I figures it'll be safe enough. I wrap myself up in the blanket thing, have a bit more chocolate. And see if I can get some sleep.

I didn't think I'd get none. It's cold enough alright – even with the blanket. And I just sit there, hunched up, looking into the dark and wondering what to do about it all. But I must've got some 'cause the next minute it's light and my neck is all cricked up. But I stay there cuddled up, maybe dozing a bit until people start coming past on their way to work.

Then I get up and head back to the burger place for some coffee. Start my day. Tell you what, it's fuckin' boring being homeless; there's nowhere to go and nothing to do. Everyone treats you like shit and you get thrown out of everywhere you stop just to try and get warm. There's no telly to watch and if you stop and look through the window at the local electric shop, some spotty work experience kid who's not much older 'n you are gets sent out to tell you to fuck off. And everyone just walks past you giving you the look like you're a piece of shit – which to them you are. And that's just how you feel and all. Then all there is to do is sit down the park with the tramps who stink of booze and piss, get riled up about nothing and then start swearing and yelling at you.

I see Sam in the distance, walking out the doctor's surgery. The one over behind the swings. I think of mum, and worry a bit. But I don't want Sam seeing me, not like this, trampy and that, and I've got enough on my plate just now, so I duck down and she don't notice me – Like no one else does that day.

To be honest, I'm glad when twelve thirty comes round. I'm ready and waiting for them there in Richmond Alley, wearing the rug round me, over my shoulders like a cape, looking like one of them fuckin' warrior blokes Albie draws – although I don't feel like no kind of warrior at all.

The Beamer we robbed yesterday pulls up beside me and the window buzzes down. It's Bollock Brain, on his own.

'Jesus fuck. You look like shit,' he goes. 'Out on the tiles all night were we?'

I don't say anything but walk round the car and slide into the passenger seat.

'On the drink. Picking up the birds, eh?' He starts laughing.

I don't.

'Look at yer. C'mere.' He drags the blanket off me, pulls at my clothes to tidy 'em then spits on a dirty hankie that's on the dash before rubbing it over my face.

'Gerroff.'

'State of yer. Fuck's sake. Now sit there and shut up.'

Now he's annoyed me. Sometimes, if I'm really pissed off about something I feel like acting nasty to people just 'cause I'm pissed off and not 'cause they've got anything to do with what I'm pissed off about. I was in a mood anyway and the hankie thing kinda just did for me, so I sit and sulk for a bit then start whingeing at him like a snotty kid. Dunno why I'm doing it really. Just baiting him 'cause I know he can't do much to me. They need me today.

Anyway, the way I feel right now, even if he goes mad and fuckin' kills me – like, really kills me, kills me dead and that – I'm not sure I care that much anymore.

So, after a while I go, 'Got any sweets?'

'No. Shut up.'

'Can I get some then? Some sweets?'

'No. Fuck up.'

He switches on the CD to drown me out. Good player actually but the CD is total crap. Drive Your Bollocks Off or some shite like that. One of them they advertise on the telly with loads of shit heavy metal music on. He loves it of course and is singing away in his horrible voice.

When he pulls into a garage and goes out to get some petrol and fags, I fiddle with the player to get it to play a decent radio station instead and turn it up. We pull away and as soon as we get back onto the motorway he turns the player back and some decent sounds come belting out.

'What've you done, you little shit?'

'Didn't you get me no sweets?'

'No. Fuck off. And leave the CD alone.'

'Where's my sweets?'

He slaps me a backhander above my ear. Don't hurt much though. And then he puts his crap CD back on and lights a fag. Doesn't offer me one. He's just lazing there, arm out the window smoking his fag and listening to his music, giving it the Charlie Big Potatoes in the car *I* fuckin' got him.

I look at the window for a bit. Concrete and concrete and bits of shitty little towns all looking the same. And I'm getting restless.

'This is shit,' I say, and switch it back to the radio.

'Right,' he goes, 'that's fuckin' *it*.'

There's a hooting of horns as he pisses everyone off by swerving across two lanes and straight onto the hard shoulder. To be honest with you, I was a bit jumpy myself, wondering what he was gonna do. If he didn't kill us both in a motorway pileup first that is. You know what I said before about them situations when you know you've gone too far and you just can't stop. Like with that fat squashhead round my mum's. Well I think this is one of them times and he's really lost it with me now. And you know I said I didn't care if he killed me? I think I do.

He pulls up with a squeal of tyres, gets out without even looking up the road and comes round to my side and pulls open the door.

'Get out.'

Shit.

I don't move, so he leans in and unbuckles the seat belt and drags me out, me trying to hold onto the car to stop him. He just yanks harder and then thumps me knuckles to make me leave go. I start bleating 'cause I'm wondering what he's gonna do and he is a big fuckin' brick-shithouse after all. I'm crapping it a bit, to be honest. I start blathering, 'Dean's gonna be pissed if you leave me here. What about the job? You can't – '

He pulls open the back passenger door. 'I'm not leaving you here. Get in, you little bollocks.'

And he shoves me in, forcing me into the kiddie seat and buckles me in with the child belt. And pulls it tight. Really fuckin' tight so's my belly's all squashed.

'Now,' he says, leaning back and smacking his hands together pleased with his handiwork. 'You sit there and shut the *fuck* up. Don't wanna hear no more out of you. Right?'

He slams the door leaving me sitting there in the back like a little gimp, gets back in and drives off. Oh. And he puts Drive Yer Bollocks Off back on. And turns the music up and all. Prick.

We pull off into one of the big service stations. Up a slip road and off at a roundabout. It's all on its own. Well big. Bigger than a supermarket and the huge car park is already packed. He parks up and then comes round and drags me out the door. He holds me by the hood and dusts me off none too gently, getting rid of some of the dirt I picked up on me sleeping rough last night.

'Come on.' He keeps a grip on me as we head across the car park, his fingers digging into my upper arm, pulling me along with him.

I try and shake him off − 'I can walk by my fuckin'*self*.' His grip's too strong and I don't make no difference. But he says, 'Okay, but if you try anything funny I *will* break your legs. Both of them.'

He gives my arm one last tug. 'And this bony thing, and all. Savvy?'

I nod, pouting a bit. He lets go and I rub my arm a bit but walk along beside him towards the automatic doors of the service station.

As it's Christmas − not that either of us are feeling very merry − there's a big automated Santa outside going 'Ho, ho, ho' and rocking from side to side. There's also one of them fellas selling mobile phone covers. There's a boss one of the England flag. White with the red cross on it. Quality.

Just for a laugh, I say, 'Hey, Dad. Get me one of them.'

He spins round then. 'What?'

'Get me one of them… Dad.'

He gives me a real evil then. And he snarls at me. 'Listen, you little gimp, stop fuckin' around or you'll be getting a slap that'll put you in the mortuary. Whatever Dean says. Geddit? Gottit? Good.'

I nod. 'Mmmm'. I'm happy just to have riled him a bit. For some reason that makes me feel better again.

We wander round the over-lit restaurant, packed with old couples, younger couples with kids and gangs of blokes going off for the soccer. No colours in case of trouble but you can tell 'em a mile off. When else d'you see gangs of blokes in places like this 'cept when the football's on?

'Can't we have burgers?'

'No, we're eating in here. Siddown there, I'll get you something.' He pushes me into a table. The seats are hard plastic and bolted to the floor so they're really uncomfortable, however much you wiggle about.

Bollock Brain goes up to the counters, gets a tray and joins the queue of old folks and mums with whingey kids, every few minutes shooting a look over his shoulder at me – daring me to move. I don't dare.

Instead, I tear open the packets of sugar someone else has left on the table and empty them, trying to make a picture out of the sugar grains by swirling them round on the table top with my finger.

Bollock Brain comes back with a pot of tea, a cola for me and two plates of chips.

'That all?'

'We won't be staying long.'

Still chips is better than nothing and I dive in. Bollock Brain looks at me like I'm a weirdo.

'Jeez, ain't you eaten since yesterday or something?'

No. Actually. 'D'you want yours? 'cause if not…'

He shoves 'em my way and looks at me like I'm some kind of animal in the zoo or something.

Then I'm aware of a couple of people standing over my shoulder. Two big blokes in long leather jackets like Dean's. Bollock Brain sits up straight.

'Anyone sitting here?' says one.

'Help yourself.'

They sit down at the next table, squashed up next to us. I can smell their aftershave. It's nasty and it's interfering with my chips. One of the blokes gets up to get some teas and us three just sit there in silence, 'cept for me eating my chips. The guy comes back with the teas and some biscuits wrapped up in sparkly Christmas paper and sits back down. Funny thing is, no one's drinking or eating 'cept me.

Then one of the guys reaches down by his feet – Bollock Brain jumps a bit as he does so, but I carry on eating – and puts a kiddie's backpack on the table. 'There you are.'

'Cheers.' Bollock Brain opens it a bit, nods, then leaves it on the table between us. He puts his hand in his pocket and puts a packet of cigarettes on the table beside it, as if he's thinking he might jump up and go and have a fag in a minute.

The other guy, the one who put down the backpack, puts out his hand and picks them up. He opens the cigarette packet, and I see there's a big wad of cash inside. He nods at his mate, then back at Bollock brain and puts the pack back down.

Then we all sit having tea like it's the most normal thing in the world. Like we're a bunch of mates or some kid and his dad and his uncles on a nice day out. But no one's talking. We're just drinking tea – the little cups looking funny in their big hands – and looking kinda cross, not saying anything and staring around the restaurant at nothing. Seems weird but actually, looking round, everyone else seems to having about as much fun as us. So, to be fair, we fit in pretty well.

Then Bollock Brain swigs down the last of his tea with a big glug, his Adam's apple jumping in his neck, and gets up.

'Right,' he goes.

He turns to me. 'You carry that,' nodding at the backpack.

'It's a kid's thing.'

He looks at me, all sarky. 'Your point being?'

'I'm not walking around with that.'

'You fuckin' are,' he hisses, 'now fuck up.' He's embarrassed, 'cause I'm showing him up in front of the other blokes, and he leans over, yanking me up by the hood of my top which is becoming a bit of a habit with him now. He nods to the geezers and we leave, as happy together as any other father and son I can see in here. His cigarettes he's left on the table which, I suppose, was part of the plan all along.

He don't say nothing, just drags me out to the car park.

'Can I sit in the front on the way back then?' I say.

'No.'

He rams me in the back of the car. In the fuckin' babies' seat again. Seat belt on. Really fuckin'tight. And locks me in with the child locks. Prick.

And he's just about to start the engine and pull out when this car screeches up in front of him, blocking his way. We both jump and he looks behind – scared – but he can't get out that way either 'cause someone's parked behind him. We're trapped.

Totally stuffed.

I wasn't worried they were gangsters or nothing. You can tell they're cops. Even CID and plain clothes. The young ones all have this scrubbed rosy Christian look on them and the older ones just look fucked. Like walking cancer. And they got us bang to rights and there's nothing we can do.

Bollock Brain jumps out the car and tries to leg it but they nab him and get him on the ground. A good old knee in the back and all when they put the cuffs on. I can't fuckin' get out can I? 'cause he's put the bastard child locks on the back doors and I can't get through to the front, so I have to sit there in the back and wait. Just sitting there with the stash on my lap. Nothing I can do.

The sergeant opens the car door.

'Oh shit,' he says when he sees me.

I'm still clutching my backpack tight to me chest. Hugging it really.

'You'd better give that to me, son,' he says, reaching his hand out towards me. As I loosen my hold on the backpack, he leans in and lifts it out of my arms, opens it and looks inside.

Then he looks back at me, slowly. And he sighs like he's too tired for the world.

THE END OF DAYS

To be honest, in the end, it was a bit of relief getting lifted. I mean it weren't at first. When they actually nicked me. No way. You get that icy panic in your guts and that wobbly feeling when it's as if your belly and your throat have swapped places. And it fuckin' hurt 'cause they were none too gentle when they finally got hold of me and dragged me out. But once I'd got in the car and gone down the station and gone through the old rigmarole and they'd took all my stuff off me and shut me in a cell-like room with no laces in my shoes and a shitey old stinking tin loo in the corner to piss in, I felt better.

Sure it ain't nice but it was kinda peaceful. Early in the day, before the drunks come in. And I waited while they tried to get hold of my mum. It was like a bit of a rest to be honest. I just sat back on the hard old bed and looked at the wall. Not really thinking of anything. Just blanking out. I mean I kind of knew this would happen one day. Where I'm from, you kinda know you're gonna end up inside the cop shop one day. Everyone does, just about. It's like one of those songs that Marlene used to play I heard once. If you do the crime you've got to do the time – or something like that, the bloke said. I think he was singing about being in love or something girlie like that. But where I'm from, that's how it goes, so I'm doing the time now, even though from where I was thinking, it wasn't a crime I did. But as far as the cops go, it was. And that's just how it is, so the end of the story is me sitting in a cell, looking at a wall.

And I was there for hours, or seemed like hours and then the social workers started coming in and umming and ahhing and giving me that stupid 'poor you' look. Honestly, I think they get off on it sometimes, I really do. And the bullshit started all over again. Mum crying, cops moaning, social workers flapping. The usual shite.

I just carried on looking at the wall, just numbed out and let them get on with it. Anyways, they remanded me to a young offenders' kids' place, which is okay. That's where I am now. It's not too bad. Some of the kids are alright and the food's okay. My room's tidy and we get to play football every afternoon. Of course there's the odd pain in the arse about it but you get that everywhere.

I'm still on remand waiting for my court date. My solicitor said it should be okay what with the social workers' reports. I just have to say I was led astray and bullied by Dean Amery and his lot, but I ain't saying that. I ain't saying anything about anything. Can you imagine? I mean, I have to come out sometime, so I'm not saying nothing.

I'm expecting to be banged up back in here to be honest – for some time and all. Maybe I'll get one of those tagging things but I don't reckon I will even though I'm young. I reckon it'll be a good few month's locked up ... or more. And I'll have to go on one of those assessment things, child psych and that. But in here. Not outside. I reckon I'll be here for the long haul.

I won't mind that too much. It's alright in here. Kind of like a relief in a way. And I can handle talking to those questioning psych people a couple of times a week. I know what they want to hear and you get a cup of tea and nice biscuits when you go for your little chats, as they like to call them, so t's not too much hassle really. Whatever sentence I get, as long as I keep my nose clean, I'll prob'ly only have to do a third so I reckon I can hack it. Piece of piss really.

I miss Albie though. He was like.... I dunno. My nan used

to say, *'everyone needs someone to let them have a bit of cry, give 'em and cuddle and make 'em a cup of tea when things go wrong... like they always do.'* Someone to tell you things would be alright even if they didn't know. But they'd say it anyway. Just 'cause they wanted them to be. For you.

And that's what he was to me – like that. And there ain't none of that here. There ain't really none of that nowhere, is there?

But we had that. For a while.

I remember.

I know.

Sometimes, I think about him. Well I kind of do a lot. And what we did. And it's funny, you know, his name. Albie, Albion like he said. And that being some old word for England, like 'cause that's what we did. We kind of tried to build our own Albion in the middle of the shit. But in the end, it was just dreams. His dreams. And dreams ain't enough.

Thing was with him, he wanted to make them dreams in his head real. He fuckin' wanted to be the guy he drew all the pictures of and that and thought he could just save everyone and we'd all ride off in some fuckin' space ship or something to some whole new world. To infinity and beyoooond!

Well I knew we wouldn't. But it was alright what we did, you know. It was alright. And, yeah, dreams ain't enough. But maybe they're a start 'cause I know I learnt stuff off him and his fuckin' dreaming. I really did.

But sometimes, you have to keep the dreams, dreams. Learn from 'em, like. But not live 'em. It's like, you don't go and see Batman and think you can fuckin' jump off the top of a building with a cape on and live. Well, this bloke round here did, jumped off the shopping centre but he ended up in bits on the pavement and it turned out he was mental anyway, so there you go.

But you can go and see Batman and decide not to be a big twat 'cause the bad guys who act like pricks always end up in the kind of shit you wouldn't want for yourself. And that's how I kind of look at it now.

*

This young offenders' kids place is the second one I been in now. I got moved from the first one which was miles away to one round here, near home. I like this one better 'cause I know more people here. Or their families, like, on the outside. I didn't know hardly anyone at the last one and then you tend to get ganged up on. I got a couple of beatings just for not being from the right area, you know. I gave good back, but that meant I got banged up all day and lost some of my privileges so it backfired in the end.

Dean got a message to me while I been here. Through the other lads. He said he'll see me on the outside, which is alright... I suppose – depending on what that means.

The day they moved me to here, we went past the flophouse. I was sitting there with my cuffs on staring out the window 'cause there weren't nothing else to do. And we went past Sned's so I could see my flats and then up the dueller and round the back, 'cept the back weren't there no more. There were just a pile of rubble and a couple of big bulldozers. The flophouse was totally gone. Not even a pile of bricks left. And I thought about Albie then, and where he would be.

I still thought about him a lot, to be honest. But, there weren't much I could do about it, sat in the back of a meat wagon between two screws on my way to my new place, another gaff in the middle of lovely countryside I'd never see 'cause I was locked up with a bunch of other shitheads. And not much I could do about it there either. Except think.

I got moved here 'cause my solicitor said I should be closer to home so Mum could see me more. And the courts said that was okay, so they moved me out the other place. And though it was better 'cause of knowing people and that, Mum was a pain in the arse, to be honest. She just used to come and cry and feel sorry for herself, so t was quite a relief when the doctors said she shouldn't come any more for the depression; 'cause it was making her worse, seeing me, they said.

They took her into hospital for a bit and Sam come up on her own after that. And she was sound. I liked it when she came up.

Sam said mum liked it in the hospital 'cause there was loads of people who she could talk to about herself and that was all she ever wanted. Just someone to take a bit of an interest. And she got loads of that there. I said they were paid to take an interest, like in the young offenders' where they all come and talk to us all the time. Them little chats and that. But Sam said that didn't matter to mum. She said she didn't care as long as she got a bit of interest from someone, so I s'pose that was okay for her, then. Sam said mum was actually happy sometimes, which was fuckin' amazing. I was glad then for her. She deserved to be happy, even if that was the only way.

Sam stayed living at home by herself when mum went in the hospital and that was cool. That's where I'll be going when I come out. Sam's really done it up now and she says it looks different. She's even done my room and all. She's having a kid from Kevin, so she wants the place all nice. Like it should be.

The other person who came and seed me was Marlene. That was nice of her. She even bought me magazines and CDs and stuff. I always thought she was sound. And it was funny I guess 'cause she was with Dean who didn't give a shit about her really and mum didn't give a shit about me, sowe were kind of similar like that.

I told Marlene that if she ever ended up in a place like here – well not like here 'cause she wouldn't end up in a young offenders', would she? – but say like hospital, I'd come and visit her, too. It was meant to be nice but when I said 'hospital' I wish I ain't said nothing at all 'cause she looked scared for a minute and I knew she'd thought about it already, what with Dean being a bit quick with his fists and that, so I said quick, when I came over I'd bring better stuff than the shite she just brought me. And then her face stopped being so sad and she smiled, the smile I liked. The proper one she has, not the one where she looks like she's just stretching her mouth.

See, like, it's important that stuff. Caring for people. That's what Albie taught me, I guess. About…. I dunno what the word is. Like love. But it ain't love. Mum said she loved me all the time and she did jackshit. Dean says he loves Marlene but kicks crap out of her. Katie said she loved Albie but fed off him like a fuckin' vampire and then fed him that shit, so who wants that?

And Albie and me, well it weren't love, like not gay or anything, but whatever it was, that's what you need. Like Marlene loves me like that. I know that sounds wrong but I know what I mean. It's like, with Marlene, I know whatever shit she has going on, I know she'd look out for me and watch my back. She did. Even with Dean. And I know, if she needed anything, I'd be the same. Like Albie. At the start.

So maybe we need a new word for it. Instead of love. Like having mates. Proper mates. Not hanging out mates. But life saver mates. And you don't get many of them, do yer?

And what we did, what we tried to do was make that

ourselves. And we nearly did it – no, we *did* do it, before things started going wrong. I know what I said about dreams and what Albie wanted with his fuckin' Albion nonsense and the dream was too big, but for a bit we made something like that place Albie was talking about – not a kingdom, but a home. And it worked. It worked for all of us. For me, for Albie, for Homeless and his mates, and Paul, and Jerry and all the others, it *was* a home. And I know Homeless didn't have one – well, he did but he didn't wanna be there I guess and the rest of us had so much shit at home we didn't wanna be there either or we just thought what we did was better. And it was. Even if there weren't no real kings or knights or all that shit. It was good enough.

But I don't hate Mum for having the depression and not looking after me, and I don't hate Albie for when everything went wrong. At the end of the right, whatever we thought he was – me, Katie, the rest of 'em – or even what *he* thought he was, King fuckin' Arthur or something, he was just a mad kid with a bad ankle and shit dad. Like the rest of us, although most of us did the double, shit mum *and* dad.

One day, I got a postcard. I coulda guessed who it was from by looking at the front of it. It didn't say nothing on the back and I couldn't read the postmark. Just the picture of us, the Children of Albion.

So I knew it was from him.

And I hoped he was okay, and doing alright, wherever he was.

But I have to get on with things now. I'll be the man of the house when I get out. Sam's baby's due in a few months and I'll have to be a kind of dad to him as well as an uncle 'cause Kevin's not much cop. He shacked up with some other girl who's got a flat down Sned's parade. To be honest he's a bit of player really and he'll prob'ly be off with some other girl soon enough. He's not evil or nothing. He just gets bored. Sam's alright about it. She knows she's better off by herself. And as long as he pays for the kid and comes to see him sometime, that's okay 'cause I can do the rest.

Yeah. I'm gonna be there for him, this little nipper.

I won't let him down. I'll look after him.

And I'm gonna make sure I teach him everything I know.

ABOUT THE AUTHOR

Jill Turner began writing as a three year old. What started out as 'little stories' about horses and cats developed over the years into teenage novellas and romances, which are still in a bedroom drawer (and should probably stay there).

A love of writing was fulfilled by a very successful and fast paced career as a Fleet Street journalist at The Sunday Times, The Daily Mail, The Guardian, and The Daily Mirror among others. Working in journalism fed Jill's interest in the individual human experience, and developed Jill's storytelling abilities. The pursuit of journalism exposed Jill to many complexities, tragedies and socio-political contradictions of the human condition.

Jill now lives in the beautiful coastal countryside of South West England, where she writes full time, still writing periodically for the national press, and increasingly dedicating her time to writing fiction. She lives with a very clever little boy, who adds infinitely to her life.

A voracious reader, she is passionate about encouraging young people to engage with literature, and has worked as a mentor with Youth At Risk, and Fairbridge / Prince's Trust.

When not working, she likes to be out on the beach with her son, or at the nearest riding stables.

JILL TURNER

LITTLE BIRD PUBLISHING
www.thelittlebirdbookstore.

If you enjoyed reading this novel, then you may also enjoy reading works by Jill's fellow Arthurian enthusiast, Katie M. John.

Her series, The Knight Trilogy, (A Contemporary Young Adult Romance series) is an award winning, bestselling YER series.

You can read more about The Knight Trilogy and Katie's other works at her website www.katiemjohn.com

You can discover many more unique works by the Little Bird author family at the official Little Bird Publishing website. www.thelittlebirdbookstore.com

Little Bird Publishing house is an innovative boutique press, committed to publishing works of quality and individuality, and the presence of more diverse voices in the literary world.

We are a community of authors who care deeply about storytelling and encouraging reading for all.

Made in the USA
Charleston, SC
21 November 2016